# MAIN STREET STORIES

a Novel

by

Phyllis LaPlante

Genoa House
www.genoahouse.com
books@genoahouse.com


First Edition



Published simultaneously in Canada, the United Kingdom, and the United States of America. For information on obtaining permission for use of material from this work, please submit a written request to:
books@genoahouse.com

ISBN 978-0-9813939-1-9

For Kenneth

# JUNE 1954

# CHAPTER ONE

"Now, what are we going to do today?" Nadine Coulter ran experienced fingers through Kathryn Parker's wet brown hair.

"Oh, Nadine, I don't know. Something pretty?"

"Maybe a little shorter." Nadine bunched the hair around Kathryn's cheeks to illustrate the change.

"Well, actually, I was thinking about letting it grow out. I think Ray might like it better long." Kathryn sought Nadine's face in the mirror, hoping that she would have a good idea. She depended on Nadine's advice.

Nadine's rich, hearty laugh ended in a cough; she took a last drag on her cigarette and crushed it in the ashtray. "Honey, I guess there's not a man alive who doesn't like long hair." Her own dark red hair was shoulder length.

Although Kathryn's mother hadn't wanted her to pal around with a girl like Nadine, the two had been friends since high school, where Nadine proved to be a prime source of information about petting, French kissing, and smoking cigarettes like movie stars. Many boys flocked around Nadine, and hearts were broken when she married Bobby Coulter. Bobby himself was an alluring figure, darkly handsome at 25, back home in Massey after a stint in the Army. That summer people watched them rocket up and down Main Street on Bobby's motorcycle, Nadine's arms around his waist, her red hair flying out behind her. Nadine reported they went out to the river bottom at night where they lay on a blanket to look up at the stars. "Course," Nadine laughed, "that isn't all we looked at." Nobody was much surprised when Nadine got pregnant and a hasty wedding followed. But Bobby couldn't seem to stay put. After only a year of marriage, he rode his motorcycle out of town, leaving Nadine and baby Renee. Nadine divorced him, went to beauty school in Gainesville, and established Massey's only beauty shop.

"You never cut your hair, did you?"

"No, I like it long. You used to wear a pageboy."

"With bangs."

"Well, I don't think you want bangs now. Okay, I got an idea." She reached for a magazine and showed Kathryn a photograph.

"Oh, Nadine, that would be perfect."

"Yeah, this is long but sophisticated."

"I think Ray might really like it." Ray and Kathryn had been married only two years. They started dating in high school, but it had looked like Ray was never going to pop the question. Kathryn had pretty much resigned herself to being an old maid until Nadine told her to go to the Frederick's of Hollywood shop in Amarillo for some sexy underwear, and to make an appointment with Doc Lomax to get fitted with a diaphragm. Kathryn had about died of embarrassment in both establishments, but Nadine's advice had led to Ray's proposal and their wedding.

Nadine began scissoring. "How is Ray doing?"

"Oh, he's real busy, getting ready for football. He's already started early morning practices. He's out of the house before I wake up and sometimes he's not home before I go to bed. I almost never see him."

"I hope he can field a better team this year. Last year was downright terrible."

"I know, and it about killed Ray. Only his second year of being head coach and the team just went to pot. He's been moody ever since."

"Well, you know this town lives and breathes football. Now tilt your head down." Nadine's scissors snipped.

"Nadine," Kathryn said.

"Yep?"

"I saw something in Reader's Digest, and I wondered what you thought."

"Shoot."

"From what you hear and everything, is there ever a time… I mean, do you think men sometimes lose interest in…the bedroom?"

"You mean lose interest in sex? Not in my experience, honey." Nadine laughed and coughed.

"Oh. Well, this article said that some men might if they're under a lot of pressure."

"Only pressure most men feel is pressure to get laid," Nadine said. "Well, you got no worries there. You and Ray are still honeymooners."

A deep flush suffused Kathryn's face and neck. She bent her head and put her hand over her mouth.

"Oh, honey, did I say something wrong?"

Kathryn sat silently, face shielded.

Nadine put down the scissors and handed Kathryn a tissue. She poured a cup of coffee and brought it over. Kathryn buried her face in the cup.

"Take comfort, honey, you're not the only woman with problems who's sat in this chair."

Kathryn blew her nose. "I guess you hear all kinds of stuff."

"Well, you know Massey, it's the grapevine capital of Texas."

The door to Nadine's shop opened to admit Virgil Harmon, the town pharmacist. Kathryn quickly wiped her eyes.

"Morning, Nadine. Oh, hi, Kathryn. You busy, Nadine?"

"As you can see, Virgil," Nadine said.

He proffered a paper bag. "I just brought over your order of chemicals."

"Just leave it on the table."

Virgil hesitated, shifting from foot to foot.

Kathryn said, "I see you got Jesse Eliot working for you this summer."

"Oh, yeah, he's a real good kid," Virgil replied. "I got him stocking shelves and running the soda fountain."

"How is his daddy?" Nadine asked.

"Well, just between you and me and the gatepost, I reckon Joe's not so good."

Kathryn said, "I heard he was acting strange again."

"Well," Virgil said, "that doesn't surprise me. When he came home from the hospital he had a prescription he was supposed to take every day. But he didn't ever get it refilled."

"I feel sorry for Marilyn being married to someone like Joe," Kathryn said.

"Oh, Marilyn Eliot is a saint," Nadine said. "Unlike her sister. Don't quote me."

Kathryn smiled. Everybody knew that Marilyn's sister, Maureen Woodson, went to Amarillo every week to get her hair done.

"I see Renee is working at Woodson's," Virgil said.

Nadine nodded. "Yeah, I told her she wasn't going to lay around the house all summer. I asked Roy to give her a job. He's a good person. Unlike his wife."

"We know, don't quote you!" Kathryn laughed.

"Speaking of the Woodsons," Virgil said, "I saw something funny this morning when I took Brother Robbins' prescription over to the church. Didn't think he was at church, cause I had seen his car over to their house."

"Whose car?" Kathryn asked.

"Brother Robbins' car. But he was at church, even if his car wasn't. It was the funniest thing. When I asked him, he didn't seem to know what I was talking about."

"Virgil, *I* don't know what you're talking about," Nadine said. "What exactly happened?"

"Well, this morning I was taking his heart medication to the church, and on the way there I saw his car, you know that big old black Packard, parked in front of Roy and Maureen Woodson's house."

Nadine's comb clattered to the floor. "Dang," she said, bending to retrieve it.

Virgil said, "So I thought, well, heck, he's not at church. But here is the funny part, when I got there, there he was, after all. Mary Pickens was there, too, and she asked him where his car was. He said he'd left it at home and walked over to church."

"Walked? That's a pretty long way," Kathryn said.

"Yeah, eight or nine blocks. Said Doc told him to get more exercise. But it was funny about the car," Virgil mused.

Nadine fastened a net around Kathryn's rolled-up hair and shepherded her over to the dryer. "You want a manicure?"

Kathryn looked at her nails. "Probably a good idea."

Nadine said, "Was there anything else, Virgil?"

"No. Well, yes. I wanted to ask you about the Elks' dinner dance."

"Virgil, I believe I already gave you my answer."

"Oh, okay, I wasn't sure. Well, I got to go. See y'all." He hurried out.

Kathryn giggled. "Poor Virgil. He's had a crush on you since grade school."

"God help me," Nadine said.

"You weren't very nice to him, Nadine."

"Wasn't I nice?" She laughed and coughed.

"Oh, he looked like a whipped puppy."

Nadine coughed and coughed. When she could catch her breath, she took a tissue and wiped her eyes carefully, so as not to disturb her mascara.

"Nadine, isn't there anybody in town you want to date?" Kathryn asked.

"What do you think? Bunch of losers."

"What about Daryl Tomlin? He's single now."

"Daryl! It's been more than a year since Carolyn left him, and he is still pining away for her. It'd be like going to a funeral. How about Redder than Rubies?" Nadine picked up a bottle of nail polish.

"No, no, Ray hates red nails. Just clear or maybe a little pink."

Nadine selected Pink Cloud.

Kathryn said, "I think I saw Brother Robbins' son yesterday. You know, Adam. I guess he's home for the summer. Maybe he's graduated from what's-it-called, Bible College?"

Nadine shrugged.

"He is one cute boy. I'll bet Renee thinks he's good looking."

"I don't think Renee cares what they look like," Nadine said. "I'm kind of worried about her."

"Really? How come?"

Nadine looked as if she might say something but reached for a cigarette instead. "Oh, I guess she's just boy crazy."

"We were all boy crazy when we were sixteen, Nadine."

"Well, I wish she'd outgrow it."

"You did, didn't you?" Kathryn said.

Nadine didn't smile. She took a long drag on the cigarette, looking away.

~ ~ ~

Across Main Street and down the block from Nadine's, Wayne Pickens was putting price tags on Levi's and observing Renee Coulter. He selected a yellow tag, licked it, and centered it on the back pocket of each pair, pressing it into place with his thumb. Since he could tag merchandise with his eyes closed, he could focus fully on Renee, who was painting her fingernails.

Apparently oblivious to his scrutiny, Renee leaned over the check-out counter in deep concentration, her little pink tongue at the corner of her mouth, as she brushed polish on her left thumbnail. Her finely penciled eyebrows tense, her mascara-filled lashes unblinking, she painstakingly applied scarlet liquid. She blew breath on the nail, then waved her hand in the air. He imagined her breasts under the purple fabric.

Wayne forced his eyes away to prevent himself from getting too excited. For distraction, he looked around Woodson's Department Store. Overhead, three big ceiling fans turned slowly, enlivening the air. He was working at one of the square wooden counters in the center of the store. At the back were half a dozen racks displaying women's and girls' dresses. There was a big three-way mirror between two little curtained booths where customers could try on clothes. There was a storeroom in the back next to the flight of stairs leading up to a little balcony, where Mr. Woodson had his desk.

Wayne was proud of the store. Main Street was lined with stores, and Woodson's was the best. He felt he was the one who kept it humming. He unpacked and marked the new merchandise, kept track of the inventory, hand-lettered the signs, and arranged the display cases and windows. He had been working at the store 12 years, since he graduated from high school, class of '42. He had shown Mr. Woodson the ropes when he bought the store from Mr. Hurst.

Lucky I didn't get drafted, he thought. Lord only knows what would have happened to the store without me here.

Wayne was also proud of Massey, where he had lived all his life. Located in the west corner of the Texas Panhandle, practically in New Mexico, Massey was booming. The war had restored prosperity to the town lost during the dust bowl days. America needed cotton, wheat, and cattle, and wartime demand for natural gas and petroleum skyrocketed. Massey was the county seat, a good-sized town, over three thousand people.

Wayne allowed himself another peek at Renee by casually shifting the stack of Levi's toward the check-out counter. She yawned and stretched her arms above her head. The purple fabric outlined prominent little nipples. No bra! His excitement rising, Wayne was torn between the enjoyment of the moment and the urgent desire to go for the second time that morning to the little toilet at the back of the storeroom where he could relieve the throbbing of what he called his manhood into a wad of toilet paper.

No, no, he had made Jesus a solemn promise only two hours ago that he would give up that carnal habit. He sternly reminded himself that self-abuse and immoral thoughts were sinful. He was going to stop lusting after women, allowing concupiscent images into the picture show of his mind. No good Christian, especially one who contemplated going to Bible College, could engage in either the lustful looking or the shameful act. Either one could send you straight to hell.

He recalled Wednesday night prayer meeting at the First Baptist Church. Brother Robbins had waxed eloquent on the cure for the licentious eye (pluck it out) and the wicked hand (cut it off).

He turned his body away from Renee and slapped on the price tags, spanking the bottom of each pair of Levi's. When Mr. Woodson arrived, he would expect to see those Levi's stacked neatly on the front counter, with a fresh hand-lettered sign.

Within a few minutes, however, Wayne began to muse. It seemed unmerciful to condemn a healthy thirty-year-old with manly needs. Hadn't Jehovah created male and female so that they could cleave to each other? Was it fair to accuse a man of sin just because he admired God-given feminine beauty? Wayne visualized himself in the pulpit. Brothers and sisters, Jesus commanded us to love one another.

Reassured by Holy Scripture, he allowed himself to gaze unhindered at Renee, who now was seated on the counter, running her fingers through her luxuriant red hair. Had she been frightened away from love by threats of hell fire? Poor thing, poor sweet girl. A holy joy rose in him.

"Renee," he said, "you look mighty pretty today."

Renee's perfect little mouth curved downwards as she hopped off the counter and turned her back on him. Creep, she thought. But she said sweetly over her shoulder, "Wayne, would you be nice and watch the cash register. I'll just run over to the P.O. and see if there's any mail yet."

Before Wayne could tell her it was too early, she had taken the key to the Post Office box and skipped out the front door. He watched her go.

Outside it was already hot, another scorcher. Squinting against the sun, Renee wished for sunglasses. Movie stars wore sunglasses all the time, even indoors. But it was cool next door inside Harmon's Drug Store. She paused at the cosmetic counter to study herself in the make-up mirror. She pulled at her hair. Maybe I could get some gold highlights.

"Hi," came a voice from the soda fountain.

"Hi yourself," she said, her eyes on her reflection. "Make me a frosted Coke."

"Say pretty please," the boy said.

"Pretty please with sugar on it." Renee sashayed over to a counter stool. Jesse Eliot scooped vanilla ice cream into a glass, added syrup and dispensed seltzer water. He set the glass on the counter in front of her. "Fifteen cents."

Renee gave him a dime and a nickel. With a straw she sucked in the cold sweetness.

"You working today?" the boy asked.

"Course." She licked foam from her lips.

"What time you get off?"

"Six."

"Want to go to the picture show tonight?"

"With you?"

"Who else?"

"Maybe. Maybe not."

Jesse took a rag to wipe the counter. He grinned as he brushed his knuckles against her right breast.

Renee moved out of reach. "I'll holler and you'll get fired."

"Nobody here but you and me. Mr. Harmon is making deliveries."

"Is that so."

Jesse came from behind the counter and stood beside her. She turned her head toward him and they kissed, tongues touching. He cupped one hand around her breast, but she thrust it away. "Huh uh," she said.

The door chime rang, signaling the entry of a customer. Jesse quickly slipped back behind the counter. Renee guided the straw to her mouth.

"Eliot," came a booming voice.

"Hi, Coach, how you doing?"

"I want to know if I can count on you for practice tomorrow morning? Six sharp?" said Coach Ray Parker.

Renee turned toward the big beefy man in a baseball cap who stood with legs apart, arms across his chest. "Hi, Coach," she said.

He ignored her.

"Sure, Coach, I'll be there," Jesse said.

The man swung himself onto a stool. "What's that?"

"Frosted Coke," she said.

"Make me one of them," he instructed Jesse.

"Coming up, Coach."

Renee finished her drink and slid off the stool. "Got to go back to work."

Jesse set a glass in front of Coach Parker, his eyes on Renee. "Six o'clock," he called.

"Seven," she corrected and strolled out the door.

"That going to keep your mind off football?" Coach nodded toward the departing Renee.

"No, sir."

Coach spooned ice cream out of his glass. "You want to be my quarterback, you better keep your pecker in your pants."

"Yes sir."

Coach threw back the rest of his drink, banged down coins on the counter, and was out the door, wiping his mouth with the back of his hand. Jesse hustled back to the pharmacy to snatch a package of Trojans. He put them in his back pocket, whistling.

~ ~ ~

Sheriff Calvin Tuttle put down the telephone and whistled softly. He motioned to his deputy, "Come on, we got to go out there."

Deputy Sheriff Pete Mosley followed Cal out of the court house. "What'd she say?"

"She says he's cutting down all the trees with the tractor."

"Jeez! What's he want to do that for?"

"Beats me." The two men climbed into the 1953 white Chevy pickup with "Plains County Sheriff" stenciled on the side. Cal backed out of the parking space and gunned it across the railroad tracks out to the highway. The land was so flat and the air so dry you could see all the way to the horizon. The Eliot place was three miles out of town, but when they turned onto the highway, they could already see plumes of dust rising. As they turned down the drive to the farm, they saw Joe Eliot on his tractor, felling the young trees he had planted last year. About a dozen poplar trees now lay splintered on the ground as the tractor mowed them down, one by one. Branches littered the road, and the air was thick with dust and exhaust fumes.

Cal had seen Joe out at Brown's Implement, buying the new John Deere 50 diesel tractor with a front loader. Cal wondered how he could afford it because he had heard tell that Joe had mortgaged the farm and was behind in his payments.

Joe had inherited the farm free and clear when his mother died, about ten years previously. He had always been his mother's favorite, but she about disowned him when he and Marilyn ran off to get married. She told anybody who would listen, "That girl got herself pregnant and trapped my son." She thawed a little after Jesse's birth and willed the farm to Joe, but left the bulk of her estate -- the ranch, the horses, the money -- to Pat, Joe's older sister.

At first Joe settled down into farming, raising wheat and hogs. It was after he came back from Korea that he became strange, erratic in his doings. Last spring Marilyn had to take him to the psychiatric hospital in Amarillo. And now this.

Cal stopped the pickup as Marilyn Eliot came flying out of the house toward them. She jumped on the running board and thrust her head through the open window. "Thank God you're here! Maybe you all can stop him. I couldn't."

"Now, you just calm down," he soothed. "Marilyn, I can't open my door till you get off the running board."

"Oh, I'm sorry," she said and jumped off. Cal and Pete got out of the pickup and the three of them watched Joe wildly circle the tractor around to make another pass at a tree which had resisted his first assault.

Marilyn clung to Cal's arm. "He said they were coming to get him. He said he wouldn't be able to get a clear shot because the trees blocked his view."

"Does he have his gun with him?" Pete asked, shading his eyes to look.

"No, it's in the kitchen," she said. "He said he had to knock the trees down first and then he could get a clear shot."

"Okay," Cal said, freeing his arm, "you just stay here and we'll go talk to him."

The tractor backed up fast, spun around, and plowed into another tree, which withstood the violent battering and remained standing. Joe again slammed the bucking tractor into the trunk. This time the tree fell, and he rode the tractor over it, butting up against the chain link fence. The tractor's new green finish was dirty and scarred.

Cal marched forward. "Hey there, Joe," he called.

As he got closer, he could tell that Joe's expression was fixed, his eyes weirdly locked on the horizon beyond the trees and the fence. Joe jammed the gear into reverse, but the wheels spun and the engine whined.

"Joe!" Cal yelled, and Pete added his own shout.

The engine died, and Joe cried out, "Goddam junk! How can a man…"

"Hey, Joe!"

Joe looked down at them from his perch, face flushed, sweat staining his hat and shirt. His eyes darted from one man to the other.

"Hey, Joe, it's me, Cal Tuttle."

"Howdy," said Pete.

Joe frowned as if he didn't recognize them. He pulled a pack of Luckies from his shirt pocket, but his fingers jittered. Cal caught the pack, shook out a cigarette to Joe, and offered up the flame from his Zippo lighter. Joe pulled smoke into his lungs and stared toward the horizon.

"Hey, Joe," Cal said and waited for Joe to look at him. "What's going on here?"

"Well, you can see how the damn things block my view of the highway."

"Is that so?"

"They could get purt near up to the house without me seeing them."

"Who would that be, then?" Pete asked.

Joe scowled at him. "Well, I'm not gonna let them get right up to my front door, am I? I got a duty to protect my family, don't I? Y'all'd do the same, if you was me." He looked at his wife, who had crept up beside Cal. "Marilyn, honey, where's your shoes?"

"Let's go into the house, Joe," Cal said. "How about making us some coffee, Marilyn?"

Joe shook his head. "I got work to do, Cal. They'll be here before dark."

"Come on, Joe, get down now and let's go into the house."

Cal turned to Marilyn and lowered his voice. "I think you ought to call the ambulance now. You run in and do that, and we'll be in directly. Pete, you go with her and put the gun away."

He turned back to Joe and put his hand on the tractor's hot metal hood. "How you like your new John Deere, Joe?"

"Good. Looks nice, don't it? It's brand new. Old one couldn't handle these trees, not enough power. Once I got word they were coming, I knew I needed a new one."

"Okay, buddy, just come on down now," Cal said.

Joe swung down from the tractor. He stumbled over a branch and would have fallen if Cal had not grabbed his arm. Joe swayed and Cal put his arm around his shoulder.

"Cal, I just get so tired fighting them off."

"I know, Joe, I know you do."

Later, Cal and Pete followed the ambulance down to the highway and watched it turn away from town, toward Amarillo.

"Sheriff," Pete said, "what the hell is wrong with that man?"

"Beats me," Cal said, turning the pickup toward town. He was thinking that they should notify the family. Pat Eliot ought to know that they had sent her brother to Amarillo again, and Maureen Woodson would be worried about her sister Marilyn. "Pete, I reckon we ought to tell Pat and Maureen about this. You call them when we get back, okay? I'll go over to the drug store and talk to Jesse. Poor kid."

# CHAPTER TWO

In the kitchen of their home, Dorothy Harmon confronted Pat Eliot. "Were you going to hide it from me?"

Exasperated, Pat answered, "Dorothy, if I was going to hide it from you, why would I leave it on the kitchen table?"

"I didn't read it. I just looked at the envelope."

"Go ahead, read it. All it says is that she got married."

"Cynthia got married?"

"Read it yourself."

"No, I don't read other people's mail." She gathered the frilly white nylon negligee around her waist.

Pat poured coffee. "You want coffee?" she asked.

"No. Well, I guess so. Yes."

Pat added sugar and cream and brought the cups to the kitchen table. She sat down heavily and opened the envelope. She held the paper in front of Dorothy's face.

"She says, 'I got married last month to a really wonderful man. His name is Steven Armstrong, and we're very happy. Steven is from New York and is working on his Ph.D. in international relations.' That's it."

Dorothy took the paper. "Hm, that's a surprise. Although when she went east to college, you said she was gone for good."

"And she is."

Dorothy sipped coffee and pondered. After a long silence, she asked, "What are you going to do today?"

"I thought I'd go out to the ranch to see my new horse. You want to go?"

"Lord, no. I think I'll go down to Woodson's and see if they have anything I can use to make new bathroom curtains."

"What for?"

"Pat, what we have are tacky."

"You put them up when we moved in. You didn't think they were tacky then."

"That was years ago. Plus, they're ruined from the damp. If you would remember to turn on the fan when you take a shower."

Pat drained her coffee and stood. "If they got any Levi's like these, get me a couple pair, 34-34's."

"All right." Dorothy waited a minute and then asked, "What did you think about Cynthia getting married?"

"I didn't think anything about it." Pat stuffed her billfold into the back pocket of her Levi's and patted her shirt pocket for cigarettes.

"She was over here all the time when she was in high school. She about lived here."

"She loved horses. She loved to ride."

"It was more than horses," Dorothy said.

"I'm going," Pat said.

"Mark my words, Pat Eliot, some day you're going to get into trouble..."

The door bell rang, and Pat strode through the hall to open the front door.

"Hi, Miss Eliot," came a girl's voice.

Dorothy clicked her tongue in irritation.

"Well, Miss Laura Tuttle! Come on in!" Pat boomed.

"I just came by to tell you I really liked those record albums."

"Is that a fact."

"Oh, yes, especially Glenn Miller."

"Yeah, he was the best. I thought you'd like him. So what are you up to today?"

"Oh, nothing really."

"Well, I'm going out to the ranch to see my new horse. You want to come?"

"Oh, that would be great!" The girl moved with Pat into the kitchen. "Oh, hi, Miss Harmon."

"Hello, Laura. Say, I heard you were dating Jesse."

"Oh, sort of, not really," Laura said, blushing.

Dorothy smiled blandly at Pat. "Coach's going to start him at quarterback this year, right, Pat?"

"Okay, Dorothy," Pat said. "Come on, Laura, we'll take the pickup."

Dorothy slumped at the table and put her head in her hands.

~ ~ ~

Cal Tuttle walked slowly from the court house the three blocks to the drug store, rehearsing exactly what to say to Jesse Eliot. He wondered what Jesse thought about his father's condition. Tongues wagged about Joe Eliot. Of course, in a small town like Massey everybody gossiped. People found out about everything, especially the things you wished you could keep secret. Cal was convinced that people knew everything about his wife, Janice, too.

God, what happened to people's minds that caused them to think and do crazy things? Watching Joe Eliot violently careening around on his new tractor and whacking down the young trees recalled to his mind the beginnings of what he now thought of as Janice's condition. It began sixteen years earlier, just after their daughter Laura was born. Mary Pickens, who cleaned house for them, had called him at work to tell him that he should come right home.

When Cal got to the house, Mary was outside in the yard, holding baby Laura. He found his wife in the house, agitated and pacing. Twisting her hands together, Janice told him she wanted to give Laura up for adoption. Flabbergasted, Cal tried to reason with her. Nobody had wanted a baby more than Janice. But things had gone sour from Laura's birth. Janice hadn't been able to nurse right, and the baby regularly screamed with hunger and frustration. By the time she put Laura on the bottle, Janice had started acting strange. Many days she didn't get dressed. Her hair got matted and greasy, and she smelled stale.

That day, Janice told him she wanted to give the baby up because she couldn't take care of her. She said she was afraid she would hurt Laura. Cal argued, but Janice became more and more frantic. She screamed at him that she would kill the baby and herself. Scared, he asked Mary Pickens to take care of Laura. He forced a raving Janice into the pickup and took her out to Dr. Lomax's clinic.

Doc told Cal to take her to the state mental hospital. He packed a suitcase for her and drove her to Gainesville. The hospital buildings were ugly red brick, and filled with frightening noises. The odor alone turned Cal's stomach while he sat in the admitting office filling out papers. He left Janice there six weeks for shock treatments. When he brought her home, she was calmer, but a different person – remote, blank. Cal would find her standing stock still in the house, a million miles away. She took care of Laura's physical needs but didn't hold her much or play with her. The old Janice, the sweet and lively girl he had loved since eighth grade, was gone and probably wasn't ever coming back.

Over the years Janice had become almost a complete stranger to him. One day he came home to find that she had moved her clothes and other things to the third bedroom, where she slept alone. Every time he left the house he felt uneasy, wondering if she would be all right. He supposed that every soul in town knew all about it because people were sometimes careful with him, as if they thought he might be crazy, too. He understood their feelings; living with Janice was like camping on the edge of a volcano which had once blown you sky-high and was still rumbling. Even now, during what had been a relatively long calm period, he felt edgy around her. When he came home from work he always felt mildly anxious, hoping that nothing had gone wrong. These days Janice rarely left the house and often stayed in her room from morning to night.

Cal thought that Laura had seemed to grow up all right. He hoped she was all right, but couldn't be sure because she was so quiet. Little by little, Laura had taken over most of the housekeeping. She did the laundry, cooked supper, and after she got her driver's license did all the shopping. He wondered about Laura's feelings. He had never really spoken to her about her mother. Maybe he should have. But what would he have said? Your mother is crazy? Your mother wants to kill herself? Because she sometimes still did. Not to him directly, but he would hear her whispering threats.

What could he say to Laura? For that matter, what was he going to say to Jesse? He was relieved to find the store empty of other customers.

"Hi, Jesse," he said, coming over to sit at the soda fountain.

Jesse stiffened. Cal wondered if he had already heard.

"Yes sir?"

"Well, son, I was out to see your folks this morning."

Jesse eyes widened in alarm. "My folks?"

"Yeah, your mom called me. About your dad."

The fear faded from Jesse's face; he seemed almost reassured. "Yeah?"

"Uh, they had to take your dad to the hospital in Amarillo this morning."

"Was he knocking down the trees?"

Cal was surprised. "Why, yes, he was."

"Yeah, he said he was going to."

"Your mom went along in the ambulance."

"Okay," Jesse said, not quite shrugging his shoulders.

"I don't know when they'll be back."

"Okay."

Cal forged ahead. "So, I was wondering where you're going to stay. While they're in Amarillo. They probably won't be back for awhile."

"I don't mind being out there by myself. Or I could probably stay at my aunt's."

"Good idea. Why don't you do that, stay with Pat."

Jesse nodded.

"Well, you just let me know if you need anything."

"Yes sir."

Cal put his hat on and left the drug store. The boy could certainly stay with Pat and Dorothy. He hadn't thought about that. So that was settled. Jesse was sure a cool customer. He hadn't seemed a bit upset.

Jesse watched him go. Jesus, I thought he was going to ream me out about Laura.

~ ~ ~

"Good morning to you, Miss Harmon," Wayne Pickens said, welcoming Dorothy into Woodson's Department Store.

"Morning, Wayne."

"What can I help you with today?"

Dorothy paused at the counter with the Levi's. "Are these on sale?"

"Yes, ma'am, dollar off."

"Are these the ones Pat buys?"

"Yes, ma'am, Miss Eliot she likes this particular cut."

"Okay, give me a couple of – let's see, 34-34's."

"Uh, no, ma'am. I believe Miss Eliot had to get 36's last time."

"Well, that doesn't surprise me. Give me the 36's then."

"Yes, ma'am. Here we are, two pair, 36-34's. And what else this morning, Miss Harmon?"

Dorothy wandered over to the piece goods counter. "I need something for bathroom curtains," she said, fingering a bolt of figured cotton fabric.

Wayne scooted behind the counter. "Yes, ma'am. Take a look at this shiny percale. Just came in. Won't shrink, stays crisp. Comes in four solids and multi-color." He lifted a bolt of pink fabric and shook a length of it out on the counter.

"Not pink," Dorothy said. "What is that, green?"

"That is lime, yes, ma'am. Also comes in azure, wheat, and multi-color."

"Lime. I don't know." She fingered the material.

The door bell jingled, and Pete Mosley hurried inside.

"Dorothy, I thought that was you."

"Hi, Pete, how you doing?"

"Dorothy, I need to talk to Pat. Do you know where she is?"

"She's out at the ranch, Pete. What's the matter?"

Pete Mosley hesitated, looked at Wayne Pickens, then back to Dorothy. He dropped his voice. "It's Joe Eliot. We had to go out there this morning. He, uh, well, he was knocking down his trees with his tractor."

"Good Lord!"

"Yeah, it was pretty bad. Sheriff thought Pat ought to know. I called your house but no answer."

"No, Pat went out to the ranch this morning."

"Is there a phone out there?"

"No, there isn't."

"Well, maybe I should go on out there."

"Pete," Dorothy said, "tell me what happened."

"Well, Marilyn called the sheriff and we went out, and sure enough he was knocking down them poplars. Beats me why. Sheriff talked to him, and he kinda calmed down, and we called the ambulance, and they took him to Amarillo."

"Just this morning?"

"Yes, ma'am. Around nine or so, I guess."

"Lord, lord. Where is Marilyn now?"

"She went in the ambulance, too. She was pretty tore up."

"Does Maureen know? "

"No, I tried to call her, but no answer. Thought I'd better stop here, tell Mr. Woodson."

"Mr. Woodson's gone to the bank," Wayne put in helpfully.

Pete gave Wayne his official face. "Wayne, this here's confidential information."

"Oh, sure, I understand," Wayne said. "My lips are sealed."

Pete looked at his watch. "Reckon he'll be back soon?"

"Why, here he comes now."

Pete went to meet Roy Woodson at the door. "Mr. Woodson, sir, could I speak to you privately?"

"Hi, Pete. Well, sure. Hello, Dorothy, you being waited on?"

"I'm showing Miss Harmon the new percale," Wayne said.

"Okay, then. Come on back, Pete," Roy said.

The two men conferred in low voices near the cash register. Roy said, "No, she's there, probably turned the ringer off. She's got one of her headaches."

"Sheriff thought she probably ought to know," Pete said.

"Oh, yeah, she'll be real worried about Marilyn. I'll run home, tell her."

"Okay, thanks, I appreciate that," Pete said. He put his hat on and walked toward the door.

"Pete," Dorothy called, "you want me to run out to the ranch and tell Pat?"

"Would you? Sure it's not too much trouble?"

"No, no trouble, really. I thought I might go out there anyway. Pat wanted me to see her new horse."

"Well, if you would, I'd sure be grateful to you."

"Just the Levi's, Wayne. I'll wait about the material," Dorothy said and took her billfold out of her purse.

"Yes, ma'am. I'll just ring these up."

Roy took his car keys out of his pocket. "Where's Renee?" he asked Wayne.

"Post Office," Wayne replied. "Second time this morning," he said under his breath.

"When she gets back, tell her I want her to help me with the display windows."

"Yes sir," Wayne said, not entirely able to disguise his surprise and disappointment.

~ ~ ~

Adam Robbins peeled off the rubber and tossed it in the toilet. He looked appreciatively at his naked body in the full length mirror in Maureen Woodson's bathroom. She had taken a chance, calling him up like that. What if the old man had answered? Of course, his father had already gone over to the church, and his brothers Abel and Seth were at Bible camp, so Adam had been alone when the phone rang, and there was that soft, sexy voice: "You can come on over now."

He hadn't thought he'd hear from her again so soon. It was only Tuesday that she had picked him up in her Cadillac to go with her to Amarillo. While she had her hair done, he walked around the city. Afterwards, in the air conditioned car they kissed and touched. She was something, outwardly so ladylike, but inwardly wanton. She was like Potiphar's wife, who cast her eyes upon Joseph and said, "Lie with me." Like Deborah Kerr in *From Here to Eternity*, that movie he wasn't supposed to have seen.

Most movies were forbidden in the Robbins household, along with television, tobacco, alcohol, eating in restaurants, dancing, and of course sex. Adam thought it an amazing fact that his mother had given birth to him and

Abel and Seth. Hard to imagine, that pious couple giving in to the weakness of the flesh. Probably that's why his mother had died, when Seth was born, from mortification.

Adam had never seen such a bathroom. The tub and toilet were peach colored with crystal hardware. There were fluffy peach towels stacked in a white wicker stand and tiny soaps in a cut glass dish on the tile counter near the basin. The tub had a little pillow attached to the porcelain at the end opposite the faucets, and there were candles and bath salts in a jar along the back edge. Above the basin was a mirror ringed with pink light bulbs. He gazed appreciatively at his reflection in the mirror. People said he looked like Jesus, if Jesus had been clean-shaven with blue eyes.

Suddenly, the bathroom door opened and Maureen threw in Adam's clothes and shoes. She hissed, "You stay here and be very, very quiet. And put your clothes on."

She closed the bathroom door and quickly buttoned the peach silk housecoat and tied its belt around her slender waist. She slipped into little silver mules and ran her fingers through her hair. She closed the bedroom door and entered the living room just as her husband came through the front door.

"Sweetheart," Maureen trilled, "I just got up. I feel so much better." She kissed Roy on the mouth. "I think those new pills really work. When I woke up, poof, no more bad old headache. Is it time for lunch?"

"I didn't come home to eat. Something has happened." He took her hands in his. "Now you have to be brave. I think probably you should sit down. This is going to come as a shock to you."

Maureen sank onto the sofa, her eyes wide. "What is it, Roy?" Her mind was racing. Through the picture window she could see the big black Packard parked in front of the house. The fool!

"It's Joe. The sheriff and Pete had to go out there this morning."

"Is he dead?"

"No, no. But they had to take him to Amarillo in the ambulance. Looks like he had another one of his spells."

"Did he hurt Marilyn? My God, I wish she could get away from him."

"No, Marilyn is okay. He didn't hurt her. He was knocking down those poplar trees beside the road to the house with his tractor."

"Knocking down the trees? What in God's name for?"

"I don't know, Maureen. You know he gets these crazy ideas. Anyway, Cal and Pete got him calmed down and they called the ambulance and took him to Amarillo."

"What about Marilyn?"

"She went with him in the ambulance."

"For God's sake, Roy!"

"I know, I know, it's bad. Pete said he tried to call you but I guess you had the ringer turned off. So I decided I had better come home. I thought it would be better if you heard it from me."

She smiled brilliantly at him. "Oh, Roy, you are the sweetest man."

"What do you want to do? Do you want to go to Amarillo? We'll do whatever you want to do."

"I don't know. I have to think. Poor Marilyn, poor baby! I need a cigarette."

"Where are they? I'll get them for you."

"No, no, I'll get them. I want to wash my face anyway. You just sit still."

Back through the bedroom, she slipped inside the bathroom and closed the door behind her. Adam was dressed, sitting on the edge of the tub. She turned the sink faucet on full force. "Now, listen," she whispered. "You are going to go out this window and through the side lot. Walk down to the filling station and tell them you need a gallon of gas. Bring it back to your car and put it in and then get in and drive off. If anybody says anything to you, tell them you ran out of gas and had to leave the car. You didn't see me. I didn't see you. You understand?"

Adam nodded, stood in the bathtub and opened the window. He turned to try to kiss her, but she dodged away and gave him a push. "Go on, go on," she urged. He hoisted himself through the open window and dropped down outside the house.

Maureen closed the window and splashed water on her face. She saw the little gray balloon floating in the toilet and and flushed it down. In the bedroom, she pulled the satin coverlet over the tangled sheets. She took a quick look around, took her cigarettes from the bedside table, and returned to the living room. Roy was looking out the picture window.

"Maureen, whose car is that out front?"

She came up behind him. "Give me a light, honey."

He flicked his lighter and ignited her cigarette.

She looked at the car. "It kind of looks like Brother Robbins' old Packard."

"What's it doing here?"

"I have no idea. Shall I make us a sandwich?" She turned away from the window and he followed her.

"Do you want to go to Amarillo?"

"I guess so. Now, Roy, you don't have to go with me. You can go back to the store and I'll go to the hospital. I want to bring Marilyn home with me."

"I should go with you. It's a long drive."

"Not that far, and I could do it in my sleep. They're probably going to send him right back home like they did that other time." She went into the kitchen and peered out the window. There was no sign of Adam.

Forty-five minutes later, when Roy pulled his Ford out of the driveway so Maureen could back her El Dorado out of the garage, the Packard was gone. Maureen waved to Roy and blew him a kiss before heading off. He waved back, then drove to Main Street and parked in front of his store.

The business district on Massey's Main Street was three blocks long, and Woodson's was in the center of the middle block, with Harmon's Drug Store and the First National Bank on one side and Frederick's Jewelers and Dunn's 5 & 10 on the other. Across the street were the Farmers State Bank, Leroy's Diner, the Royal Theatre, Loretta's Dress Shop, and a vacant building on the corner where Franklins Shoes had been before they went out of business. A few other retailers and Nadine's Beauty Shop were in the first block, down toward the court house, alongside office buildings. His only direct competition, J.C. Penney, was in the third block, next to Bradshaw's Photography Studio and across from the Post Office.

It was a good location. If anybody had business on Main Street, they would have to walk by his store. When he bought the store from Homer Hurst, seven years ago after Homer had his stroke, Roy felt confident he could make the business a success. Homer had never done any modernizing and the interior was dark and dingy. Roy had the walls painted and the floors refinished. He put up a new sign and brought in fashionable new lines of merchandise. He hoped to win the business of those ladies who drove to Gainesville or Amarillo for their clothes and shoes, while supplying the men their Levi's, Nocona boots, and Stetson hats. He bought new manikins for the display windows. Still, he wasn't making any money. The store had yet to break even.

He looked at the display windows. It was time to change the women's apparel. He hoped Renee could help him with the window. He wasn't going to let Pickens handle the female manikins again after what had happened last time. Roy wondered if anybody else had seen Pickens rubbing himself against the naked model – right there in the display window. Sometimes Pickens gave him the willies. But, all in all, he was a good employee. He knew the merchandise, and he was helpful to the customers.

Roy's thoughts nagged at him. He wondered about Maureen's state of mind. Today she had been affectionate, but she could be so distant. He felt fortunate that she had married him. Why, she was so pretty, she could have had anybody. But she had married him. He wondered if she was sorry.

He had bought her the house she wanted and given her a free hand to decorate it. It troubled him that she always shopped in Amarillo, never liking what he had in stock at the store. Well, she should have what she wanted. He could afford to give it to her. Never mind that the store wasn't making money. There was plenty of money from his father's estate. Father had been a smart businessman, had bought up all that farmland people couldn't hold onto during the dust bowl, mineral rights, too. Now tenant farmers paid him rent, and the natural gas wells kept pumping out money.

But was Maureen happy? He faced the more precise question, was she happy with him? She had never been satisfied with him in the bedroom, had called him "timid" and "inhibited." Well, he guessed he was, but he couldn't help that. His mother had raised him to be a gentleman. Lately Maureen had had so many headaches. It was probably a month since she had invited him into her bed. He was content enough sleeping alone in his own spartan room, because he felt claustrophobic in her bedroom with all her stuff. But he wondered if she would ever be happy married to him. Roy shook himself and went inside the store.

❧ ❧ ❧

Mary Pickens had just set the big pitcher of sweetened iced tea on the table when Wayne rode his bicycle into the yard.

"Hello, Sonny," she called.

"Hello, Mama."

"It's all ready. Just wash your hands and come sit down."

He did so, and they folded their hands when they took their chairs at the table. "You say grace, Sonny."

Wayne closed his eyes, furrowed his brow, and intoned: "Oh, Lord, make us truly grateful for thy bounty, which we enjoy today. Bless your servant Mary who prepared our food. Bless all who are troubled, especially Mr. Joe Eliot and his wife. Bless Brother Robbins, the First Baptist Church and all its members. Heal the sick and convert the sinful. In Jesus' name, Amen."

"Amen," echoed Mary. She passed the bowl of mashed potatoes to Wayne. "I declare, Sonny, you pray so well. I think you pray almost as well as Brother Robbins."

"Thank you, Mama. I think the Lord just tells me the words to say." He forked himself a fried chicken breast from the platter, ladled gravy over the potatoes, added a big spoonful of lemon Jello to his plate, and began to eat.

"How was your morning, Sonny?"

"Just fine, Mama. How about you?"

"I cleaned the church. And Sonny, I hope you don't mind, but I spoke to Brother Robbins about you. I told him I believe you have the call."

"You did?" Wayne smiled, pleased.

"I did. I told him about your Bible study and your prayers and everything."

"What did he say?"

"He said he knew you were a Godly man. I must say he didn't seem a bit surprised. I think he's been watching you, Sonny, watching you grow into a Godly man."

"What else did he say?"

"Well, he said that he wanted you to talk with Adam – he's home for the summer – about Bible College."

Wayne frowned. "I don't know about talking to Adam."

"Well, Brother Robbins said he wants to talk to you himself. I think he could help us figure out a way for you to go to Bible College."

Wayne felt a pleasant excitement in his chest. He saw himself preaching, bringing lost souls to repentance.

"Sonny, what was that in your prayer about Joe and Marilyn Eliot?"

He hesitated. "Well, Mama, this is confidential information. Your lips will have to be sealed."

She nodded, and pinched her lips together with thumb and forefinger.

"I believe that the Lord has seen fit to afflict Mr. Joe Eliot again."

"Lord have mercy!"

"You may well pray that, Mama. Although the Lord is merciful and slow to anger, he will reprove the wicked in order to turn him from his sinful ways. You know, Mama, the Eliots do not go to church."

"I thought they were Methodists."

"Well, yes, they belong to Memorial Methodist, but I hear tell they never attend. It is my belief that they have never truly repented their big sin."

"Well, Sonny, that was a long time ago, when Joe and Marilyn had to get married."

"Exactly my point, Mama. That was fornication, and you know what the Bible says about fornication." Wayne poured himself another glass of iced tea.

"Well, Sonny," his mother asked, "what exactly was the affliction?"

"Lips sealed?"

"The Lord is my witness."

Wayne told her what he heard Pete Mosley tell Dorothy, with the addition of a few dramatic details – "completely wrecked the tractor" and "was raving like a madman" and "had to put him in a strait jacket." By the time he finished, her eyes were bugged out and she had dropped the chicken bone on her plate. “Oh, may the Lord have mercy!”

“Amen.”

“I wish I'd known, I could have told Brother Robbins – in confidence, of course – just so he could be praying over this.”

“I'm sure he'll hear about it, Mama.”

“Well, if that don't beat the band,” she said. Then she reached out to grab his arm. “Oh, Sonny, that reminds me! I wanted to ask you what you thought!”

“About what, Mama? Is there dessert?”

“Yes, there's peach pie from last night. I'll just dish you up a piece.”

When she brought him his pie, she said, “Well, you know, sometimes I have to wait to get in to clean the church if Brother Robbins isn't there. They never used to lock the church until somebody stole the silver communion ware from the Presbyterians. Isn't it terrible, to steal from the church?”

“Sinful,” Wayne agreed.

“Well, this morning when I drove past Brother Robbins' house, his car wasn't in the driveway, so I knew that meant he was already at the church, and I wouldn't have to wait on him. I think, Sonny, I should just get a key from him, I'm there to clean every other Friday morning, so it makes sense I should have a key, don't you think so?”

“Go on, Mama, you were saying.”

“Oh, yes, I was saying, well, when I saw that his car wasn't at his house, I reckoned he would be at the church already and I could get right in, but what do you think? When I got to the church, his car wasn't there!”

“So you had to wait on him to get there?”

“No, and this is the interesting part. He *was* there. He said he left the car at home and walked to the church. In this heat. At his age. I hope it didn't hurt him. So then I thought well, Abel probably had the car, he's old enough to drive, but he says no, Abel and Seth are over to Gainesville to Bible Camp. So I'm wondering where his car could be. And then, Sonny, here comes Virgil Harmon delivering Brother Robbins' prescription, you know, for his heart condition. That's why I worry about him walking over to the church, God bless him. That's probably why Virgil delivers to Brother Robbins, doesn't want him to have to exert himself to come down to the drug store.”

Wayne waited as his mother drank more iced tea. “And you were saying, Mama?” he prompted.

“Oh, yes, well then, Virgil says he didn't think Brother Robbins was at the church because he didn't see his car there, and Brother Robbins says to Virgil same as he said to me, that he walked over to the church and left the car at home. And what do you think Virgil said then?”

"I don't know. What?"

"He said he saw Brother Robbins' car at the Woodsons' house. Now don't that beat all, after what you told me you saw on Tuesday?"

Wayne pondered. Tuesday before noon he had seen Mrs. Woodson driving her Cadillac out to the highway and there was somebody with her, and he had thought that somebody was Adam Robbins. The person was all scrunched down in the passenger seat, but it sure had looked like Adam. He and his mother had chewed over this information at supper but had concluded he must have been mistaken. The Woodsons were Methodists, and there wouldn't be any reason for Mrs. Woodson to be taking Adam somewhere.

"Brother Robbins was at church, and he said he left his car at home," he said slowly.

"That's right."

"But you noticed that the car wasn't at his house," he continued. "And then Virgil Harmon says that his car was at the Woodsons' house."

"That's exactly right. Now don't that beat all? Don't that just beat the band?"

~ ~ ~

Pat Eliot walked the quarter horse around the inner ring. She and Junior Thompson, her hired hand, looked him all over. "I think maybe he's a winner," she said.

"You gonna take him to race at Ruidoso?" Junior asked.

"I might just do that, Junior. Or Raton. I'll have to see what Spence thinks." She turned to Laura. "Spencer Ames over to Morgan has been working with him. He says he has promise."

Pat gave the horse a carrot and caressed his neck. "You're a good boy, Silverado. Come on, Laura, you can help me groom him in the stable. Say, Junior, you might as well go on to town and pick up that order at the feed store."

Junior picked his teeth. "Well, I could, but we don't really need it till next week. I can groom him."

"Nah, we'll take care of him. You go on to town now."

After Junior racketed off toward town in his old pickup, Pat led the horse back into the stable and put him in his stall. Laura followed. After removing the bridle and bit, Pat took a curry brush from the wall and handed it to the girl.

"Here, you remember how to do this." Pat guided Laura's hand to demonstrate the correct pressure on Silverado's glossy coat. "Just easy like that."

While Laura brushed, Pat rested her other hand lightly on the girl's neck.

"So what's this about you and my young nephew?" she asked.

"Jesse? We just went to the picture show."

"The drive-in?"

"No, the Royal. I'm not allowed to go to the drive-in."

"Do you like Jesse, Laura?"

"Oh, yes, Miss Eliot, he is really cute. All the girls think so."

"Did he get fresh with you?"

The girl ducked her head. "Like what?"

"Here, brush him down his flank. Oh, I don't know, like did he kiss you?"

"Well…yes."

"Is he a good kisser?"

"I don't know. I guess."

"How did he kiss you?"

Laura flushed. "Just the regular way, you know."

"Did he use his tongue?"

"Miss Eliot, Jesse is a nice boy!"

"Well, that's good, I'm sure his mama would be glad to hear that. So he didn't get fresh?"

"Well," Laura said.

"Come on, you can tell me. Did he use his tongue?"

Laura blinked. "Kind of."

"Did you like it?"

"Golly, Miss Eliot…"

Pat stroked the girl's cheek, then put her forefinger on Laura's lips, touching them lightly. "Laura, you are so beautiful," she breathed. "I just love you to pieces."

"Oh, Miss Eliot."

From outside came the sound of a car. Pat went quickly to open the stable door.

"Dorothy?"

Dorothy hauled herself out of the car and walked up to Pat. She looked beyond her and saw Laura. She chewed on her lower lip, then said, "Laura, could you please wait over at the house. We need to have a private talk."

"Sure, Miss Harmon."

"Surprised to see you," Pat said.

"I came out here to tell you that your brother has gone crazy again."

"What happened?"

Dorothy told Pat word for word what Pete had said. She then embellished, reciting previous events relating to Joe. She speculated about Marilyn. "So I think we need to go to Amarillo."

"Let's do it."

Dorothy shielded her eyes from the sun and looked at Pat, then to where Laura sat, and back to Pat.

"Something wrong?" Pat asked.

"I just..." Dorothy's voice trailed off.

"You been acting funny all morning."

"Sometimes, Pat, I wonder about you and these little high school girls."

"Now, Dorothy, you know you are my only true love."

Dorothy wavered among indignation, confusion, and pleasure. "Oh, phooey, Pat."

They stood together after Pat closed the stable door, Dorothy in flowered dress and high heels, Pat a head taller in worn Levi's and muddy boots. Pat grinned down at her. "You do look pretty today."

"Oh, Pat, you are the limit."

"Listen, I'll drop Laura at her house and meet you at home. We can go to Amarillo directly."

"Your clothes are filthy."

"I'll get cleaned up. Laura, come on, we're going back to town. Dorothy, you better gas up on your way home."

Pat started the pickup and peeled out of the gravel drive onto the road. She took a Pall Mall from her shirt pocket and pushed in the lighter on the dash.

"Is something wrong, Miss Eliot?"

Pat held the burning lighter to the tip of her cigarette. She took a long drag and flicked ashes out the window. "Wrong? Why would anything be wrong? Don't you worry your pretty little head. Everything's just fine."

~ ~ ~

"Jesse!" Pat strode behind the counter. "Listen, I just talked to your mama. They had to take your daddy to..."

"I know, Amarillo."

"Who told you?"

"Sheriff."

"Oh, okay. Well, I just talked to your mama in Amarillo. She is going to be there for awhile with your daddy, and she wants you to stay with us."

"I could stay at home."

Pat gripped his shirt collar. "Jesse, I told her you were going to stay at our house. End of story. Savvy?"

Jesse indicated that he savvied.

"Okay, that's settled," Pat said, relaxing her grip. "Now, chapter two. Dorothy and I are on our way to Amarillo right now. We won't be home until late tonight. Or if it gets too late, we'll stay over and come back tomorrow. So here's a key to the house."

Jesse took it.

"You got football practice tomorrow?"

"Yeah, six o'clock."

"There's an alarm clock in the guest room. You'd best set it in case we don't get home tonight. There's food in the fridge. You got money?"

"A little," Jesse said.

"Well, here's five bucks. You working late tonight?"

"Maybe."

"Okay, Jesse, I got to go. You want me to tell your mama anything? Or your daddy? No? All right."

After she left, Jesse smiled down at the key in his hand.

# CHAPTER THREE

Brother Robbins sat at his desk in the church office and wrote in his careful longhand: "…the devil-blinded, self-hardened condition attained in this life by the worst of men, who, in their willful, blasphemous and high-handed opposition to God and holiness, show that they are spiritually possessed by the devil. Beloved children of the Heavenly Father, let us pray that you may be spared the eternal death which is the consequence of Adam's sin, through the mercy and sacrifice of our Lord and Savior Jesus Christ, Amen."

He read the last sentence aloud, nodded with satisfaction, and put down his pen. He gathered into a neat stack the twelve hand-written sheets of paper which comprised his Sunday sermon and placed his O.C.B.C. glass paperweight on top. He closed the volume of Boyce and his Bible, bookmarked at the first chapter of Romans. Five o'clock. He switched off the desk lamp, stood and stretched. On his way out of the church, he paused briefly at the door to the chancel. Good, Sister Pickens had put new candles on the altar, and the candelabra gleamed in the dim light. Hymnals and Bibles stacked tidily at the end of each pew. Sister Pickens was a good steward in the house of the Lord. A virtuous woman, her price above rubies.

His brow furrowed as he recalled Mary Pickens' request that he talk with her son about the ministry. He stroked his chin, methodically turning Wayne Pickens over in his mind. He calculated that Wayne must be almost thirty. He had worked at Woodson's Department Store for a long time, even before Roy Woodson had bought it from Homer Hurst. Wayne hadn't served in the military. 4-F or something. Perhaps a little old to begin ministerial studies. Still, he seemed devout, faithful in his attendance at Sunday morning worship and Wednesday night prayer meeting. Quiet. Kept to himself. Didn't have a girlfriend, as far as Brother Robbins could tell. Nothing wrong in that. Marriage, while an honorable estate before God, was not required in a minister. If Wayne has kept himself chaste in order to serve God, so much the better.

Well, he would examine him, see what Wayne had to say for himself. He made a mental note to speak to Wayne after Sunday worship. He locked the church door and turned expectantly to the parking lot.

Where was his car? Oh, yes, he had walked over this morning. Dr. Lomax prescribed exercise. He had completely forgotten. Well, exercise was good for the body and possibly also for the soul. He strode through the parking lot out to the sidewalk.

What was that Virgil Harmon had said about his car? That he had seen it – not at his own home – but at the home of Mr. and Mrs. Roy Woodson. Surely Virgil was mistaken. There was no earthly reason for it to be there. It had been in the driveway this morning, and the keys were right here in his trouser pocket. Impossible. Seth and Abel wouldn't be home from Bible Camp until tomorrow. Virgil must have been mistaken.

Adam. Well, yes, Adam was home. He could have driven the car. There was another set of keys somewhere in the house. Adam could have taken the car. Well, that was all right, Adam had his license, was a good driver. Why shouldn't he take the car? But surely he would not have driven to the Woodsons' home. The Woodsons were fine people, but Methodists.

The subject of Methodism never failed to rouse Brother Robbins' indignation. It was his conviction that the Methodist church allowed people to believe and do whatever they wished. Don't believe in the Virgin Birth? Throw it out. Doubt the doctrine of election? Forget it! Want to get a divorce? Fine!

Quickened by his ire, he felt a sermon coming on. The Methodists held no firm convictions; they were namby-pamby Christians, tepid in the faith. They were…lukewarm. Yes, yes, "Because thou art lukewarm, I will spew thee out of my mouth." He would have to be subtle, though, it wouldn't do to take on the Methodists directly in a sermon, there were so many of them in town, and Reverend Dressler would likely hear about it and might take offense.

Well, he didn't want to offend Reverend Dressler, who was a fine man, if steeped in deplorable liberality. Therefore, the sermon would have to be a call to the pious, urging them to cling fervently to the principles of the faith. He would draw a distinction between those who cling fervently and those who are lukewarm. The congregation could draw its own conclusions.

"I will spew thee out of my mouth." That was from Revelation, but exactly which chapter couldn't recall. He would go straight to the concordance when he got home. Once he had the whole text, he could prepare the sermon Monday and preach it Wednesday night. Or if it turned out particularly powerful, he would save it for next Sunday.

He rounded the corner and strode briskly toward his home. There was the Packard in the driveway, exactly where he had left it. Virgil must have been seeing things. "Because thou art lukewarm, I will spew thee out of my mouth."

"Blessed afternoon, Adam," he said, finding his son in the living room, Bible in his lap.

"Blessed afternoon, Father. Did you have a good day?"

"Yes, yes. Adam, a Bible quiz."

"Yes sir?"

"Because thou art lukewarm, I will spew thee out of my mouth."

Adam grinned. "Revelation 3:16."

Better than a concordance, Brother Robbins thought contentedly.

~ ~ ~

Nadine sat at home in the recliner, her feet up, bourbon and water and cigarettes close by. She was bushed after twelve shampoos and sets, three colors, and six manicures. Tomorrow would be even busier.

Renee was holed up in her bedroom. Nadine wondered if she was planning to go out, and if so with which worthless boy. Renee seemed to collect boys with greased-back ducktails who sat sullenly in their hot rods, honking for her to come out. Regular hoodlums, Nadine thought.

However, on the bright side, Renee reported that she had helped Roy with the display window and that he had been pleased enough with her work to take her to the diner to eat. Nadine had noticed the window on her way home, and sure enough, it looked better than usual. So Renee was actually helping Roy. That was one worry off her mind.

A more major worry popped up to fill the space. Nadine kept meaning to have a talk with Renee. About boys and sex. There were things she needed to tell her. Should she tell her about birth control? Would that just put ideas into Renee's head? Nadine was pretty sure that Renee's head was already full of those ideas. She suspected that Renee had stopped wearing underwear. Nadine herself sometimes went without (she didn't like feeling confined), but Renee was too young. A 15-year-old ought to wear underwear. Especially on a date. Boys get the wrong idea. Especially boys from Gainesville in black leather jackets with that honky-tonk music blaring out of their car radios.

What if Renee got p.g.? Was Renee already going all the way? And if she was, would she have the sense to use a rubber? Not that a rubber worked every time – Renee herself was a rubber baby. Boy, if you could just take a pill to keep from getting pregnant. Should she take Renee to Doc Lomax and get her fitted for a diaphragm? Wouldn't that just encourage Renee to have sex?

Nadine sighed. I don't want to think about this. She drank from her glass and lighted a cigarette.

"Mama, I'm going now," Renee said.

"Renee, come here."

"What?"

Nadine gave her the once over. Renee wore a sleeveless red blouse, a red and yellow circle skirt over several stiffly starched petticoats, and Nadine's purple cinch belt. The combination looked good, even though they say red and purple clash. She's got a flair, Nadine thought. Her hair teased into a bouffant, wearing a ton of makeup, Renee could have passed for twenty-five.

"What?" Renee repeated.

"Where are you going?"

"Picture show."

"I hope not with any of those Gainesville boys."

"Relax, Mama, Jesse Eliot is taking me to the picture show."

That was a relief. Jesse struck Nadine as being a nice boy. "I didn't know you liked him."

"It's more he likes me," Renee said, patting her bouffant. "I thought he was dating Laura Tuttle."

Nadine took a closer look at Renee's chest. "Renee, you're not wearing a bra."

"So what?"

"So go put one on."

"Mama, I don't need one. I'm not that big. Plus, the straps cut into my shoulders."

"We'll have to get you some that fit. Now, tell me the truth, are you wearing underpants?"

Renee reddened. "I certainly am!"

"Promise?"

"Mama, I am! Swear on a stack of Bibles."

Nadine gave in. She wasn't going to ask to see. "Is Jesse picking you up?"

"Course. Here he is now."

Sure enough, through the picture window Nadine could see Jesse getting out of his 1939 Ford. He and his daddy had got the old car in running condition, and Jesse had painted it maroon and gold, the school colors.

Nadine called, "Come on in, Jesse."

"Howdy, Miz Coulter. Hi, Renee."

"Where y'all going?" Nadine asked.

"Picture show," he said.

"Which one?"

"Probably the Royal," Renee said.

"Renee, I want you home by ten-thirty. Jesse, you hear?"

"Yes, ma'am."

"Okay, Mama. Bye now."

They made a cute couple, Nadine thought. Jesse had his daddy's build and his mama's amazing eyelashes. And nice manners. Called her ma'am.

Out in the car, Jesse said, "We're not going to the Royal."

"I know, silly, but she doesn't need to know that."

"We're not going to the drive-in either."

"We're not? Where are we going?"

"Just wait and see. First we're going to Benny's to get something to eat. I'm starving. Then you'll see. It's a surprise."

She scooted next to him, thinking maybe she had a surprise for him, too.

Nadine drained her drink and lighted another cigarette. Seeing Renee and Jesse together set off a lonely longing. Wish I was all dressed up to go out with my boyfriend. Boyfriend, she snorted. Well, that'll never happen. Imagine what people would say if they saw us together! I'd probably be run out of town.

Maybe he'll call. Yearning tugged at her belly and a hot tingly memory played with her. She lay back in the recliner, cigarette forgotten in the ashtray, moving rhythmically as the fantasy became real, capturing her.

~ ~ ~

Coach Ray Parker sat at his desk in his little cubbyhole office at the high school gym, sweating and gnawing his fingernails. He thought he might have the flu, he felt so miserable. It was hard to catch a breath, and his chest hurt. His skin was clammy and his heart was pounding. Maybe I'm having a heart attack. The thought consoled him. He pictured himself in the hospital, at death's door, doctors and nurses hovering. A crowd of people clustering around his bed, Kathryn and the whole team in tears.

All those sons of bitches down at the diner, especially old Lloyd Tomlin and that jackass L.W. Foster, would be there, apologizing for calling him a sorry coach with a sorry team. The whole faculty and administration would be there. Mr. Pointer, the principal, and Mr. Arnold, the superintendent, those sour-faced old men who had never played a lick of football in their lives, who had criticized his coaching. They would beg his forgiveness. We didn't realize, we didn't know, they would say. Everybody would be pleading with him to live, to come back and coach the team again. Win or lose, Ray, you're our man! Without you, this town is nothing!

He was ashamed to feel so weak. He had never once been this scared fighting the Japs. Look, his hands were shaking. Maybe I'm having a nervous breakdown. He saw himself in a strait jacket, like poor old Joe Eliot, being carted off to Amarillo in the ambulance. No, he backtracked, heart attack was better. Nobody wants to visit poor old Joe in the hospital.

Now, Ray, he said to himself, there is no reason to be so scared now. Last year was last year. Got rid of those goddam seniors, thought they were too good to practice. Got a good offensive line and pretty good defense. And Jesse Eliot. Throws the football like his daddy did.

Never forget Joe and me in that game against Gainesville, it was colder than hell, the last quarter, we were behind 17-7, and Joe threw me that long pass all the way down field, right in my hands, and I took it in for a touchdown. Then it was 17-14, and only about two minutes to play, and they fumbled and we got the ball back again on their 35, and that time Joe just ran it in himself. 21-17, over Gainesville, and they were state champions three years in a row. I think that was the best night of my whole life.

I am glad I told Kathryn I wouldn't be home for supper. I can't stand her pity. She feels sorry for me, I can see it in her eyes. She thinks I'm pathetic. Hell, the whole town thinks I'm pathetic. If I had a gun, I'd shoot myself. Put the barrel in my mouth and pull the trigger and blow my head off. Then they'd be sorry, they'd be crying at my funeral. Oh, Ray, we never meant to call you a sorry coach with a sorry team.

Now, Ray, pull yourself together. It's a long time before our first game, and it's only with Sanford, we can certainly lick Sanford. They are the lousiest team in the district. We even beat Sanford last year. I hope I can count on Jesse. We'll see, tomorrow morning at six a.m., we'll see. He damn well better be there. Or I'll bench him, I swear I will. Well, maybe not bench him, but I swear I'll make him do a hundred push-ups. He has got to show up.

Who was that girl this morning? Was that Nadine's daughter? Man, has she grown up. Little flip tail. I saw him with his hands on her when I came in. He had better put his mind on football, not pussy. If I catch him with his pecker out, I'll cut it off, I swear I will. Pussy, it's all these boys ever think about. Telling jokes, swapping dirty pictures, jacking off.

He felt better, his mind easier, his body more relaxed. I'll go out and run some laps around the lake now. It was almost eight o'clock and much cooler. Then I'll go home, watch some TV, go to bed early. No, I better wait till Kathryn's asleep. She'll be after me, and I can't think about pussy during football season.

~ ~ ~

Supper dishes finished, Laura Tuttle found her father in the living room reading the newspaper. "Paper says Morgan got half an inch of rain, and we didn't get one drop," he commented.

"Do you want me to turn the sprinkler off?" she asked.

"I already did," he said.

"Where's Mama?"

"In her room." Cal put the paper down. "You made us a good supper. What are you doing tonight?"

Laura slumped against the sofa. "Nothing."

"You want to watch wrestling on television? You take the guy in white shorts, and we'll make a dime bet." He expected her to smile, but she didn't.

"I don't know. I thought I might listen to records."

From upstairs came the sound of mirthless laughter. Laura looked up the stairs. Cal said, as if he hadn't heard it, "What records?"

"Glenn Miller. Miss Eliot has a whole stack of albums from the '40's. She gave me two by Glenn Miller."

"Oh, yeah, 'In the Mood,' 'String of Pearls.'"

Laura was surprised. "Did you use to listen to Glenn Miller?"

"Honey, everybody used to listen to Glenn Miller. Especially during the war."

"Papa, tell me about the war."

"Well, you know, I wasn't in it. Deferred. It was bad though even at home. Rationing. Worrying."

"I remember when the war was over."

"Do you?"

"People hollered and sang and banged on pots and pans. Everybody was so happy. Even Mama."

There was a silence, broken by Janice's loud laughter upstairs.

Laura said, "In history class we talked about us dropping the bomb on Japan. I think it was the right thing to do."

"Well, lots of people think that. Others think the war would have ended without us doing that."

"Papa, are the Russians going to drop a bomb on us?"

"I surely hope not."

The sound of laughter rose and fell.

"What's she doing up there?" Laura asked.

"Laura, I don't know. Want me to go see?"

"No. I just wonder what's so funny."

"Laura, honey, sometimes people get sick in their bodies and sometimes they get sick in their minds."

"Like Jesse's daddy."

"What did you hear about Jesse's daddy?"

"Everybody at the grocery store was saying that he went crazy again. That they took him to Amarillo in the ambulance."

Cal winced. Word gets around, he thought. "Well, honey, Jesse's daddy can't help what happened. There is something wrong with his mind. He doesn't mean to go crazy, it just happens. In fact, he doesn't know he's gone crazy. He thinks he is fine. That's because his mind doesn't work right. When people get sick in their minds, they sometimes do things that make sense to them but don't make sense to anybody else. They can't help it."

Now go on, he told himself. Go on and talk to her about her mama. But Laura had risen, was wandering away from him.

"I think I'll go over to Miss Eliot's house."

"Honey, it's almost dark."

"I know, Papa, but it's not far. I just want to go somewhere."

"Okay, honey, but turn the porch light on. And don't stay too long."

She was already out the front door. More laughter from upstairs. Cal sighed. His thoughts wandered to Pat. Ever since she took riding lessons from her, Laura had liked to hang around Pat. Cal recalled when she and Dorothy moved from the ranch into town. Built their own house, fixed it up. Yard always looked good. Dorothy had a green thumb, grew flowers and vegetables. They had eaten some of Dorothy's tomatoes last year. Pat played golf better than most of the men out there on the little old nine-hole course out at the lake. He wondered why neither of them had ever gotten married.

Glenn Miller records. Music these days wasn't the same. He'd like to hear those songs again himself. Maybe when Laura got back.

~ ~ ~

Miss Eliot had said Laura could come over any time, she had a standing invitation. However, Laura wasn't absolutely sure about that. Miss Harmon seemed to be in a funny mood whenever Laura was there. Not exactly a bad mood, but funny, like she had been out at the ranch today.

Laura didn't know Miss Harmon well because she hadn't been in Miss Harmon's fourth grade class. She had been in Mrs. Dale's class. Laura had loved Mrs. Dale. In fact, she loved all her teachers, from Mrs. Wells in first grade on up. Once when her mama had to go back to the hospital, when Laura was in second grade, she had stayed with Mrs. Arnold, her teacher. It had been fun, sleeping and eating meals at Mr. and Mrs. Arnold's house. Mr. Arnold was superintendent of schools and always looked gruff, but it turned out he was nice. He taught Laura to play dominos. The three of them played dominos every night after supper. Laura was almost sorry when her mama came home.

All her teachers seemed to love her, probably because she was a good student. It was vital to Laura that her teachers love her. Once, in sixth grade, when she got a C on an arithmetic test, it about killed her when Miss Collier said, "Laura, I'm disappointed in you. You can do better than this." Laura had cried her eyes out that night, her heart broken because Miss Collier, whom she loved with all her heart, was disappointed in her. She worked hard on her arithmetic, and the next test she got an A. Miss Collier had beamed at her: "I knew you could do it!" Laura had been relieved no longer to be a disappointment.

Laura hugged to herself what Miss Eliot had said to her that afternoon. She said that she loved Laura, loved her to pieces. Well, Laura loved Miss Eliot to pieces. She loved spending time with Miss Eliot. Miss Eliot had taught her how to ride and although she rarely rode these days she loved going out to the ranch. And today had been really special. She had to admit she felt funny when Miss Eliot asked about Jesse. What questions! Did he get fresh? Did he kiss her? Was he a good kisser? Did he use his tongue? Laura blushed to remember it. It had been embarrassing. But it had been exciting, too. Miss Eliot's fingers on her lips made Laura feel all shivery.

Jesse. She had about died from pleasure when he asked her to go to the picture show. He was so cute and popular. All the girls wanted to go out with Jesse Eliot. But the evening got off to a bad start. He was irritated by her refusal to go to the drive-in. He said, "Your folks won't know if you go to the drive-in or to the Royal."

"But I would know," Laura said, "and I would feel guilty."

He called her a goody two-shoes, but he took her to the Royal. Afterwards, he parked out at the lake. At first it felt nice when he kissed her, but then he stuck his tongue in her mouth. When she pulled away, he drew her closer and put his hand over her breast. Panicky, she shoved him away. "Stop!"

"Okay, goody two-shoes," he said and drove her straight home. He didn't offer to walk her to the door, just sat looking disgusted while she got out. Then he floored it, tires squealing, as if he couldn't wait to get away from her.

At home, deflated, she agonized over his accusation. Was she a goody-two-shoes? She liked kissing, but she didn't like his tongue in her mouth. Was this what boys expected? Did other girls let boys use their tongues and touch their breasts? She had heard that Renee Coulter would let a boy do anything.

She came to the corner of Pecan Street where Miss Eliot lived and looked down the block. The house was dark.

When the street light illuminated the maroon and gold car coming around the corner, she almost cried out. It was Jesse! He was looking for her! He had probably come by her house and Papa had told him she was at Miss Eliot's. Jesse had come to find her! That proved he liked her!

The car pulled up in front of Miss Eliot's. She wanted to call out to him, tell him she was there on the corner, but then she saw Jesse put his arm around Renee Coulter and walk her into the darkened house.

"This is really a nice house." Renee paused inside the front door, taking in the velvet draperies, the brocade sofa and tufted armchair, the mahogany side table. She examined the bronze cowboy on the credenza. "This is beautiful."

"I guess. Come on back." He tried to lead her down the hallway.

"Wait a second." Renee lingered over a delicate figurine of a ballerina. "What is this? I have never seen anything like this."

"Do you want a beer?" Jesse asked.

"No. Golly, they have lots of beautiful things." She picked up a deep blue velvet pillow from the sofa and rubbed her cheek against it. "I love this color. Jesse, I love this house. Did your aunt decorate it herself?"

"How would I know? Come on, Renee."

"This is a real oil painting," she said, stopping to look at the still life on the wall.

"Renee, come on." Jesse turned off the living room lights and maneuvered her down the darkened hall.

"Is this your aunt's bedroom?" she asked, pausing at the first door and switching on the light. "I want to see it."

Renee skipped over to the bed, Jesse following in mute protest. She exclaimed over the brocade draperies, matching bedspread, and contrasting pillows. She slipped off her sandal to experience the dense carpet. "This is a gorgeous room!"

Jesse switched the light off and shoved her back into the hallway.

"Oh, my gosh, look at the little bathroom! It is darling!"

"Renee..."

"Show me Miss Harmon's bedroom, Jesse. I'll bet it's beautiful, too."

"The only bedroom I'm going to show you is this one." He propelled her into the guest bedroom and closed the door behind them.

"Well, turn on the light, Jesse."

"We don't need any lights."

"Jesse, I can't see a thing."

"You don't need to see."

He put his arms around her, found her mouth and kissed her. She had been hot as a firecracker in the car, all over him, but now she twisted away. "There's throw pillows on this bed, too," she said triumphantly. "Do they match the drapes? Jesse, turn on the light so I can see."

"Come on, Renee..."

Headlights swept across the front of the house as a car pulled into the driveway. Jesse started. "Oh, shit, they're back! God damn it!"

They froze in the dark bedroom as they listened to Pat and Dorothy entering the house. "Maybe he's asleep," came Dorothy's voice.

"I doubt it. Jesse, you here?"

Down the hall Pat bulled, turning on lights. She opened the door to the spare bedroom and flicked the switch. Jesse and Renee blinked at her.

Pat grinned broadly. "Well, well, well, Miss Renee Coulter. What a pleasant surprise."

# CHAPTER FOUR

Reverend William Dressler raised his hands in benediction over bowed heads at Memorial Methodist Church. "And now unto him that is able to keep you from falling, and to present you faultless before the presence of his glory with exceeding joy, be glory, both now and forever. Amen. We will close our worship with hymn 268, 'Are Ye Able, Said the Master.'"

An usher put his hand on Cal Tuttle's shoulder and whispered in his ear. Cal nodded and said to Laura, beside him in the pew, "I have to go. Can you get home okay?" She nodded. He moved quickly down the side aisle to leave the chancel. Six ushers hovered at the back of the church. One said, "Doc Lomax said it was urgent."

"Okay, thanks very much, gentlemen." What now? Not Joe Eliot; he was still in Amarillo. Janice? Anxiety cut a path through his innards. He and Laura had left Janice that morning at the kitchen table with coffee and a library book. Nerves twanging, he urged the pickup out to the Lomax Clinic.

Dr. Albert Lomax, short and big-bellied, met him at the door, pipe in his mouth and golf shoes on his feet. He came outside and shut the door behind him. "We got something here, Cal. I think we might ought to get L.W. out here, too." L.W. Foster was the County Attorney.

Not Janice. "What's going on, Doc?"

"It's a baby. Was a baby, now deceased."

"Whose baby?"

Doc puffed on his pipe. "Danny Tomlin's. And his girlfriend's."

"What happened?"

"I'm not altogether sure. Without an autopsy, I can't tell how she died. But it looks funny to me."

"You think..."

"Don't know what to think." Dr. Lomax wiped his face with his handkerchief. "Hot out here. I want to take you round back first so's you can see the baby."

They walked around the building to the back door. "Who all is here?" Cal asked.

"Danny's family, and Danny and the girlfriend. Lloyd came out to the golf course to get me. After I examined the baby, I decided I better call you."

Inside, Cal saw a small figure on an examining table under a sheet. Doc pulled the sheet back. They bent over the body of a baby, wearing a diaper and undershirt. Cal took a long look. "Can't see anything that looks like an injury. No bruises."

"Right, but look, see her eyes." He pulled one eyelid up. "See, bloodshot. And take a look at these little red spots around the eyes."

"What does that mean?"

"I'm just not sure. But somehow it doesn't look natural to me. She seems to have been in good health, normal weight. But, you know, Cal, in cases like this, I'm required to do an autopsy to determine the cause of death."

"Yeah." Cal straightened up. "Well, I guess I'd better talk to the parents."

Lloyd Tomlin, Danny's grandfather, and Daryl Tomlin, Danny's father, sat in the waiting room. Lloyd, a permanent fixture on the county council, lifted his hand in a little wave to Cal. Lloyd had recently retired, leaving his son Daryl to run Tomlin's Lumber Yard. Daryl was a youthful 40 with a crew-cut. Across the room stood a young woman Cal guessed to be Danny's girlfriend. Her yellow sundress showcased her voluptuous body. Dirty blonde hair partially shielded her face. Danny Tomlin stood in her general vicinity. Tall, handsome, and insolent, he methodically cracked his knuckles.

Cal had had many encounters with Danny over the past three or four years for speeding, two DWI's. About a year ago he caught Danny and two of his buddies breaking into Lamb's Cash-and-Carry at Four Corners. That had resulted in jail time.

Cal recalled that Danny had always been a problem. His parents, Daryl and Carolyn, had trouble controlling him. Even Lloyd, who was said to be partial to Danny, called him "hell on wheels." After numerous discipline problems in the Massey public schools, Danny had been sent away to a military school in Missouri, from which he was expelled. He hadn't finished high school and as far as Cal knew was unemployed.

The year before, Carolyn Tomlin divorced Daryl and moved from Massey to Santa Fe. Folks felt sorry for Daryl, but there was little sympathy in the community for Danny.

Cal heard that Danny and his girlfriend had a baby last winter and were living in a trailer on land Lloyd owned near Four Corners, but he had never seen the girlfriend or the baby. He figured that the Tomlins, as well as Carolyn's parents, Jim and Mavis Atkins, were all ashamed that there was a baby born out of wedlock.

"So, folks, if I could just get some information." Cal tried and failed to get eye contact with any of the four.

Daryl Tomlin leaned forward. "Jeannie called me this morning from the trailer. She said there was something wrong with the baby." Daryl paused and looked at Jeannie and Danny. "I didn't know what was wrong, but I thought Doc ought to have a look at the baby. So I decided to go out there."

"What did you find out when you got there?" Cal asked.

Daryl rubbed his mouth. "The baby was in the crib. I picked her up and..." He looked helplessly at Cal. "I put them all in my car and we came here."

Lloyd said, "Daryl called me, and I went out to the golf course to get Doc."

"Yeah, I was just finishing up," Doc said.

Cal asked, "Danny, what happened to your baby?"

Danny's shrug was eloquently insulting. "*I* don't know," he muttered.

Cal crossed the room to Jeannie. She shrank away from him, her eyes wild and her nose streaming. "Doc, could we get her some water?" Cal offered Jeannie his handkerchief. "Now, Jeannie, blow your nose and wipe your face. I need to ask you a few questions, okay?"

Dr. Lomax brought a glass of water which Jeannie gulped down. Cal took her by the arm and sat her down in a chair. He squatted down beside her and looked into her face. She looked away.

"Now, Jeannie, what happened to your baby?" he asked softly.

Daryl started to say something, and Danny muttered under his breath. Then Lloyd's deep voice rang out. "Hold on a minute, Cal. I think it would maybe be a good idea for us to have a lawyer here before anybody says anything else."

Cal looked up. "Why, sure, Lloyd. That's fine."

"I'll call Don Paulson," Daryl said. "Okay to use your phone, Doc?"

"Sure, Daryl, go ahead."

Cal stood up. "Daryl, why don't you tell Don to meet us at the court house. I would appreciate it if all of y'all would come on down to my office," Cal said. He lingered at the door, his hat in his hands. Nobody would look at him.

~ ~ ~

Brother Robbins stood at the big front door of the First Baptist Church, shaking hands with his flock. Encountering the fiery midday heat, most did not linger but got in their cars and drove away. When Brother Robbins went back inside, Mary Pickens took his hand.

"That was an inspired sermon," she said.

"Thank you, Sister."

"It was powerful. I felt the Lord was present."

"The Lord is always with us, Sister."

She pushed Wayne toward him. "Brother Robbins, I wonder if you would want to talk to Wayne now."

Blushing and sweating, Wayne heartily shook Brother Robbins' hand.

"Why, certainly. Wayne, your mother has been telling me about you."

"Yes, sir, thank you, sir," Wayne said.

"Why don't we go to my office and make an appointment for you to come and visit with me, Wayne?"

"I'd be grateful, sir." Wayne followed Brother Robbins down the aisle.

Mary Pickens smiled as she walked down the aisle, looking for discarded bulletins and misplaced hymnals.

"Why, Adam," she said. "I didn't have a chance to greet you."

"Hello, Mrs. Pickens. How are you?" Adam Robbins rose from the pew where he had been sitting with bowed head.

"I'm sorry, did I interrupt your prayers?"

"I was finished with my prayer, thank you, ma'am."

"You home now for awhile?"

"Yes, ma'am. I will return to my studies in the fall."

"My, my," she said, her bright eyes taking him in. "You're looking very well, Adam."

"Thank you, ma'am."

"I was saying to your father that it is very nice to have you home again, although I reckon Massey must seem pretty quiet to you, after living in the big city."

Adam hesitated. "It's always nice to be home."

"I expect you have many friends here, Adam?"

"Yes, ma'am. Friends from high school."

"Oh, I didn't mean only your high school friends, Adam. I expect there are many others here in town who are glad to see you."

"Yes, ma'am, I hope so. Well, it was nice to talk to you, Mrs. Pickens." Adam moved away. "I should go. I think my father may be waiting for me."

"Oh, no, Brother Robbins is speaking with Wayne in his office. You and I can chat while we wait on them."

Adam cleared his throat. "Well, how have you been, Mrs. Pickens?"

"Oh, I have been so busy. I said to Wayne I don't know where the time goes. You know I always clean the church every other Friday."

"Yes, ma'am."

"Friday I came over to clean the church and I thought your father wasn't here because I didn't see his car." She paused and twinkled at him. "But he *was* here after all. He told me he had walked over here that morning."

"Yes, ma'am. The doctor suggested that he get more exercise."

"That's what he said. I suppose he also wanted to leave the car free for you, Adam."

Adam was silent.

"I wish Wayne would learn to drive," she went on. "Somehow he just never wanted to learn. But you drive, don't you, Adam?"

"Yes, ma'am."

"I thought you did, but I wasn't sure. Well, that would explain it."

"Ma'am?"

"Oh, nothing really, Adam. I was just trying to unravel a little mystery."

Adam started to turn away from her, but she detained him with her voice. "Now Bible College is in Oklahoma City, isn't it?"

"Yes, ma'am. That's right."

"I have never been to Oklahoma City. Just wondering how it compares with Amarillo. You are familiar with Amarillo, aren't you, Adam?"

Adam slapped his forehead. "Oh, I just recalled something I forgot. I'd better take care of it now. Good bye, Mrs. Pickens." He backed away from her to the end of the pew and walked swiftly along the side aisle to the front of the church.

"Always nice to talk with you, Adam," she called after him. "Welcome home."

~ ~ ~

The Hotel Worth Coffee Shop was brimming over, mostly with Methodists and Presbyterians fresh from church. The few Baptists there had either missed or disregarded Brother Robbins' sermon concerning the dubious practice of dining away from home, "where no one says grace and the Lord is forgotten."

Gentlemen in dark suits and colorful ties left their hats on a rack at the door. Ladies in summer hats were happy not to be in their hot kitchens. Children were delighted by the cafeteria line, where you could take more than one dessert if your folks didn't notice. People pushed their trays and loaded their plates from steaming pans filled with slabs of chicken fried steak, fried chicken, and roast beef. Next came trays of mashed potatoes, gravy, okra, snap beans, and corn on the cob. There were dishes of coleslaw and saucers of quivering Jello with canned fruit suspended inside. An amazing selection of desserts: peach, coconut cream, and chocolate pies, devil's food and angel food cakes, and chocolate and tapioca puddings. People took large sweating glasses of iced tea or lemonade, paid the cashier, and made their way to tables of four or six set with napkins, flatware and condiments.

It was a time for families and friends to visit. Crowded around a table for six were Roy and Maureen Woodson, Marilyn Eliot, Pat Eliot, Dorothy Harmon, Virgil Harmon, and Jesse Eliot. At the next table were Mayor Collier and his wife and Jim and Mavis Atkins. Jim owned an insurance company, and the Mayor was in real estate. The room rang with conversation. Jim Atkins and Vance Collier discussed needed improvements to the golf course, with Pat Eliot chiming in. Mavis Atkins complimented Maureen Woodson on her outfit.

Virgil Harmon sat next to Marilyn Eliot. "When are they going to let Joe come home?" he asked.

Before Marilyn could answer, Maureen said, "We just don't know yet, Virgil."

"Have you talked to the doctor?" he asked Marilyn.

"No, we haven't." Maureen's flinty stare didn't deter Virgil.

"Is it Dr. Siegel?" he persisted, looking at Marilyn.

"Yes," she answered.

"I hear he's very good," Virgil said.

"We appreciate your concern," Maureen said repressively.

"If there's anything you need, Marilyn," he said, "anything at all."

"We are just fine, thank you so much," Maureen snapped.

Marilyn's eyes were wet. "Thank you, Virgil," she whispered.

"How's the football team, Jesse?" Roy Woodson called across the table.

Jesse paused from shoveling chocolate pudding into his mouth. "We had practice again yesterday morning."

"Which you would have missed if I hadn't hauled you out of bed," Pat boomed, cuffing her nephew's arm.

"I hope to heck you boys can do better this year," Vance Collier put in. "Last year was just pitiful."

"Is Coach Parker starting you at quarterback?" Virgil asked.

"How's the defense?" Jim Atkins asked. "I guess anything would be an improvement over last year."

Jesse ducked his head. "We're gonna work real hard," he mumbled into his pudding.

"Well," Pat said, lighting a cigarette and stretching her legs out to the side of the table, "Coach has got his work cut out for him. My opinion, Jesse will do okay, if he gets any kind of blocking at all."

"I remember your daddy playing football," Virgil said to Jesse and then addressed the table. "You all recall that game against Gainesville, when Joe threw that pass to Ray Parker?"

There was enthusiastic assent from the men, Pat, and Marilyn. Jesse looked up, interested for the first time. "My dad and Coach Parker were on the same team?"

"Boy, they *were* the team," Pat said.

"Gainesville thought they were going to be state champions again, but we knocked them out of first place," Virgil confirmed.

"We were the underdogs, but we fought tooth and toenail to win," Pat crowed.

A suddenly animated Marilyn called across the table to Jesse, "What I remember is how cold it was that night! We cheerleaders were freezing! But then we stopped noticing the cold, we were cheering so hard."

"What was the score?" Jesse asked.

"Twenty-one to seventeen," chorused Virgil, Pat, and Marilyn.

"We were behind 17-7, and it was the last quarter," Virgil continued. "Joe threw that Hail Mary..."

"Right into Ray's hands," Pat continued. "We got the extra point and then after the kickoff, Gainesville fumbled."

"And Joe ran it in and it was 21-17, and time ran out," finished Virgil.

"I never cheered so hard in my life," Marilyn said.

"We carried Joe and Ray off the field on our shoulders," Virgil said.

Marilyn's face glowed. "I will never forget that night," she said, and her eyes rested on Jesse.

Pat leaned over to stub out her cigarette. "Those were the days, young man," she said, slapping Jesse on the back, "those were the days."

~ ~ ~

Cal locked up his office and walked out to his pickup. It was still hot, and he was tired and hungry. It had been a long frustrating afternoon. He hadn't been able to reach L.W. Foster. With attorney Don Paulson objecting to almost everything he asked, Cal had learned nothing more about what had happened to the baby. Jeannie and Danny had given almost identical statements, without any explanation of how the baby came to die. All they said was that the baby had been fine in the night and that they had discovered her in the crib this morning, not moving, not breathing, and that Jeannie had called Daryl.

Cal mightily wished he had been able to question Jeannie alone. By the time everyone arrived at the court house, Jeannie had pulled herself together and seemed walled off. She wouldn't even look at him. She was the key to this, Cal was sure, but it didn't look like she wasn't going to say anything. There wasn't anything more he could do until after Doc performed an autopsy and he could talk to L.W. Foster about a hearing.

Cal puzzled over Danny and Jeannie, living way out in the country in a trailer. He wondered why they hadn't gotten married, like most people did with a baby on the way. He had learned that Jeannie's last name was Backus, that she was 18, and that her folks lived in Sanford. Jeannie said she had been waitressing at the Steak House Saturday night. She said she had come home about ten and that the baby was fine then. Danny said he had given the baby her bottle and put her to bed about eight. They both insisted that they had no idea what happened to the baby to cause it to die.

The thought of the baby girl lying dead on the table at Doc's clinic filled Cal with pity and despair. He drove home, feeling worn out.

❧ ❧ ❧

Daryl parked his car in front of Benny's, and he and Danny and Jeannie walked in and took a booth. The waitress came over, her pen poised over her book. "What can I get y'all?"

"Double burger, fries, chocolate shake," Danny said.

Daryl said, "Regular burger, fries, and Coke." He nodded toward Jeannie. "Jeannie, how about you?"

"I'm not hungry," she said.

"Come on, you got to eat something. How about a burger?"

She shrugged. He said to the waitress, "Bring her a regular burger, fries, and a Coke."

He turned in his seat toward Danny. "Now, Danny, I want you to show up for work tomorrow morning."

Danny stared out the window.

Daryl continued in a low, insistent voice, "You got to straighten yourself out. If there's any more questioning, you understand what I mean, Danny, you need to be able to answer that you're working steady now."

No answer.

"Danny, I am talking to you."

"I heard you," he said. He cracked his knuckles, one by one.

They sat without speaking until the food arrived. Danny wolfed his burger and thrust handfuls of fries into his mouth. Jeannie drank some Coke but left her burger and fries untouched.

Danny asked, "You going to eat that?"

She shook her head. He pulled her basket of burger and fries in front of him.

No one spoke during the twenty minute ride to the trailer. Daryl parked beside Danny's Chevy. He said, "When I get home, I'm going to call your mother, Danny. Probably she will want to come out here."

Danny shrugged.

"Now, Jeannie," Daryl said, "you be all right? You want to go down to Sanford, spend some time with your folks?"

"Maybe," she said.

"You just let me know. I can take you. You maybe want to go there for awhile."

"Maybe. I don't know," she said.

"You just let me know, okay?"

"Okay."

"Now, Danny, I mean it, I want to see you at the lumber yard at nine o'clock tomorrow morning. You can help Eldon."

"Yeah, okay," Danny said.

Daryl climbed in the car and drove down the dusty road to the highway.

~ ~ ~

"What's for supper?" Renee asked.

"I could make pancakes. With maple syrup. And bacon. What do you say?"

"I say yes," Renee said. Nadine put her magazine down and went into the kitchen to make the pancakes. Soon the smell of frying bacon drew Renee into the kitchen. Renee laughed when Nadine flipped a pancake in the air.

Nadine dished up their plates and they ate for awhile before she said, "I have to congratulate you. You got home way before your curfew last night."

Renee put her fork down. "I swear, boys can be so dumb!"

"You can say that again," Nadine agreed.

"I really mean it. Jesse is the dumbest."

"Why do you say that?"

Renee considered, her head on one side. "Well," she began, "you know about what happened with Jesse's daddy."

"Yeah, I heard they had to take Joe to the hospital in Amarillo."

"So Jesse was staying with his aunt. You know, Miss Eliot."

"Yeah? And?"

"So he wanted to take me over to show me her house."

"Were they home?"

"Uh…"

"No need trying to think up a lie, Renee. When Dorothy cancelled her appointment with me, she said they were going to Amarillo."

"Well, I didn't know that," Renee said, but without aggression. "I thought he was just going to show me their house."

Nadine's eyes narrowed. "Right, I'm sure real estate was tops on Jesse's mind."

"Yes," Renee said, chin out, "that's right, to show me their house. But turns out they weren't home when we got there. They weren't back from Amarillo."

"You mean you and Jesse went inside their house, when you knew they weren't at home?"

"Have you ever been to their house?" Renee sidestepped.

"No, but…"

"You ought to see it. It is beautiful. You should see the furniture and the drapes. The bedspread matches the drapes and there are little matching pillows."

"Renee, what were you doing in the bedroom?"

Renee tossed her head. "Just looking."

"Right. At night. With Jesse. Just looking."

"I was! Anyway, Miss Eliot and Miss Harmon came home right after we got there. And they were real nice. Miss Eliot especially. She gave me a ride home."

"Why didn't Jesse bring you home?"

"Yeah, that's the point. Miss Eliot seemed real glad to see me, but she told Jesse he had to go straight to bed because of football practice. Then she said she'd drive me home. She was real friendly to me."

"She found you and Jesse in a bedroom?"

"Well, yes, but we weren't doing anything."

"What were you doing in a bedroom, Renee?"

"We didn't *do* anything. Honest." Renee cleared the table. "Boys are so dumb!"

"Listen, Renee, I don't want you going into any bedrooms with any boys. You hear me?"

"I hear you." Renee looked at her mother. "Was my daddy a dumb boy?"

Surprised, Nadine turned toward her. "Your daddy? Why no, baby, your daddy was the exception to the rule."

"Mama, do you ever think about him?"

Nadine's face grew soft and unguarded. "Why, sure I do. Do you?"

"Well, I sort of wonder about where he is now."

"Yeah, me, too."

"I wish," Renee said, chin quivering, "I just wish he hadn't left us."

"Oh, honey, he just wasn't cut out to be married and raise a family. I didn't altogether blame him." Nadine reached over to pat Renee's hand.

"He was really handsome, wasn't he?"

"Handsome! He was the handsomest man I ever saw, bar none."

"Better looking than Tab Hunter?"

"Honey, your daddy was more the Rock Hudson type."

"Mama, tell me more about him."

"Okay," Nadine agreed. "What do you want to know?"

The telephone rang, and Renee picked up the receiver. "Hello. No, this is her daughter. Just a minute." She handed the phone to Nadine with a shrug.

Nadine cradled the receiver between ear and shoulder as she lighted a cigarette. "Hello? Just a minute. Renee, go outside and turn off the sprinkler."

She watched Renee go, then said, "Well, I thought you died."

"Oh, you're mad."

"I am not mad."

"Well, that's good. What are you doing?"

"Nothing."

"Good. Let's get together."

"Tonight? Now?"

"I've missed you."

"Where?"

"You know where. Fifteen minutes."

"Okay," Nadine said. "But be…"

"What?"

"Careful. It wouldn't do for anybody to see you."

"I'm always careful."

Nadine stubbed out the fresh cigarette in the ashtray and threw off her apron.

"Hey, where are you?" Renee called.

Nadine was in her bedroom, brushing her hair and checking her makeup. "Honey, I have to go out."

"Go out? Now? What for? Who was that on the phone?"

"Nobody. I've got to go down to the shop and take care of something. I clean forgot about it and it won't wait. I'll be back soon."

She sped downtown and parked in the alley behind the beauty shop. She let herself into the building, leaving the back door ajar. It was pitch black inside her shop and it took a minute to find and turn on the little lamp in the back room. She cleared the couch of some magazines and the sack of chemicals Virgil had brought her, then took the little atomizer from the shelf and sprayed perfume on her pulse points. She ran her fingers through her hair. Her body felt pleasantly agitated and alive.

She heard the soft rattle of the back door and watched a shadow walk toward her. She melted into his embrace and opened her mouth to welcome his tongue. He led her to the couch, his hands stroking her.

"Hi, Nadine."

"Hi, Adam."

~ ~ ~

After, when she got up to fetch her cigarettes, Nadine said, "So, what have you been up to since you got home?"

"Not much. Come back over here."

She moved closer but did not lie down beside him. "You trying to make me jealous?"

"Jealous? Of what?"

"Not of what. Of who."

"Come on, lie down beside me."

"Adam, I know what you've been up to."

He gave a short laugh. "What do you mean, what I've been up to?"

"You were over at Maureen Woodson's Friday, weren't you?"

The laugh died out when she continued, "It's all over town. You took your daddy's car and parked it in front of her house."

"I did no such thing." He rose on one elbow. "I don't know where you heard that, but it's not true."

"People talk, and I know for sure it is true."

"Which people?"

"People have even been talking about it to your daddy. Mary Pickens, for one."

Adam looked alarmed. "How do you know this?"

"It's not that I know, you dummy. The whole town knows by now. But my question is, what the hell do you think you're doing screwing Maureen Woodson?"

~ ~ ~

Daryl Tomlin gripped the telephone. It was almost eleven o'clock, and he had been trying to reach his ex-wife for hours. On the fifth ring, Carolyn answered.

"Hello?"

It always surprised him how the sound of her voice could still bring on that familiar loss and longing lodged in the pit of his stomach.

"Hi, it's me."

"Daryl?"

" I've been trying to get you all evening."

"I just got in this minute."

"Are you alone?"

"Daryl, mind your own beeswax."

"Something's happened. I need to know if I've got your full attention."

"You have my attention. What's wrong?"

"It's Danny."

"What? Is he all right? Is he hurt?"

"He's not hurt. But something happened to the baby."

"To the baby? To Danny's baby?"

"Carolyn, the baby died."

"Died? Was she sick? I never even got to see her."

"Whose fault is that?" Daryl snapped. "You could have come home anytime to see her if you had wanted to."

"Daryl, I have been busy. You always seem to think I can just drop everything. I was intending to come maybe next month."

"You keep saying that, Carolyn. You say you'll come, but you don't."

"Daryl, what I do is my business. You don't own me any more."

Daryl wrenched himself away from the painful pleasure of participating in the old quarrel. He knew everything she was going to say before she said it, and he guessed she probably knew all his lines too. They had been reading each other's minds for years. He could picture her now, holding the phone. She would have removed her earring so she could hold the receiver close to her ear. He could see her long slender fingers playing with the earring. He could see her smoky hair, her eyes, sometimes green, sometimes blue. He could almost smell her. He ached with need.

"Carolyn, you need to come home. You need to talk to Danny."

"What happened to the baby?"

"I don't know. Jeannie called me this morning in hysterics and said the baby wasn't breathing. So I went out to the trailer to see, and she was right, the baby wasn't breathing. I felt her. She was cold. She was dead."

"Oh my Lord, Daryl!"

Her attention and emotion brought him pleasure. "So I put Danny and Jeannie and the baby in the car and brought them to the clinic. Doc looked at her and then he called Cal Tuttle and..."

"Called Cal Tuttle? Why did he do that?"

"Yeah, that's the point. We all ended up at the court house, giving statements."

"Statements? What kind of statements?"

"Statements to Cal, Carolyn, about what happened to the baby."

"Oh, my Lord. Did you think to have a lawyer with you?"

"Sure. Don Paulson was there."

"Well, thank God for that. They didn't keep Danny, did they?"

"No, I took him and Jeannie back out to the trailer this afternoon. I told him to come to work tomorrow. He's got to straighten himself out. Carolyn, you need to come home. He'll listen to you."

"Did you tell my folks?"

"Not yet. I wanted to tell you first."

"Do your folks know?"

"Yeah. Lloyd met us at Doc's. He went to the court house with us. I talked to Florence this afternoon."

"Are your folks upset?"

"Carolyn, we are all upset."

"Do they blame me?"

Her sudden insecurity surprised him. She had tried to make Lloyd and Florence understand her reasons for leaving. Daryl didn't know exactly what had transpired, but the meeting hadn't gone well. Now his parents never spoke her name. Loyal to him, he guessed.

"Nobody blames you, Carolyn," he lied.

"They do. They think I'm terrible."

"Nobody thinks that, Carolyn," he said soothingly. He could hear her crying. "Don't cry, honey."

She blew her nose. "What's going to happen now?"

"Well, there's going to be an autopsy."

"Oh, my God."

"But, listen, Don Paulson says even if the autopsy shows that the baby was…that the baby didn't die of natural causes, that doesn't necessarily mean they would have reason to charge Danny with…anything."

"Did you see the baby?"

"I told you, I went out there. Yes, I saw her, I held her."

"What did she look like? Did she look like…was she…hurt?"

"No, she looked fine."

"What did Danny say about it?"

"He didn't say anything to me."

"I mean to Cal."

"He just said that he gave the baby a bottle and put her to bed last night about eight, and that she was fine then."

"Where was Jeannie?"

"Waitressing at the Steak House."

"What did she say?"

"She told Cal that she got home about ten and that the baby was fine."

"Did she say anything more to you?"

"Not really."

"Daryl, I'm going to call Daddy. I think we probably need to get a different lawyer."

"Well, Don seemed to think…"

"Don Paulson is a nice man, Daryl, but he's not the smartest person in the world. Daddy will know of a lawyer in Amarillo. Daddy will know what we should do."

"Carolyn, will you please come home?"

"Maybe tomorrow. Daryl, don't you talk to anybody about this."

"I won't. Carolyn, you can stay here with me."

"I will stay with my folks. I'm going to hang up now and call Daddy."

"Okay. I'll see you tomorrow. Thank you. Carolyn, I love you."

The phone clicked in his ear. He wasn't thrilled about getting Jim Atkins involved in this, but Carolyn was probably right that her daddy would know what to do. He walked around the house, buoyed. She was coming home.

In Santa Fe, the man put his arms around Carolyn. "What's the matter?"

"Trouble," she said.

He kissed her neck and unbuttoned her blouse. "What kind of trouble?"

She let him touch her for a minute, then pushed him away. "I've got to make a phone call, Johnny. You wait for me in the bedroom."

"Okay, but don't be too long."

She smiled. "Go on, now. Light some candles for us, okay?"

He disappeared into the bedroom, pulling at the knot of his tie.

She turned back to the phone and dialed. It rang and rang.

"Daddy? Did I wake you? I'm sorry. Daddy, I need your help."

"Where are you going?" Jeannie asked.

"None of your business," Danny replied.

"It's after eleven."

"Your daddy said…"

"Shut up."

"You go to town tonight, get in trouble, then what?"

"It's not your business what I do."

"Your daddy told you to straighten up."

"Get off my back, Jeannie." He opened the door to the trailer.

"I can say whatever I want to."

He turned to her, his face twisted with anger. "You little tramp, I got no reason to be with you now. You might as well go on back to Sanford. Start whoring again."

"Maybe people might think you did something to the baby," she said to his departing back.

He was in front of her in a flash, grabbing her by the elbows, standing her up to face him. He shook her, and her head snapped back.

"Stop, Danny, that hurts!"

"Listen to me," he said, forcing her to face him. "You were the one..."

"No, you..."

He let her go. He began to crack his knuckles, one by one. He paced around the little trailer. She dropped into a chair, rubbed her elbows, gave him a defiant stare.

"Ah, look, Jeannie," he said finally. "We shouldn't fight."

She didn't answer.

"Come on, Jeannie. I didn't mean it. You and me, we're together for always."

"I was not a whore," she said.

"I know. I didn't mean that. I was just mad. Come on, Jeannie, give me a smile."

"Are you going to town?"

"Nah, I changed my mind. Too late. Come on, let's go to bed."

He shut the door and turned off the overhead light. She could hear the bedsprings creak. He grunted with the effort of taking his boots off, and they bumped on the floor as he flung them away. More noises as he got out of his Levi's and shirt. The bedsprings groaned under his full weight.

"Jeannie, come on now. Don't be mad. Come on to bed."

Jeannie sat in the dark, thinking.

# CHAPTER FIVE

Monday morning, Wayne Pickens stood looking out Woodson's front door, musing on his meeting with Brother Robbins. Although he had been over it many times in his mind and with his mother, he loved recollecting the whole event, start to finish.

Brother Robbins had taken him into his office and picked up a book from his desk. "Wayne," he told him, "this book was written in 1887 by the sainted Reverend Doctor James Boyce. For many years this book was the underpinning of our faith, next only to the Holy Scriptures. Through the devil's work, it fell into disuse for awhile, but now it has been restored to the faithful. Take it, Wayne, and open it to any page."

The book was heavy, supple and fragile, its leather binding tattered. Wayne carefully opened it. "Read what you see," Brother Robbins told him.

Wayne looked at the words and read aloud, in what he hoped was a preacherly tone: "Corruption can only be removed by a cleansing of human nature sufficient to root out all taint of sin and to restore a holy disposition and habits."

Brother Robbins interrupted him. "Exactly! You see, Wayne, it is a holy book, just like the Bible. A man can open it anywhere and receive divine wisdom. Read it again." Brother Robbins placed his fingertips to his forehead in an attitude of concentration.

"Corruption can only be removed by a cleansing of human nature sufficient to root out all taint of sin and to restore a holy disposition and habits."

"It is indeed prophetic, Wayne, that you should choose that sentence, for its beautiful simplicity sums up the duties of the ministry. We are called to remove corruption, to cleanse human nature, to root out sin, and to restore, to restore..."

"A holy disposition and habits," Wayne finished helpfully.

"Amen!" Brother Robbins took the book from Wayne and looked at the sentence himself, his lips moving over the words.

"I want you to stay after prayer meeting on Wednesday night, Wayne," he said, making a mark on his calendar. "At that time I will examine you."

"Yes sir."

He gripped Wayne's shoulder. "May the Lord bless and keep you, Wayne."

"Yes sir, thank you, Brother Robbins, I am most grateful."

Wayne had left Brother Robbins' office in a state bordering on ecstasy. He could picture himself removing corruption, cleansing human nature, rooting out sin.

"Hi, Wayne." The voice from behind him caused him to jump.

"Good morning, Renee." He began to straighten the men's dress shirts.

"You never mentioned the window me and Mr. Woodson fixed," she said.

"Didn't I?"

"No, you didn't. Don't you like it?"

Wayne gave the window a brief glance. "It seems fine, Renee."

"Mr. Woodson said he couldn't have done it without me."

Wayne kept silent. He had certainly noticed that Mr. Woodson hadn't asked him to help with the window display. He had also noticed that Mr. Woodson had taken Renee to the diner to reward her work. Mr. Woodson had never taken him to the diner, not once in all the time he had worked for him. Wayne thought of himself as the store's manager, even though Mr. Woodson called him a clerk. Who opened up every morning? Who put price tags on the new merchandise? Who swept the floors with sawdust every night? Who watched to see that no one was stealing? And how had he been rewarded? Mr. Woodson had asked Renee to help him with the window display and had taken her to the diner. Why, she was just a high school student, only summer help.

Wayne struggled to preserve his good mood. He reminded himself that working at Woodson's was only temporary. He would soon be leaving to go to Bible College. He would be a preacher, removing corruption, rooting out sin. Speaking of sin, he noticed how trashy Renee looked with her big red hair, her painted fingernails, her too-tight blouse. Suddenly it struck him that the Lord was giving him an opportunity here, to convert Renee, to – what was it? – to restore her to holy habits.

"Wayne," Renee said, "you go to the Baptist Church, don't you?"

It was prophetic. She was bringing up the subject herself. She was ready to be saved, and he was just the man to do it.

"Yes, I do, Renee. Why do you ask?"

"Oh, no reason," she said, playing with her hair. "I was just wondering."

Careful, careful, Wayne thought to himself. I have to be subtle. "Do you go to church, Renee?"

"Not regular."

"Renee, have you been baptized?"

"I don't know."

He considered how to proceed. He wanted to ease her into a confession of her sinful life. That would lead her to the necessity for cleansing. When she became convinced of her corruption, he could then proclaim the gospel to her. He would save her soul, and she would be forever thankful. He could see her in the baptismal pool, lying back gratefully in his arms while he submerged her.

"You know Adam Robbins, don't you?" she asked.

"Course I do."

"I thought I saw him the other day. Is he home for the summer?"

The vision of the baptism vanished. Wayne licked his lips, recalling the discussion with his mother over supper. She reported word for word her conversation with Adam. They were thoroughly convinced that there was hanky-panky going on between Adam and Mrs. Woodson. Wayne visualized the ensuing drama. He would inform Mr. Woodson about his wife's infidelity. Mr. Woodson, filled with gratitude, would make him manager and give him a raise. Adam would be exposed as a hypocrite and a sinner. Brother Robbins would disown Adam and take Wayne for his own spiritual son. He would pass on that holy book to Wayne. Wayne would be glorified and Adam would be disgraced.

Converting Renee Coulter and exposing Adam Robbins vied for supremacy in Wayne's mind, and Adam's fall won out.

Even greater subtlety was now required. Where had Renee seen Adam? That could be the key to his investigation. She said she thought she had seen him. Had she seen him scrunched down in the passenger seat of Mrs. Woodson's Cadillac? Or getting out of his daddy's car and going into Mrs. Woodson's house?

"Where exactly was he when you thought you saw him?" Wayne asked.

"Just around, Wayne," Renee answered with irritation.

Wayne could barely contain his excitement. If only he could get Renee to say that she had seen Adam in a compromising position with Mrs. Woodson. "Was he in a car?" he asked, craftily.

Renee, frowning, shook her head.

"Well, where was he then?"

"What does it matter, Wayne? I was just asking a simple question." She moved away toward the back of the store. He started after her, but the bell jingled and a customer came through the front door. Defeated! But there would be other opportunites.

He is such a creep, Renee thought. Restlessly, she straightened the ticket books on the counter by the cash register. She thought about going to the Post Office, but it was way too early for there to be any mail. She was definitely not going to the drug store, not after what happened at Miss Eliot's house.

Jesse looked like an ashamed little boy when Miss Eliot came steaming down the hall and found them. But Miss Eliot was so nice about it. Driving Renee home she had been completely pleasant. Renee asked her about the way her house was decorated, but Miss Eliot didn't seem interested in that.

Renee couldn't really blame Jesse for being embarrassed, standing there in the bedroom with her. But did he have to act like such a baby? She thought he was going to start bawling. He didn't even say goodbye, just turned away, his face all red and screwed up. She was through dating high school boys. They were dumber than dirt.

~ ~ ~

Jesse's face tightened into a frown when his mother came into the drugstore. Marilyn sat on a stool in front of him. "Jesse, I need to tell you I am going back to Amarillo. They are going to keep your daddy there for awhile. I may stay for a few days."

He shrugged and wiped the counter with a rag.

"Now, you're going to stay with Pat and Dorothy, right?"

Jesse shifted from one foot to the other. "I'd rather stay out at the farm."

"I'll feel better knowing that you're at Pat's."

"Aw, Mama."

"Pat said you could stay as long as I'm gone."

Jesse wanted to tell her that he couldn't stand to stay there one more day. Pat kept on making sly remarks about Renee. It had been humiliating getting caught, and Pat's joking made it ten times worse. He couldn't figure out why she seemed so tickled that she had found him with Renee.

"Aw, Mama, I'll be okay out at the farm."

"Jesse, I want you to promise me you will stay with Pat. I don't want to have to worry about you."

She looked so pitiful, he caved in. "Okay, okay," he said, taking out his frustration on the counter.

"You want me to tell your daddy anything from you?"

He shook his head.

"You sure?"

He glared at her. What more did she want from him?

Marilyn slid off the stool. "Okay, well, then I'll let you know when I'll be back."

No answer.

"Jesse," she said, "pretty soon all this will pass, and we'll be back to normal. You mustn't worry; he's going to be just fine."

He is the least of my worries, Jesse thought.

"Is Virgil here?"

"I think he's in the back." Jesse turned away from her.

She went back to the pharmacy and called, "Virgil? You here?"

He appeared from the back and beamed at her.

"Virgil, I want to thank you for cleaning up out at the farm," she said warmly.

"That's okay," he said, pleased and embarrassed in equal parts.

"Really, it just means the world to me what you all did out there. I couldn't believe it when Roy took me out there this morning. I thought it was still going to be a big mess."

"It wasn't any trouble. Mostly Pete's idea. He got some of his buddies to help."

"I'm on my way over to the court house to thank Pete in person. Virgil, I'm going to tell Joe what you all did. If he's in any shape to understand."

"Are you going to Amarillo today?"

"Right after I see Pete."

"Well, you have a safe trip, Marilyn. Tell Joe we're all pulling for him. If there's anything I can do, you just let me know."

At the court house, Marilyn finally located Pete near the clerk's office. "Pete!"

"Hi," he said shyly. "How're you doing?"

"Pete, I don't know how to thank you for what you did out at the farm."

"Oh, it wasn't nothing. Didn't take hardly any time at all."

"Y'all did a lot of work."

Pete ducked his head. She reached for his hand. "Pete, it means the world to me."

He couldn't meet her eyes. He had carried a silent torch for Marilyn in high school, and it killed him when she married Joe. This was the first time they had ever touched, and he was about to perish. When he finally could look at her, his face was on fire. "Marilyn," he said, his voice breaking like a teenager's, "I would do anything for you."

~ ~ ~

It was after ten when Danny's Chevy shot into the parking lot at Tomlin's

Lumber Yard, but Daryl was so relieved to see him he couldn't quarrel about the hour.

He met his son at the door. "Hi there, Danny. Come on into my office."

They sat in Daryl's cramped office, facing each other across his desk. "How you doing?" Daryl asked.

"Okay." Danny cracked his knuckles.

"Had breakfast?"

"No."

Daryl got up and poured a cup of coffee from the pot, added sugar and cream and handed it to Danny. "If you're hungry, you could go get something to eat at the diner."

"That's okay."

"How's Jeannie this morning?"

"Sleeping when I left."

"She going to be all right, you think?"

Danny shrugged.

It was like pulling teeth, talking to Danny. He's not like I was, Daryl thought. He remembered that with one stare Lloyd could elicit all kinds of damaging information without having to ask a single question. Not that I was ever in trouble like this. He switched gears.

"Your mama is coming to town this evening."

Danny looked up. Daryl couldn't tell if he was pleased.

"I talked to her last night. She wants your Grandpa Atkins to get you a new lawyer."

Danny said, "Looks to me like it's Jeannie who needs a lawyer."

"What's that mean?"

"Nothing. Only," Danny stole a look at Daryl through his eyelashes. "I was sleeping when she went in to get the baby. I never even woke up until she started hollering and carrying on."

"What are you saying, Danny?"

"Nothing, only whatever happened to the baby happened yesterday morning. She was fine when I put her in the crib."

~ ~ ~

"I don't think you got much here, Cal," L.W. Foster said, handing him back the file folder.

"We don't have the results of the autopsy yet," Cal reminded him.

L.W. re-lit his cigar and took several puffs. County Attorney for almost ten years, he was a tall, stooped man with a huge head and tiny hands and feet. He sat opposite Cal in shirt sleeves, bow tie, and suspenders.

"When do you expect to get that?"

"I talked to Doc last night. He said he had sent off tissue samples to the lab in Gainesville. I don't know how long it will take."

"For argument's sake," L.W. said, leaning forward confidentially, "the baby could of died of natural causes. You yourself said there were no marks on the body."

"Doc said something about hemorrhages around the eyes."

L.W. puffed out smoke. "Okay, but say that's because the baby cried a lot. Did the baby have colic?"

"I don't know."

"Well, for argument's sake, let's say the baby cried a lot because of colic. Say the autopsy shows that the baby died of unexplained natural causes."

"Like what?"

"Like, well, I don't know, but babies die, Cal. You know that. Remember when the Pearsons lost their baby. They never did find out exactly what caused it."

"So you're saying that…"

"You've got nothing to go on. The parents both state that the baby was fine Saturday night."

"Doesn't it strike you as odd, though, that a baby wouldn't have cried in the night?"

"Lots of babies sleep all through the night. What did Doc think?"

"That's why he called me out there. He seemed to think somebody might have done something to hurt that baby."

"Had Doc seen the baby before yesterday?"

"I don't know."

"Did Doc deliver the baby?"

"I don't know."

"Did you request the autopsy?"

"No, that was Doc's idea. He's the coroner."

L.W. frowned and fingered his cigar. "Maybe I better call Doc."

"Look, L.W.," Cal began.

"I know what you're thinking, Cal," L.W. said. "Danny Tomlin is a bad apple, always has been. Breaking and entering, theft, DWI's, you name it. Acts like a thug, even when he hasn't been up to anything. That damn hot rod, his attitude, the whole nine yards. That doesn't mean he killed his own baby."

"I know, but..."

"What's his girlfriend – is it Jeannie? What's she like? I hear she's a hot little number." L.W. raised his eyebrows.

"I don't know about that. She seemed mostly scared. I think she was about to say something out at Doc's, and then the Tomlins decided they needed to get a lawyer involved, and by the time I took her statement, she had clammed up. She pretty much just echoed what Danny said. I had the feeling that somebody – maybe Lloyd, maybe Daryl – told both Danny and Jeannie what to say."

L.W. leaned toward him. "Now you're talking about suborning perjury, Cal. You want to accuse Lloyd or Daryl of that? Good Lord, Lloyd's been on the county council since day one, and Daryl's president of the Jaycees."

Cal expelled breath. "I'm just telling you what I sensed, what I thought at the time. What I've been thinking since."

"Well, we'll see what the autopsy says. Still, I don't think you've got much here."

Cal was taken aback. L.W. seemed closed-minded, as if he had already decided.

"Well," Cal said, "early days. I'll just wait to see the autopsy report. You play golf yesterday?"

"Nah, Joyce's family had their reunion over at the big park in Gainesville."

"When I couldn't reach you, I figured you were out on the course."

"Not yesterday. Played this morning." He beamed. "Shot 79. First time this year I broke eighty."

"Who'd you go out with?"

"Just me and Jim Atkins. He's the only other s.o.b. in town wants to play golf at six o'clock on a Monday morning."

Jeannie rolled out of bed around noon, had a Dr. Pepper and a Hershey bar for breakfast. She washed her hair in the sink and rolled it up. Really, it was a relief that the baby was gone; she couldn't even hardly think with the baby crying and having to be fed and changed and everything. Pure and simple, a baby was a lot of work. She couldn't sleep until noon if the baby was still there. In the beginning, the baby woke up two or three times during the night and then again at six a.m. She couldn't go out or read her magazines or have any fun with a baby around.

It was like heaven when she went to work at the Steak House Friday and

Saturday nights. Waiting tables was a snap compared to taking care of a baby. Saturday night a lot of her regulars showed up, and her jokes and flirtations had resulted in good-sized tips. She picked up her pay check for the last two weeks, so she had a fair amount of cash when she got home. Danny, rich kid, never thought about money. That was one thing to be happy about. His mama sent them a hundred dollars to buy baby clothes, but then his grandma Mavis showed up with a whole bunch of stuff so she still had the hundred. Then his grandpa Lloyd slipped fifty dollars into her hand when they left the court house.

There was almost two hundred dollars in the little money box she took from the trunk. She packed her suitcase with clothes, cosmetics, hair curlers, and movie magazines. A Hershey bar, comb, brush, and lipstick went into her pocketbook along with the money and her driver's license. She dressed in her best Levi's and shirt and Levi's jacket. As an afterthought, she took half the money from the zippered compartment in her pocketbook and put some in her hip pocket and some in her shoes. Never carry all your money in one place.

Her eye fell on a framed photo of her and Danny, taken when they first started dating. She looked at herself gazing adoringly up at Danny, who was smiling broadly. That was a long time ago, she thought, and dropped it on the table. Danny said last night he had no reason to stay with her now. Well, that went double for her. With no baby, she didn't need him or his high-falutin' family. She was free to move on. She could earn money waitressing, or the other way. She knew what men would pay money for.

It wasn't far to the highway. Jeannie turned west, walking quickly. I'm certainly not going to Sanford, she thought. About a quarter of a mile down the highway, she stopped under a tree and put her suitcase down. She didn't have to wait long before she saw a car coming toward her. She stepped closer to the pavement, smiled, and put out her thumb. The big black Chrysler with Nevada plates rolled to a stop. The driver leaned over to roll down the window. "Where you headed, little lady?"

"Clovis."

"Come on then. Climb in."

She shoved her suitcase into the back seat and settled into the passenger seat.

"What's your name, little lady?"

"What's yours?" she countered.

"Me? I'm Leo."

"Call me Janine."

"Pleased to make your acquaintance, Miss Janine."

~ ~ ~

"More coffee?" Mavis Atkins waved the coffee pot at her daughter and husband.

"No, thanks," Carolyn Tomlin replied. Jim Atkins shook his head.

"So you haven't talked to Danny?" Carolyn asked her father.

"I went out to the trailer," Mavis said, "let's see, I guess it was a week ago Friday. Was it on a Friday, Jim? What day did I go to Amarillo?"

"You went to Amarillo Friday."

"That's right, I went to Amarillo Friday. So, I guess it was Thursday then." Carolyn and Jim regarded Mavis with fond exasperation. Plump and jolly, with her round face flushed from the stove's heat, she was drinking coffee, smoking a cigarette, and wracking her brain about two weeks ago.

"Mother, it doesn't matter when," Carolyn said.

"Oh, honey, I just was trying to think," Mavis said.

"So you went out to the trailer a couple of weeks ago," Jim prompted.

"I wanted to take out some baby clothes. I was at the Tot Shop, and Brenda had some darling little outfits on sale, so I bought a couple. I already had that little pink sweater and booties I knitted and a couple of crib sheets I found up in the closet. I guess they had been up there since you were a baby, Carolyn. Are you sure you don't want more coffee?"

"Mother, sit down and talk to us," Carolyn said.

Mavis perched on a chair. "Well, I just can't get over it, that poor little baby. I didn't even get a chance to hold her last time I was there. If I had known..."

"Mother," Carolyn said.

"I know, but it just makes me so sad, that poor little baby." Mavis' eyes filled with tears.

"Mother, was Danny there when you went out to the trailer?"

"Danny? No, just Jeannie. I think he had gone into town."

Carolyn turned to her father. "Have you talked to Danny?"

"I would guess we haven't seen Danny in months," Jim said.

"Well, he came over here the day the baby was born," Mavis said. "I had such a good feeling about him that day. It seemed like he was going to grow up and be a daddy to that little baby, and I thought he and Jeannie would finally get married. I had the feeling – didn't you, Jim? – you said you did – that he was going to grow up."

"That couldn't have been the last time you saw Danny," Carolyn said.

"When?" Mavis asked.

"The day the baby was born."

"No, later I went out to the trailer. Oh, gosh, Jim, when was that when I went out to the trailer to take diapers and bottles, do you remember?"

Carolyn looked at her father. "So neither one of you has really talked to Danny."

"You could say that," Jim said.

"I haven't talked to Daryl either," Mavis said. "I see him at church, and he just looks so awful. He is really suffering, Carolyn. He misses you."

Carolyn rolled her eyes.

"You know," Mavis went on, "Lloyd and Florence have literally not spoken to us since you left Daryl. I can't understand it. They just look past us, as if we weren't there. Now Daryl will talk to me. For awhile after you left, Daryl would come by here and sit at this table and drink coffee with me."

"Lloyd speaks to me," Jim said.

"Well, he doesn't speak to me."

"They spoke to you last Sunday at church," Jim said.

"Well, yes, they said good morning, but I don't mean that. I just wish there was some way we could all be friends again."

Carolyn stretched and yawned.

"Oh, honey, you're tired. What time did you leave this morning?" Mavis asked.

"I couldn't sleep, so I got up and left around four," Carolyn said.

"Car run okay?" Jim asked.

"Fine."

"Do you want to lie down for a little while?" Mavis asked. "You could sleep a couple of hours before supper."

"I think we ought to talk about what we're going to do," Carolyn said. "I think we need some good legal advice."

"I called Jack Morrison in Amarillo," Jim said. "He's willing to come out here anytime we say. I thought you and Daryl ought to decide."

"Oh, Daryl," Carolyn said contemptuously. " He will mostly be in the way."

"Why, honey," Mavis said, shocked. "Daryl is Danny's father."

"Mother, I know who Daryl is, better than anybody else." She stood up. "I think I will lie down for awhile."

Jim got up. "I need to turn on the sprinklers."

The doorbell rang. Mavis said, "Now who could that be? I'm not expecting anybody."

From the front door, Jim called out, "Carolyn, Daryl's here."

"Oh, rats," Carolyn said. "I'll come out in a minute," she told Mavis.

In the bathroom Carolyn smoothed her dark hair. She found a lipstick in the cabinet and reddened her mouth. Well, that will have to do, she thought.

"Hello, Daryl," she said.

"Hi!" Daryl cried. He started to come toward her but stopped as she sat down on a chair opposite the sofa. Jim dropped into his big recliner.

"Why don't you sit down, Daryl," Carolyn said.

He sat on the edge of the sofa. "How was your trip?"

"Fine. I left early this morning. Very little traffic."

"Car run okay?" Daryl asked.

"Fine."

"Daryl, could you drink a cup of coffee?" Mavis asked.

"Thanks, Mavis."

"Where's Danny?" Carolyn asked Daryl.

"Down at the lumber yard, helping Eldon. I'll take you down there," he said.

"That won't be necessary. How does he seem to you?"

Mavis set a cup of coffee in front of Daryl. "Daryl, you take sugar and cream, don't you? I already put it in for you."

"Thanks."

Nobody said anything. After a few seconds, Daryl offered, "When I saw Carolyn's car I thought I would stop in for a minute and say hi." He had been parked down the street for about an hour, screwing up his courage to come to the house.

"Now, listen," Mavis said, "I have a big ham ready to put in the oven and I made a chocolate cake this morning. Daryl, I want you and Danny to eat supper with us tonight. And what about your folks – will you invite them? And I guess Jeannie, too, if she wants to come."

Carolyn interrupted her mother. "I think we should talk about Danny."

"Seems to me," Jim said, "there's no reason to treat this as a criminal matter. What's the matter with Doc anyway?"

"I don't know," Daryl said. "He and Cal were real insistent."

"Some kind of burr up their ass," Jim said. "Maybe out to get Danny?"

"Maybe," Daryl agreed.

"How does Danny seem to you, Daryl?" Carolyn persisted.

"Well, I read him the riot act last night and told him he had to straighten up and fly right, beginning with coming to work today. And he did show up. I told him you were coming home, Carolyn. When I told him you were getting him a new lawyer, he said something interesting." Daryl waited to make sure her eyes stayed on him. "He said he figured it's Jeannie who needs a lawyer."

~ ~ ~

"Renee, you can go on home. Wayne can close up," Roy Woodson said.

"Okay," she said.

"Tomorrow I want to change the men's window." Roy told her.

Wayne said, "I got some ideas about the men's window, Mr. Woodson."

"I was already thinking about that," Renee said, her back to Wayne. "I read in a magazine that the preppy look is real popular with boys. I'll bring the magazine tomorrow." She paused at the door to give Roy a smile. "See you then, Mr. Woodson."

The shortest way home was past the drug store, but she didn't want to go that way in case she should run into Jesse Eliot. She wouldn't want him to think she was looking for him. After buying a pack of chewing gum at the 5 & 10, Renee regarded Main Street with discontent. I wish I lived someplace else. Nothing ever happens in Massey. Head down and lamenting the fate of being stuck in a boring little old town, she rounded the corner and there he was. She had been daydreaming about him all afternoon, and there he was right in front of her. "Well, hello, Adam Robbins. You remember me?"

"I don't remember you being so pretty," Adam answered.

She smiled. That was the way older boys talked, and she liked it. "What are you doing downtown?"

"Why, is there a law against it?"

She grinned. "Maybe there ought to be."

He grinned back. "What are *you* doing downtown?"

"I work here. I am in charge of the window displays at Woodson's."

"Is that a fact."

"Yes, it is. You want to see the window I designed?"

"Sure," he said, "show me."

She led him back down the block to Woodson's, now dark and the "Closed" sign on the door. She proudly indicated the women's display window. "I did that."

"It looks almost as pretty as you."

# CHAPTER SIX

It was like old times, Mavis thought with satisfaction. The meal finished and most of the dishes cleared, the seven of them sat around the dining table. She had set a place for Jeannie, but Danny said she was waitressing. Mavis watched lovelorn Daryl look at Carolyn. Her eyes rested fondly on Danny. He always did love her chocolate cake. She felt a pang of sadness about that poor little baby. But she couldn't help feeling happy tonight. Surely everything would be better now. Florence had seemed like her old self and had brought a pecan pie and watermelon rind pickles. It was just like old times. Mavis was relieved that Jeannie hadn't come. Jeannie had never really fit into the family. So cheap looking. Mavis had about torn her hair out when Jeannie turned up pregnant. And then, to make it worse, they didn't get married. A nice girl wouldn't have gotten pregnant in the first place, but she sure would have gotten married. Funny, Mavis thought, it was a good thing that they weren't married. Now, everything was simpler.

Florence smiled at Mavis, thinking that it felt so much better to be on good terms again. Mavis was broken up about the baby, too. Florence had always liked Mavis and Jim, but she had felt like she just couldn't excuse the divorce. The first ever divorce in Florence's family, and she believed in Lloyd's too. Daryl was still all broken up about it, and Danny – well, he had always been a handful, but he just went to pot when Carolyn left. If Carolyn had just stayed put, probably none of this would have happened.

Jim had been dubious about this get-together, but it turned out to have been a damn good idea. Although nobody had come right out and said it, Jim was sure that Lloyd and Daryl agreed with his point of view. The whole family had to stick together, let bygones be bygones. Out on the golf course, L.W. had seemed to agree with him that Cal and Doc were making a mountain out of a molehill. Still, Jim felt like wringing Danny's neck. Young devil, always in some kind of trouble. But bad as Danny was, Jeannie was worse. Sly little tramp. Maybe it wasn't even Danny's baby. If she had come tonight, he doubted he could have been civil to her.

Daryl couldn't keep his eyes off Carolyn. She was more beautiful now than ever. In high school they were nicknamed "Dare and Care." He thought ruefully that she was the one who dared and he was the one who cared. She was wearing silver and turquoise jewelry and a turquoise colored dress with silver braid on it. He guessed it was the style in Santa Fe. He wondered about her life there. He was sure that she went out with men. Jealousy surged within him.

Okay, he said to himself. It's time for Daryl to dare. He raised his voice. "I was thinking it might be kind of fun to go out to the Rondy-Voo tonight. Listen to some music. What do y'all say?"

"Oh, I'm too beat," Mavis said. "You kids go."

"Yeah, y'all three go ahead on," Lloyd said. "Do you good."

Danny's eyes widened. The Rondy-Voo was one of his favorite hang-outs. The owners had converted an old warehouse into a bar and restaurant with live music and dancing. People brought their own bottles to circumvent the county's stringent liquor laws. Danny thought he could meet up with some of his buddies out there, and if Daryl picked up the tab, so much the better. "Sure, I guess so, why not," he said.

Carolyn shook her head. "I don't know."

Daryl took her hand. "Come on, it'll be fun."

She gave him that flirty look through her eyelashes."Well, okay, but only for a little while. I got up at the crack of dawn this morning."

"You'll need this," Jim said. He put a bottle of Seagram's 7 in a paper bag and handed it to Daryl.

"Thanks, Jim," Daryl took Carolyn's hand. "Come on, beautiful. Let's go dancing."

~ ~ ~

Smoke and loud country music welcomed them to the Rondy-Voo. Daryl and Carolyn paused at the door while Danny forged ahead to speak to the hostess who laughed and patted him on the shoulder. He motioned his parents to follow them to a booth in the dimly-lit room.

"Give her the bottle," Danny instructed Daryl.

On the raised platform at one end of the room was a three-piece band and a girl in a cowboy hat who was giving "Your Cheatin' Heart" all she had. About a dozen men and a couple of women jostled at the bar.

"It's crowded," Carolyn said.

"You ought to see it on a Saturday night," Danny told her.

A waitress appeared. "Why, Danny Tomlin! Haven't seen you in an age!" She tugged at her blouse to expose a little more shoulders and bosom.

"Hi, Darlene," Danny said.

She laid coasters on the table. "Having a family reunion? What can I bring y'all?"

"Seven-sevens okay?" Danny asked.

Daryl and Carolyn nodded.

"Set ups for seven-sevens," he told Darlene.

"Who was that?" Carolyn asked when the waitress left the table.

"Darlene Shields," Daryl said.

"Shields?" Carolyn asked. "Not..."

"Yeah, the preacher's daughter," Daryl said.

"Well, he must be beside himself," Carolyn said.

Daryl looked around. "I don't recognize anybody in here."

Danny surveyed the crowd at the bar, where a roar of laughter rang out. "Well, that bunch is mostly from Sanford."

"Do you know everybody in here?" Carolyn asked.

Danny laughed. "Purt near."

The singer launched into "I Really Don't Want To Know" and Daryl drew Carolyn to the dance floor.

Darlene Shields delivered peanuts, set-ups, and the Seagram's bottle, now labeled "TOMLIN." She rested her hip against Danny's shoulder. "What you up to these days?"

"Not too much, how about yourself?"

"I heard you got married."

"Married! Reckon not." Danny poured Seagram's and Seven Up into his glass and raised it. "Cheers."

"Down the hatch." She bent over him, breasts swaying in the flimsy blouse. "I got my own place now."

"Where at? In town?"

"Yeah, little house on Eleventh Street. Come on over sometime."

Danny grinned. "I might just do that."

When Daryl and Carolyn returned to the booth, Danny poured drinks for them, then clinked their glasses with his own. "Cheers."

The fiddle player took the microphone. "We invite all you gents to bring your little ladies up here to the dance floor for 'Put Your Little Foot.'"

Danny slid out of the booth, taking his drink with him.

"Well, he's certainly in his element," Carolyn said, her eyes following Danny to the bar where he slapped a man on the shoulder.

Daryl clinked his glass gently against hers. "Here's to the prettiest woman in the world."

She smoothed her hair. "I don't know how you can say that. I am a wreck."

"You are even prettier than you were in high school."

She rolled her eyes. "I think you need glasses."

"It's nice to dance with you again. I was thinking about the first time we danced."

"When was that?"

"You remember, you wore a blue dress."

"Daddy took me to Amarillo to buy that dress," she said.

"You were the prettiest girl at the dance," he said.

"I think I still have that dress," she mused.

"I loved you then, and I love you now, Carolyn." Daryl took her hand and put it to his lips.

"Daryl, we've been all through this."

"Nothing to go through. I'm just telling you the truth." He uncurled her fingers and gently kissed her palm. She didn't pull away. He kissed the tip of each finger. When he got to her pinky, he gave it a tiny suck.

"Daryl, people can see you."

"It's dark in here." He delicately ran his fingers over her thigh, just barely stroking her through the soft material of her dress. She drew in a breath through her nostrils. "Now, Daryl," she warned.

"Shh," he said. He leaned closer to her, inhaled her scent, breathed softly into her ear. "Come home with me tonight."

"What would Mother and Daddy think?"

"That you've gone home with your husband."

When Danny came back to the booth, Daryl said, "Danny, your mother got up at the crack of dawn this morning. She needs to get her rest."

"It's okay," Danny said. "I can get a ride."

"Well," Carolyn said, collecting her purse. "I hate to be a party pooper, but..."

Daryl handed Danny a bill. "This enough?" he asked. Danny nodded and took it.

When they had gone, Danny signaled Darlene. "Another set up."

When she brought it, Danny asked, "You got any cigarettes?" She offered her pack of Marlboros. "What time you get off?" he asked.

"One."

"I could use a ride."

"Won't Jeannie be looking for you?"

"Jeannie don't own me. What I do is my business."

# CHAPTER SEVEN

"Okay, you sissies," Coach Parker said to his players, "Your drills stink, you block like girls. I figure Sanford is just going to run right over y'all. Sorriest excuse for football players I ever saw. Y'all make last year's team look good."

The boys hung their heads. Sweat soaked their bodies inside their shoulder pads and helmets.

"So I'm going to help y'all out. Try to make men out of you pansies. You are going to go run laps around the lake."

"How many, Coach?"

"How many, Coach?" Coach mimicked in a high, girlish voice. He resumed in his normal register, "I'll let you know how many. Anybody slacks off, I'll add more."

The boys groaned. The lake didn't look so big until you ran the circular path that hugged the water's edge and then circled over the dam.

"Leave your equipment here. I don't want any of you weak sisters to pass out on me."

The boys stacked their shoulder pads and helmets in the little shed on the edge of the playing field and ran out of the stadium onto Birch Street and down to Second Street, where they turned and continued out to the lake. Driving his pickup slowly along the street beside them, Coach yelled, "Pick it up, ladies!"

Jesse welcomed the breeze running created. He was out front, joined by Bill Lynch, who played end. Coach was right; they did stink. Jesse couldn't throw the ball worth a damn this morning. Feeling ashamed, he ran faster. Bill matched his pace. When they got out to the lake, they were striding more easily. Leading the pack, they headed up the incline to the top of the dam.

"I hate this," Bill said.

Jesse said, "He probably won't make us do more than three or four laps."

"No, I mean here...the lake," Bill puffed. "Keith. Gives me the creeps." He shuddered and made a face.

Jesse looked at the dark blue water. The lake was deep, many feet to the bottom of the canyon, and there were strong undercurrents. Danger and No Swimming signs dotted the shore. Jesse remembered last spring when Bill Lynch and Keith Holder skipped school. Jesse probably would have skipped, too, if he had been invited. It had been a clear, warm May afternoon, about a week before the end of school. The two boys took hamburgers and fries from Benny's out to the lake. It was rumored that they also brought beer. They stripped down to their shorts and lay under the bright sunshine. Then they decided to swim across the lake.

He heard tell when they found Keith's body it was blue. At the funeral, Keith's face looking up from the open coffin was an improbable orangey-pink color, as if he wore makeup. A week later at graduation, there was a prayer about him, and his older brother Joe Don went up on the stage to receive Keith's diploma.

Jesse hated remembering all that. He picked up speed running down the incline and started around the perimeter of the lake. Bill slowed and then stopped running. He fell to his knees on the grass beside the path. Jesse ran back to him. The rest of the team ran by, staring at them. Bill bent double and vomited.

"Lynch! Eliot! What the hell is going on?"

Jesse couldn't face Coach. He was furious at Bill and at his own throat for clogging up with tears. "He was talking about Keith," he muttered.

"Okay. Eliot, you see that everybody does two laps and then go on back. Practice is over for today." Coach bent down to Bill. "Come on, son, I'll drive you home."

~ ~ ~

"Sonny, you didn't eat your breakfast."

"I'm not hungry, Mama."

"Are you sick?" She tried to feel his forehead., but he pushed her hand away. He slouched down the hall to his room. She watched him with concern. Sonny was almost never sick. He had almost perfect attendance throughout school. Dear Lord, Mary prayed, please don't let Sonny be sick.

Wayne said, "I'm going now, Mama."

"Sonny, you never told me about your meeting with Brother Robbins," she called out to his departing back. He didn't reply.

Wayne tried to concentrate on the tasks that awaited him at the store. He had to shelve the shoes that came in yesterday. Yesterday! He had been so happy yesterday, and now everything was changed.

Nothing could have upset him yesterday afternoon, not even the sight of Renee Coulter flouncing around the store bragging about her windows. Wayne had given up on the idea of converting Renee. He didn't need her testimony to confirm Adam's sins. Wayne knew what he had to do about that, and he could do it without her help.

Yesterday he hurried through closing up the store and went home to shave. He wanted to look perfect for his meeting with Brother Robbins. He put on a fresh white shirt and his Sunday suit, knotted a sober maroon tie. Brushing his Sunday shoes, he sang "Onward, Christian Soldiers." He tried to flatten his hair, which liked to curl.

When he emerged spic and span from his bedroom, Mary clapped her hands. "Sonny, you look so handsome!"

Bible in hand, he was the first to arrive at prayer meeting. He sat in the back. When Adam filed into a pew with his younger brothers, Wayne thought, Hypocrite, how can he live with himself? Fornication was a terrible sin, but it could be atoned, whereas adultery put a person permanently in danger of hellfire. Poor Mr. Woodson didn't know he was married to Jezebel.

After the service, the "examination," as Brother Robbins called it, started off nicely. Wayne had no trouble answering questions about church doctrine. He quoted Scripture to support his points. He felt he was making a powerful impression. It was when the subject turned to living a holy life that things changed.

"Of course, Wayne, you know that a minister of the Gospel must lead a life consecrated to God."

"Yes sir, that is the Lord's truth," Wayne said.

"Have you endeavored to live a holy life?"

"With the help of the Lord."

"Can you confess to me, my son, what obstacles Satan has placed in your path to prevent you from living a God-pleasing life?"

Wayne leaned forward and clasped his hands together. "Sir, like any man, I have been tempted by the devil. The devil uses woman for his evil purposes. But it is man's duty to keep woman at bay. I am untainted by the sin of fornication. The Bible says that the body is the temple of God, and I have kept my temple pure."

Brother Robbins smiled. "Your efforts will not go unrewarded, my son."

"I know there are others, sir, others who you may know of, who have failed to keep their bodies pure. There are some who have committed the sin of fornication. But there are worse sinners who have committed adultery and they are in danger of hellfire. Those sinners deserve the wrath of God."

Brother Robbins said, "Our Lord tells us judge not, that we may not be judged."

"Nevertheless, Brother Robbins, is it not our Christian duty, as ministers of the Gospel, to root out flagrant sin committed right under our very own noses? There is sin committed here today even as we speak, sin eating away at the sanctity..."

Before he could add "of your very own home," Brother Robbins interrupted him. "Wayne, I must strongly caution you. While I applaud your efforts to keep yourself pure, I cannot condone a judgmental and self-righteous attitude."

"But, Brother Robbins..."

Brother Robbins rose from his chair, his outstretched palm demanding silence. He stroked his chin. Wayne fidgeted. He had not yet made his point.

"I fear, Wayne, that it may be premature for you to apply to Bible College. I do not wish you to be altogether disheartened. In a few months perhaps, we can talk again. In the meantime, you should humbly ask our Lord to remove the sin of pride from your heart. Satan has not been able to tempt you to contaminate your body, Wayne, but in his subtle wickedness he may have contaminated your mind. And a contaminated mind can be just as dangerous as an impure body. Pray, my son, pray, and I will pray for you."

~ ~ ~

Cal Tuttle walked from his office at the court house to the little kitchen where he poured himself a cup of thick coffee. On his way back he ran into Pete Mosley.

"Any news about Jeannie?" Cal asked after he closed the door and they sat down.

Pete shook his head. "Nosiree. The Highway Patrol put out an all-points bulletin with her high school picture. I been out to the trailer, but I couldn't find nothing to give me any idea where she might of gone to. I talked to Danny again." Pete consulted a little notebook, "He says, let's see, beyond a suitcase, he doesn't know what she might of took with her. He doesn't know what she might of wore."

"You talk to her folks?"

"Yeah, for all the good that did. Her mother said they ain't seen her in months. Seemed like that was just fine with her. She said she has washed her hands of Jeannie. They never even saw the baby. It didn't seem to faze them that the baby's dead and that Jeannie has gone missing."

"Nice people," Cal growled.

"No," said Pete, who had no ear for sarcasm, "just the opposite. Her daddy didn't say nothing, except to cuss me out for bothering them."

"How about the Steak House?"

"Talked to Milton. He sets up the waitresses' schedules. He says Jeannie hasn't been around. But said he didn't expect her since she was only working Fridays and Saturdays. I told him to let us know if he heard from her. Told her folks, too, for all the good it did."

"So the last time Danny saw her was…"

"Monday morning when he went to work. He said she was sleeping when he left."

"What about Monday night?"

"Says he didn't go out to the trailer Monday night. Says he went out to the trailer Tuesday afternoon to get some clothes and Jeannie wasn't there then. It looks to me like Danny has pretty much moved back to Daryl's house."

"He didn't report her missing until yesterday morning."

"He said he thought she'd be back. Said he thought she was probably," Pete dropped his voice, "out catting around."

"Did Daryl say anything that might help?" Cal asked.

Pete looked at his pad. "He said he ain't seen her since he dropped her and Danny off at the trailer Sunday afternoon. Said she might of run off, maybe for good."

"Did Danny think she'd run off for good?"

"He didn't say one way or the other. You know Danny. You ask him a question and he just gives you a look."

"Where was he Monday night?"

Pete considered. "Well, I talked to Miz Atkins. She didn't know nothing about Jeannie. Carolyn is in town, and the whole lot ate supper over to the Atkinses Monday."

"Who all?"

"Danny and Daryl and Mr. and Mrs. Lloyd Tomlin."

"I thought the Atkinses and the Tomlins were on the outs."

"I guess not any more."

"Jeannie didn't go to the Atkinses Monday night?"

"Nope. My guess is that Jeannie wouldn't be exactly what you'd call welcome, if you get my drift."

"Okay, thanks, Pete. You just write all that up for the file."

"Will do."

Cal took a sip of bitter and now lukewarm coffee. He re-read the autopsy report. No trauma to the body. Stomach empty. Mild cerebral edema. Retinal hemorrhage. Cause of death: Undetermined. L.W. had taken a look at it and tossed it back to him. "You got nothing here," he said.

His gut told him that somebody -- Danny or Jeannie -- had done something to hurt that baby. It didn't look good for her that Jeannie was gone missing. She was like a cornered animal Sunday morning. Was she grieving or was she guilty?

Doc had turned different, too. He said he couldn't say whether the baby had been harmed, said it could have been crib death. Said he had released the body to the family for burial. Cal thought Doc seemed in a rush to get off the phone.

What if Jeannie was dead, too? He hadn't told Pete to treat the trailer as the scene of a crime. He had better drive out there. It would at least give him something to do.

~ ~ ~

Janice Tuttle cautiously opened her bedroom door and listened. Slowly she came out and softly closed the door.

"It's okay," she said aloud. "They're gone."

She went into the kitchen. "No knives. No, I told you, no knives."

She picked up a pencil and the grocery list pad from the counter and took them over to the kitchen table. "Just so they know," she said. She wrote quickly, "Dear Laura and Calvin I love you Mama." She crossed out Mama and wrote Janice, then put an X through Janice. "Oh, well, they'll know," she said and laughed. "That's right, they'll figure it out." She placed a saucer on the pad, removed her watch and wedding band and set them on the table.

She opened the back door. "It's a pretty day. Come on, we'll go through the alley." She went through the back gate into the alley. A skinny yellow tomcat with mangy ears hunkered beside a trash can. She bent down. "Hello, kitty." He bristled and spat, then streaked away into an adjoining back yard, dead bird in his mouth.

"Oh, bad kitty, killed a bird, didn't you? They do that, you know. Can't prevent them. It's the law of the jungle." She laughed. "That's right, law of the alley."

When she got to Second Street, she turned right. She began to hum and then to sing. "Oh, give me a home where the buffalo roam and the deer and the antelope play. Where seldom is heard a discouraging word and the skies are not cloudy all day."

She looked up. There was a white pickup coming toward her. "No, it's not Calvin. It's Ray Parker." She waved cheerily as the pickup passed by. "He is nice. High school football coach. If it hadn't been for Calvin, I might have dated Ray."

She lifted her face to the luminous sky and spread her arms wide. “Home, home on the range where the deer and the antelope play. Where seldom is heard a discouraging word and the skies are not cloudy all day.”

When she got to the lake she said, “Nobody here. The water looks pretty, doesn’t it? I always liked water. Daddy one time took me fishing on the river. That was before they made the lake. You know, I really never thought about the lake until Keith.” She frowned, listening, then said sullenly, “I am. I will. Just wait a minute, can’t you?”

She walked down the sloping bank to the water’s edge. A flock of geese flew over, honking. “Go home,” she called out. “Geese know when it’s time to go home.”

She bent to unbuckle her sandals and arranged them side by side. “All right, then, I’m ready.”

When the water reached her thighs, she gasped at the cold but didn’t stop. She kept on walking.

# CHAPTER EIGHT

"Anything special you want me to do today, Mrs. Woodson?"

"Well, you could defrost the refrigerator, Mary."

"I'll do that. You going out?"

"Not right away."

"I'll just get started here in the kitchen then." Mary Pickens took the ice cube trays from the freezer. "I'll vacuum and dust before I take the laundry to the Washateria."

Maureen walked back through the living room down the hallway to her bedroom. She sat at her dressing table and looked at herself in the mirror. Her pale hair framed her face perfectly. She had gotten a particularly good set Tuesday, but it had been a let-down to drive to Amarillo alone. She had planned on Adam's company. She wondered why he had turned down her invitation. Of course they had parted on somewhat hectic terms, but that was because Roy showed up unexpectedly. She congratulated herself on how well she had handled the situation. She was sure Roy didn't suspect anything.

It was effortless getting around Roy. He was all wrapped up in that store. Besides, he had almost no interest in sex. He had been a sufficiently ardent suitor, but after the wedding he turned out to be self-conscious and awkward. One time he couldn't sustain an erection; then the next time, as if to compensate, he would ejaculate almost immediately. Face it, he was a big disappointment in the bedroom. They had been married less than a year when Maureen took her first lover.

She had always been the soul of discretion. Until Adam, she had never chosen a man from Massey. Her first lover was Max Allison, who had pursued her before she married. She would drive to Gainesville to meet Max at his house. He had never married, so that was easy. That time when Roy was in Dallas she stayed the whole week in Gainesville. Max usually managed to give her a climax, but he was unimaginative, just did the same thing over and over again.

After tiring of Max, Maureen had a brief fling with her dentist in Amarillo. He was such a cheapskate, though, he wouldn't spring for a hotel room. He just locked the door and had her spread her legs in the chair.

Then last fall during a shopping trip to Oklahoma City she had run into Adam Robbins. She had noticed him when he was in high school because he was so handsome, like a Greek god. On a whim that day in the City, she asked him to have dinner with her at her hotel, and he readily accepted. Over coffee, she proposed that he come up to her room. She was surprised by his expertise and delighted by his compliments. He had quoted poetry to her, something about her breasts looking like deer. The comparison seemed a little odd, but it was enchanting to have her body praised so extravagantly.

Now that Adam was home for the summer, she expected to see him frequently and was baffled when he stammered out a refusal to go to Amarillo. He had sounded almost unfriendly.

She wandered back into the living room, where Mary Pickens was dusting. "Mary, just out of curiosity…"

"Yes?"

"Adam Robbins is home for the summer, isn't he?"

"Why, yes, he is."

"Do you know if he's working somewhere?"

"Working? No, I don't think so."

"I was just thinking, I'd like to get somebody to wash windows, and I thought maybe some boy would like to earn some spending money, and I thought maybe Adam..."

Mary smiled. "I couldn't really say."

"If he's not working, he might be bored and needs something to occupy him."

Mary twinkled at her.

"Does he have a girlfriend?"

"A girlfriend? Very likely, he's so good-looking. Don't you think so?"

"Oh, I never really noticed. Well, I just might call over there and see if…"

Maureen returned to her bedroom, and Mary Pickens turned on the Hoover. Well, this will surely brighten Wayne's day.

~ ~ ~

Cal didn't know what he had expected to find at the trailer. It was messy, but lack-of-housekeeping messy, not messy as if a crime had been committed. Nothing suspicious, no blood stains, no newly dug grave out back. Maybe he was letting his imagination run away with him. Maybe L.W. was right. Disgusted by his lack of focus, he got in the pickup and headed slowly back toward town.

He thought about Danny and Jeannie – too young and immature to be parents. But that didn't mean they hurt the baby. He recalled that Janice had said she couldn't take care of Laura. That wasn't due to age or lack of maturity. In fact, as she got older, Janice seemed to get worse.

At the fork coming back from Four Corners, instead of coming on into town over the dam, he took the spur to the highway going out to Joe and Marilyn's place. He had heard that Joe was back. He would swing by there and see how things stood.

He sat at the table with them for some time. Marilyn couldn't keep her hands off Joe. She patted his hand and stroked his arm and the back of his neck.

"So you feeling okay, Joe?" Cal asked.

"Yeah, not too bad," Joe responded. He licked his lips.

"Here, honey, drink some water," Marilyn said, pushing his glass toward him. "The medicine gives him a dry mouth. But it seems to work."

"What's it called?" Cal asked.

Joe picked up the bottle from the table and showed him the label. "Thorazine. I don't know exactly what it does. Makes me kind of lazy," he said and laughed. "I should be out fixing that fence."

"You don't need to do a thing," Marilyn said, rubbing his shoulder.

"How long do you have to keep taking it?" Cal asked, examining the bottle.

"We go back to see Dr. Siegel in a few weeks," Marilyn said. "He said to take it regularly until then."

"Is he pretty good?" Cal asked.

"He is wonderful. Isn't he, Joe?"

"I reckon he's okay. One thing I didn't like, he told me not to drink."

"He said you could have a beer with your meal," Marilyn said.

"Yeah," Joe said, "that's what I said. One beer!"

"He wants you to get better," Marilyn said. "And you are better. Isn't he, Cal?"

"I'd say so," Cal said. "You look like you feel better."

"I feel pretty good," Joe said. "But like I said, the damn stuff makes me sleepy."

"It's no crime to take a nap during the day," Marilyn said.

Cal rose from the table. "I need to get back."

Joe stood and offered his hand. "Want to thank you, Cal."

"I didn't do much, Joe," Cal said as they shook hands.

Marilyn put her arm around Joe. "Everybody's been so nice."

The two followed him out to the yard and waited until he got in his pickup.

He waved as he pulled out onto the road. When he looked back through the rearview mirror he saw Joe bend to kiss Marilyn.

"Dr. Siegel, the miracle worker," Cal said. "Maybe he could work a miracle on Janice."

❧ ❧ ❧

Renee stuck her head into the beauty shop. "You busy?"

Nadine looked up from her magazine. "Do I look busy? How come you're not at work?"

"We finished both windows and there's no customers, so I asked Mr. Woodson if I could come over here for awhile."

"Well, come on in then, make yourself at home."

Renee threw herself on the couch. "I am so bored I could just die!"

"Aren't you going out tomorrow night?" Nadine asked.

"No. Maybe."

"No maybe," Nadine laughed. "Does that mean Jesse hasn't asked you yet?"

"Jesse?" Renee wrinkled her nose. "That'll be the day I go out with Jesse Eliot."

"You still mad at him?"

"Mama, I am permanently mad at Jesse Eliot."

"You know who I think is cute? Bill Lynch."

Renee made a face. "All those high school boys are dumb. Mama, I was just wondering…"

"What?"

"My daddy was older than you, wasn't he?"

"Oh, sure he was."

"And that didn't make any difference, did it? I mean, age."

Nadine's eyes grew dreamy as she remembered. "When we met, it seemed like we were meant for each other."

"Age is not that important, is it?" Renee asked.

"Well, it wasn't for us. I mean, he had been in the service, you know, and I was still in high school, but we…we got along just fine. It was later that he got itchy feet, had to get out of Massey. Go someplace, find his fortune. But in the beginning…."

"Do you still love him?"

Nadine considered. "I guess in a way I do."

"Is that why you don't date anybody? Because you're still in love with him?"

Nadine laughed, but the laugh turned into a cough. She coughed for a long time.

"Well, are you?"

"You are full of questions! Why are you asking me all these things?"

"Well, I been thinking…"

The wail of a siren drowned out her words. Nadine looked out the window in time to see the ambulance hurtling down Main Street, siren screaming. She opened the door of the shop and stepped out onto the sidewalk. Pete Mosley came running down the sidewalk toward her.

"What's going on, Pete?"

"You haven't seen the sheriff, have you?" he panted.

"No, I haven't."

"I need to find him."

"What's happening, Pete?" she called, but he had already gone.

"Is Miss Harmon here?" Laura asked.

Pat said, "She went downtown. How come you ask?"

"I don't know, I just sometimes get the feeling she doesn't want me to come over here so often."

"Laura, you're imagining things. Miss Harmon likes you a lot."

"She does?"

"Sure she does. Everybody likes you, Laura."

Laura blushed and smiled. "I just never want to bother anybody."

"You are definitely no bother. Now come on in. You want something to drink?"

"Is there lemonade?"

"Look in the refrigerator."

"Yeah, there's a pitcher. Do you want some?"

"Sure, pour us both a glass and come sit down." Pat stretched out her legs beside the kitchen table and lit a cigarette.

Laura brought two glasses to the table and sat down.

"So, you looking forward to going back to school?"

"Oh, yes. This summer has been so boring."

"Boring? I would think a young lady like you would have lots to do. What about your girlfriends?"

"They're all on vacation."

"So, you're about to start your senior year."

"Yeah."

"Then what?"

"Oh, college, I guess. Papa wants me to go to college."

"Well, you should. Where do you want to go?"

Laura sighed, ran her finger around the edge of her glass. "I don't know. It's hard to think about going away."

"You get good grades, don't you?"

"Yes, but I hate to leave Papa. I worry what he will do without me."

"You said he wants you to go."

"Yeah, but then it will be just him home alone…with Mama."

Pat asked, "How is your mama?"

"Okay, I guess. I don't know, really. She's up in her room most of the time. She only comes down to eat."

"Who cooks?"

Laura laughed. "I do."

"I knew you did the grocery shopping but I didn't know you cooked, too."

"Yeah, well, somebody has to. I mean, Papa's got to work. I don't mind, really. It's not the cooking that bothers me…." She stopped, her eyes down.

Pat leaned toward her. "What does bother you?"

"I guess it's the laughing mostly."

Pat looked puzzled. "The laughing?"

"She'll be up in her room by herself, but you can hear her laughing, like she's with somebody and having a good time. Papa says it's because she's sick, and I know it shouldn't bother me, but sometimes I just can't stand it. I wish she would stop it." Laura put her hand over her mouth. "I'm sorry, I shouldn't have said that."

"It's okay, you can tell me. I won't tell anybody," Pat soothed. "He's probably right about her being sick, but that doesn't mean you have to like it."

"I hate it!" Laura burst out. "The girls never want to come over to my house, and I really don't want them to, either, because of the way she acts. Laughing and talking to herself. It really drives me crazy." She clamped both hands over her mouth. "I'm sorry, I'm sorry."

Pat reached over to put her hand on Laura's shoulder. "It's okay, it's okay," she said.

"I'm sorry, I'm sorry," Laura sobbed.

"Nothing to be sorry about. You just cry."

The back door opened. Pat turned to see Dorothy's ashen face.

"Oh, you've already heard," Dorothy said. She came over and put her arms around both of them. "Laura, honey, I am so sorry."

# CHAPTER NINE

Vance Collier placed his ball on the tee and looked out over the first fairway. In the early morning light it was hard to distinguish the fairway from the rough brown prairie on either side. He took his driver from his bag.

The other three men stood quietly behind him as he took a practice swing and then hit the ball. "Good shot, Mayor," Jim Atkins said as the ball arced down the fairway.

"Better than good," said L.W. Foster.

"Can't hit 'em like I used to," Vance complained, stooping stiffly to retrieve his tee.

"I can't hit 'em like you do now," Don Paulson said, stepping up to the tee. He swung, the ball duck-hooked, veering sharply left. "Damn. Swinging too fast," he admonished himself. "Slow it down."

"One thing about this course," L.W. Foster said, stepping up to take his turn. "You can usually find your ball."

"Yeah," Vance said. "I can see Don's over there in the sagebrush."

Jim Atkins watched L.W. hit his ball directly down the fairway. "Good shot, L.W.," he said. "You been taking lessons?"

L.W. grinned.

"This old boy beat the pants off me Monday morning," Jim told Vance and Don. "What'd you shoot, a 78?"

"Seventy-nine," L.W. said. "Once in awhile I get lucky."

Jim drove his ball down the fairway, replaced his driver in his bag, and the four men wheeled their pull-carts down the fairway, Don heading left and the other three together down the middle.

"Sorry to hear about your loss, Jim," Vance said.

"Yeah, well, Mavis's taking it pretty hard. Funeral's this morning at ten."

"We should be done here by nine," L.W. said.

"Carolyn here?" Vance asked.

"Yeah, she came in Monday."

"How's she like Santa Fe?"

"She appears to like it fine. Course we wish she wasn't so far away."

"Yeah," Vance said, "kids grow up, but you never stop worrying about them."

"Well, her mind's on Danny now," Jim said. "So's mine, for that matter. Sheriff seems to be treating this as a criminal matter."

"Is that right?" Vance asked, surprised.

"Well," Jim said, "Danny's been in trouble before, but the idea that he could have done something to a baby, well, none of us think that's even a remote possibility. But it looks like Cal's got a bee in his bonnet."

"That so?" Vance asked. He looked at L.W.

"Maybe he's just blowing smoke. L.W. knows more about it than I do."

L.W. shrugged. "Y'all know Cal, he's a stickler for details."

"Cal's got his own situation now," Vance mused. "Here's your ball, Jim."

Jim took a nine iron from his bag, looked, waggled, and hit it right over the flag onto the back fringe.

"Looked good for awhile," L.W. commented, and then walked on to his own ball.

"Sounds like you got nothing to worry about," Vance said to Jim.

"We'll see, we'll see."

When the three got close to the green, Don joined them and they all chipped up to the pin. "How much would it take, you think, to replace these damn things with grass?" Don asked.

They regarded the oiled sand. "Not much to begin with," Vance said, "but there's the matter of keeping the grass alive. You'd have to install underground sprinklers, or hire somebody to water."

"Like to see the council look into that," Don said.

"Take it under advisement," Vance said.

They putted and walked toward the second tee. A ball bounced up within twenty yards of the first green.

"Who the hell's that?" L.W. asked, shading his eyes to look into the sun.

"It's Pat Eliot," Don said.

"Damn," Jim said. "Was that off the tee?"

"Oh, hell, yes," Don replied. "Some times she hits it right onto the green."

"Our own Babe Didrikson," Vance said.

L.W. snickered. "Well, y'all know what they say." The other three leaned in to hear the joke.

~ ~ ~

"Good shot, Sis," Joe said. "You got a birdie easy. Me, I can't hit the damn ball anymore."

"You're just out of practice, Joe," Pat said. They replaced their drivers in their bags and started pulling their carts toward Joe's ball.

"Feels good to be outdoors," Joe said. "Seems like I been sleeping so damn much."

Pat looked at him. "You feeling okay?"

He yawned and rubbed his face with his free hand. "I don't know, Sis. So damn lazy. Can't seem to get anything done. I got all this work to do on the farm and I get up in the morning and purt soon the day's over and I ain't done shit."

"Well, give it some time, Joe. It hasn't been that long."

"I know, but I don't have any energy. Feel like an old man. Cotton mouth," he groused. "And I can't have more than one beer."

"How come, because of the medicine?" Pat asked.

"Damn straight. I think the stuff is bad for me."

"What does Marilyn think?"

"Oh, Mare thinks it's a miracle pill. She's thrilled. But she don't have to take it."

Joe took out an iron and swung at his ball. It trickled only about thirty yards down the fairway. "God damn it! I swear, Pat, I'm gonna throw those goddamn pills away."

Pat chewed her lip. They walked to his ball and this time he put it nearer the green, but still behind Pat's first shot. After they chipped on, Joe three putted, finally holing out for a triple bogey seven. Pat's putt just slipped past the hole and she tipped it in.

"I may as well just throw these goddamn clubs right into the goddamn lake," Joe fumed.

"You hear about Janice Tuttle?" Pat asked as they walked toward the second tee.

"Oh, yeah, I heard. Poor old Cal. You know, I think he was out at our place about the time it happened."

"He was?"

"Yeah, he just came by to see how I was doing."

"He's a good old boy," Pat said.

"Yeah. Wonder what he's going to do now?"

Pat put her tee in the ground. "Have a life, I hope," she said.

~ ~ ~

"If only I had thought to stop her when I first saw her." Ray Parker turned his anguished face to his wife.

"Ray, you can't blame yourself," Kathryn said.

"I saw her walking out toward the lake. She waved to me. I thought, that's funny, Janice Tuttle out walking on the street. I hadn't seen her for years, practically forgot about her. If I had just stopped then and asked her where she was going."

"You couldn't have known what she was going to do." Kathryn took Ray's icy hands and massaged them.

"Kat, it is so strange. I had the team out running laps around the lake and I had to take Bill Lynch home. He got to thinking about Keith drowning out there and..."

"Oh, that's right. Bill was out there with him that day."

"Seems like he's been holding himself responsible for Keith's death. He was crying and saying it was all his fault. That it was his idea to swim across the lake. I talked to him for awhile at his house, and then I drove back out to the lake to see if the team had finished their laps. When I saw they were gone, I was heading back to school and then I saw Janice."

"You couldn't have known."

"Well, I must have known something was up. Otherwise, why did I go back out there? I had this really bad feeling about her."

"You didn't see her go in."

"No. But I walked down to the edge and then I saw her shoes. I waded into the water and hollered her name. But you know it gets so deep so fast." His eyes were agonized, as he recalled the moment. "So then I jumped in the car and drove back to school and called the ambulance. I went back and waited for them down by the water's edge. I thought it might not be too late to get her out, if I could just only see her. But I couldn't see her. I should have gone in after her."

"Sweetheart..."

Miserably, he drew his hands away and tucked them under his arms. "I wish I had stopped when I saw her. She waved at me. She looked like she used to look, before she got sick. Young, cheerful. She was smiling. Why didn't I stop and talk to her? I could have stopped her."

"Ray, don't torture yourself."

He put his head down. When he finally spoke, she could barely make out the words, they were so soft. "I bet you Cal blames me."

"Ray! Cal would never blame you. Nobody would blame you. If you hadn't gone out there when you did, it could have been days before they found her."

Ray burst out, "Kat, what makes a person want to die?"

Her eyes were brimming with tears. "Oh, honey, sometimes we just get mixed up about what's important and what's not."

He rubbed his face, reached out and took her hands again. "You're so warm."

"You're shaking all over."

She put her arms around him, her strength and warmth finally quelling his shudders. "Hush," she whispered, as he started to speak. "Just let me hold you."

~ ~ ~

Carolyn carefully folded the black sheath dress she had worn to the baby's funeral and laid it in the suitcase. Mavis sat on the edge of the bed, watching her daughter pack.

"Let's see. I'm going to want my silver crescents." Carolyn took a pair of earrings from her jewel case.

"I just wish you wouldn't leave so soon," Mavis said.

"There's really no reason for me to stay."

"Are you sure about that?"

Carolyn selected a silver bracelet from the jewel case and clasped it around her right arm. "Yes, Mother, I'm sure."

"It just seems to me that Danny might need you here for awhile. Even if nothing is going to happen, as you say. We don't really know what the sheriff will decide."

"This probably will sound heartless, but right now Cal Tuttle is in no frame of mind to decide anything."

"That poor, poor man. And his poor little girl. I just feel so sorry for them. You know I hadn't seen Janice in…I guess it's been years. I just kind of forgot about her. I told Daddy they should drain that lake. Two drownings in one year. It's not safe."

"It's not the lake's fault," Carolyn said. She examined her face in the mirror. "I can't believe it – I'm getting a pimple!"

"Is it time for your period?" Mavis asked.

Carolyn dabbed the offending area with powder and applied lipstick with a little brush. "Well," she said, looking at herself from all angles, "I guess that will have to do."

"You look lovely," Mavis said. "I was looking at you at the funeral. Daryl has aged, but you look as young as you did when you got married."

"Mother, you need glasses."

"I wish I had your skin. And your figure. You never gain an ounce, do you?"

Carolyn stood up to scrutinize herself in the full length mirror. She was Santa Fe smart in slim denim pants and cowboy boots.

"That is a darling outfit," Mavis said.

"I got these at a little boutique in Santa Fe."

"Carolyn, Daddy told me to ask you. Are you doing all right for money?"

Carolyn brushed her hair. "Well, you know I get alimony, and then there's the money Grandpa left me."

"Daddy doesn't want you to spend Grandpa's money."

"Well, I haven't spent all of it, but I did have to buy a house in Santa Fe."

"Well, Daddy said to tell you that if you need money you should let him know. We just worry about you, Carolyn, all alone there in a strange place."

"Mother, Santa Fe is not a strange place. It's my home now. I have friends there."

"I suppose you…go out with men?"

"Oh, sometimes."

"Any one special?"

Carolyn smiled.

"Oh, there is someone special, then! When do we get to meet him?"

Probably never, Carolyn thought, and the thought brought irritation. "Don't pry, Mother. It isn't becoming."

"Well, I was just asking. Don't you sometimes miss Daryl?"

"Mother, it is all over between Daryl and me."

"Well, I just thought – you all looked so cute going out to the Rondy-Voo."

Carolyn banged shut the suitcase and snapped the fasteners.

Mavis said, "Well, if you're sure you have to go, I'll make you some ham sandwiches for your trip."

Carolyn took her suitcase into the living room and set it down by the door. Jim laid his newspaper aside. "Where are you going?" he asked.

"Home," she said.

He sighed. "I wish you would stay awhile. We haven't had much chance to visit."

"I know, Daddy. How have you been feeling?"

"Okay, I guess. Still have some heartburn. Doc told me to take Pepto Bismol. Other than that, I'm fine."

"Why don't you and Mother come out to Santa Fe to visit me?"

"Well, we might could. Maybe your mother could come by herself."

"I'd love it if *you* came," Carolyn said. She sat on the arm of Jim's recliner and smoothed his hair. "Daddy, I don't want you to worry about me."

"Well, sweetheart, you're so far away. How are you doing for money?"

"I told Mother, I'm okay."

"Just okay?"

She laughed. "Well, you know me, I like pretty things."

He reached into his hip pocket for his wallet. He handed her a check. "You just put this in the bank."

She looked at the amount. "Oh, Daddy, this is too generous."

"More where that came from if you need it."

"Oh, Daddy," she said and kissed his cheek.

~ ~ ~

Daryl leaped out of his chair when he saw Carolyn's turquoise and cream Oldsmobile through the window. He hurried outside to help her out of the car.

She said, "Is Danny here? I'm here to say goodbye."

Daryl stared at her. "I thought you were going to stay awhile."

"Where is Danny?"

Daryl had no idea where Danny was. "He'll probably be back soon. Sit down. Why are you leaving?"

"Daryl, there is no reason for me to stay. I need to go home."

"Carolyn, we need you to be here. Please."

His hangdog look irritated her. She had always been contemptuous of his weakness. It would be good to get away from him, from Massey, from all this trouble. It had been stupid to go to bed with him. Now he had expectations, which she was in no way going to fulfill.

Daryl said, "Why don't you sit down? How about a Coke?"

She shrugged. Daryl put a nickel in the machine and brought out a bottle. He popped the cap off and handed it to her.

"Don't you have a glass?" she asked.

"I don't think so. There's some coffee cups, but I think they may be dirty."

Carolyn took a dainty sip from the bottle.

"Does Danny know you're going?" Daryl asked. "He didn't say anything to me."

"I don't think he expected me to stay forever."

Daryl ran his fingers through the stiff bristles of his crew cut. He tried to take her hand, but she eluded him. She looked around the office and said, "This place is a mess."

"I know," he said humbly.

She set the bottle on his desk and fished car keys out of her purse. "I need to get started."

"What about Danny?"

"Tell him I had to go. I'll call him later."

Daryl followed her out to her car and watched in misery as she slid behind the wheel. "Carolyn, I wish you wouldn't go."

"Goodbye, Daryl." She slammed the door and started the engine. Without looking back, she drove away.

~ ~ ~

Reverend Dressler looked at his watch. After one. He had not sufficiently recovered from this morning's funeral, and now it was almost time to meet with Cal Tuttle to plan another one. Two difficult funerals in one week. He wiped his face with his handkerchief while paging vaguely through his hymnal. It had been bad enough this morning saying a few words and offering prayers concerning the death of an infant girl.

No one at the funeral seemed to mourn Baby Angela or to notice that her mother wasn't present. There had been an almost festive air when the Tomlins and the Atkinses trooped into the sanctuary and arranged themselves in the front pews near the tiny white coffin draped with a spray of pink roses.

He had chosen Matthew 19:14 for his text. Now he wished he had chosen Matthew 18:6 as a rebuke to Baby Angela's relatives, who grinned and whispered in the pews. Not even the tender-hearted Mavis shed a tear. Everyone treated Danny as if he were the heroic survivor of an ordeal. The men slapped him on the back, and the women petted and hugged him.

After the brief service, Maynard Keyes and he loaded the little coffin and the flowers into the hearse for the trip to the cemetery. On the way, Maynard told him much more than he wanted to hear about the effort he had gone to, in case the family wanted to view the body.

"You can't imagine what an autopsy does to a body, Reverend," Maynard said. "You can cover the body with clothes, but there's no disguising the fact that the skull has been cut open, particularly on a baby who had no hair.

What a relief they didn't want a viewing."

The hot wind whipped and stung while they stood around the gravesite, and grit found its way into everyone's eyes. When it was over, the Tomlins and Atkinses quickly drove away. Maynard's man filled in the minuscule grave, and Maynard arranged the pink roses on top of the freshly piled earth.

"Rest in peace, Baby Angela," Reverend Dressler murmured, "And may God have mercy on us all."

Now he sat at his desk, hymnal in his hands, pondering. He had been young when he went to seminary, young and idealistic. He had purposed to become a minister in a small town. Memorial Methodist was the fourth church he had served in twenty-five years, and at each congregation he had seen membership and stewardship increase. People regularly attended worship, served on committees, and spearheaded campaigns for new buildings and foreign missions. Musicians played the organ and other instruments; choirs sang cantatas; youth leaders planned activities for the youth groups; secretaries prepared the bulletins and newsletters; and members helped maintain the building and grounds. Ladies took care of the altar and his robes, organized church suppers and bazaars. Men took leadership positions as elders and deacons.

For his part, he tended the sick and the dying, performed baptisms, marriages and funerals, and preached countless sermons. He had counseled people, prayed with them and for them, shared meals with them at their homes. All the outward signs pointed to success and fulfillment.

At 50, doubt became his constant companion. During the war he had been troubled by the Bible-thumping that accompanied saber-rattling. Many folks seemed to assume that God was on America's side. He watched religion become the willing handmaid of war and politics. The bombings of Hiroshima and Nagasaki sickened him. Yet many seemed confident that God desired the destruction of Japan.

Reverend Dressler wondered what God really had in mind for the world. In occasional conversation with Brother Robbins, he envied the other man's rock-solid convictions and unshakeable beliefs. In contrast he found himself less certain of anything. The familiar beliefs he had formerly espoused no longer seemed pertinent. Even the words of the Lord's Prayer now seemed like a foreign language to him, one he didn't know and couldn't learn.

He seemed to have endless questions about God. Why had He made it almost irresistible for man to disobey Him, and why was the punishment for disobedience so severe? How did it help anything for Jesus to die on the cross? What kind of God could arrange His Son's terrible suffering and death? Question piled upon question, and he knew no answers.

What troubled him most, however, was whether being a minister held any real significance. There were times when he thought religion completely irrelevant, not only to him but to the world. He tried to pray, but his thoughts wandered, and he had little confidence that God attended to prayer. If God knew everything that was going to happen, what was the use of prayer? It seemed like going to a movie and hoping for an ending different from the one that had already been filmed.

In spite of his own doubt and dilemmas, he had tried to offer comfort to a grieving family this morning. He and Emily were childless, but he loved children, especially babies. He loved performing baptisms of tiny sweet-smelling bundles in his arms. Children flocked to him, hugged his neck, and sat on his lap at church suppers. His cheer, girth, and gray hair suggested Santa Claus or a jolly grandpa. He agonized for folks who had lost a child.

But he couldn't fathom the Atkinses and the Tomlins. Did these good Christian folk believe that it was better to have a dead baby than to have an illegitimate baby? The thought angered him, but he worried that he might be partly responsible for that kind of attitude. He had preached many sermons about the importance of correct moral behavior. Wasn't that what God expected of ministers of the church, to teach morals and ethics?

Was it God's will for Angela to die? Did He want to make a point about babies born outside of marriage? Did God take Angela away from this family in order to punish them? If so, God must really have His nose out of joint now, because these people were in a celebratory mood.

And where did love fit in? God so loved the world. Love one another. The greatest of these is love. If God was so loving, how come He was also so bloodthirsty?

He shook himself back to the task lying ahead. In fifteen minutes, Cal Tuttle would walk into his office, and he would be faced with a thorny theological dilemma. The church taught that suicide was the unforgivable sin; those who took their own lives could not possibly enter the Kingdom of Heaven. Furthermore, during the eight years he had been the minister at Memorial Methodist, Janice Tuttle hadn't once attended church or Bible study or helped with a church supper.

He was positive that Brother Robbins would know what to do in a case like this. He would likely quote some damning passage from scripture to support his certainty that there was no place in Christendom for suicide.

Trying to pray, he clasped his hands together, shut his eyes, bowed his head. "Oh, God, help me," he said aloud. "I don't know what is right or pleasing in your sight. I don't know what you want from me." He sat in this position of prayer, waiting, hoping for something. "Please, God."

No answer came. God seemed absent. So he was on his own. Somehow that realization came as a tremendous relief. He released his hands, opened his eyes, and raised his head. Now relaxed, he waited for Cal Tuttle.

# CHAPTER TEN

~

Adam Robbins stood outside Woodson's studying the men's display window as if contemplating a purchase. After a bit, he moved over to the women's display window and inspected its contents with the same concentration. The door to the store opened and Renee joined him.

"Thought you left town," she said.

"That was only a rumor," he replied.

"Come on in," she urged. "I'll sell you something."

"I'll bet you would."

She looked him over. "You probably need some new clothes to take back to Oklahoma City with you."

"What's wrong with these clothes?"

"Oh, nothing, I guess. Don't you own any Levi's? You dress like a city boy."

He grinned at her. "I guess you like boys from the country."

She wrinkled her nose. "Boys are stupid."

"And some girls are too smart for their own good," he said.

"Say," Renee said, "do you like frosted Cokes?"

"Favorite thing in the whole world. Want one now?"

"Wait a minute." She stuck her head in the door and called out, "Wayne, I'll be back in a couple of minutes."

Jesse glowered at them as they approached the counter. "Two frosted Cokes," Adam said. "Bring them to the booth."

Renee took a straw, bit off one end of the paper wrapping, and blew into the straw. The paper hit Adam's throat. "Bulls-eye," she said.

Adam imitated the action, and the paper bounced off Renee's cleavage. "Bulls-eye," he said.

Jesse banged the two glasses on their table and stomped back to the counter. Renee giggled.

She tasted her drink. "Sweet," she said.

"Like you." Adam said.

"You don't know whether I am or not."

"Maybe I can find out."

"Maybe."

Adam leaned toward her. "You smell sweet." He picked up her hand and brought it to his tongue. "Taste sweet, too."

Renee shivered and took her hand back.

"You cold?" Adam asked.

"No."

"I'll bet you're not."

"Maybe you can find out."

Renee licked her lips. Adam ran his tongue around his open mouth.

"You are naughty," Renee said.

"You don't know whether I am or not," he said.

"Maybe I can find out. What are you doing tonight?" Renee asked.

"Why?"

"Thought you might like to go to the picture show." She noted his hesitation. "Scared?" she asked.

"Should I be?" he asked.

"Maybe you should be real scared," she said. "That's okay, you don't want to go to the picture show with me, that's okay." She slid out of the booth.

"See you later?" he asked.

"Not if I see you first."

~ ~ ~

Wayne met Renee at the door. "Was that Adam Robbins?" He already knew that it was, because he had watched the two of them.

"Or his twin," Renee retorted. "What are you staring at?"

"Your face is all red," he said.

"It is not. It's hot outside. Stop staring at me." She brushed past him. She needed time to think about what had just happened. It seemed Adam had turned her down, but maybe he was just playing hard to get. She needed to think and to plan. She wasn't about to give up, not yet anyway.

Wayne followed her to the back of the store. "I should warn you about Adam Robbins," he said.

"Leave me alone, Wayne."

"You should stay away from him. He's not what he seems to be. He's an unrepentant sinner."

"Oh, shut up, Wayne."

"Everybody thinks he's a saint. But he's a hypocrite, the worst kind of sinner. Until I stepped in, he was even fooling his daddy. But his daddy knows now. Pretty soon the whole town will know. You'll be grateful I warned you."

Renee turned. "Warned me about what?"

"About Adam Robbins. He's an adulterer."

"He's a what?"

"He has committed the sin of adultery. He is going to burn in hell for that."

Renee's eyes widened. He imagined that she was already grateful and swelled with righteous pride. He pictured himself baptizing her, restoring her to a holy disposition.

He raised his voice. "Adam Robbins has transgressed. He has brazenly committed adultery with a married woman. He will be most certainly be punished."

"What do you mean, Wayne?"

"I mean that Adam Robbins has committed adultery with Mrs. Roy Woodson."

"You better shut up, Wayne," Renee hissed. But it was too late.

Roy Woodson leaned over the balcony. "Pickens," he thundered, " you get up here right now."

❧ ❧ ❧

Marilyn touched Joe's shoulder. "Supper's ready."

He jerked in his chair, looked up at her. "Already? Seems like we just ate."

"It's 6:30. Aren't you hungry? I made chicken fried steak."

"Where's Jesse?"

"He just got in."

Joe bent down, grunting, and pulled on his boots. He stood up, swaying slightly."Tired," he said.

"Well, no wonder. You got up before six to play golf."

"Pat beat the pants off me."

"Pat beats the pants off everybody," Marilyn said. "Jesse, we're sitting down."

"No, she skunked me. I couldn't hit the damn ball." He took a chair at the table. Marilyn shook a pill out of its bottle and handed it to him. "Take your pill."

He reached for his water and took a swallow. Marilyn went to the hallway and called, "Jesse! Time for supper."

Joe took another mouthful of water and swallowed hard. “Ugh,” he said.

“I know, they’re hard to get down,” Marilyn said. “But they’re working a miracle.”

“Did you wash up?” Marilyn asked Jesse.

He showed her his hands and plopped into a chair.

“How was practice?” Joe asked him, as Marilyn ladled food onto their plates.

“We didn’t have a practice.”

“How come?”

“I don’t know. We were waiting for Coach to show up, and finally he came and said we should just do warm ups and go home. He said out of respect to Mrs. Tuttle.”

“Mrs. Tuttle?” Joe looked at Marilyn, confused.

“Honey, don’t you remember, I told you, Janice Tuttle drowned in the lake.”

“She probably came out there yesterday after we did our laps,” Jesse said.

“Out where?” Joe asked.

Jesse gave his mother a look and then answered, with exaggerated patience, “Out at the lake, where she drowned.”

“The boys were running laps around the lake,” Marilyn explained.

“Did you see her out there?” he asked Jesse.

“No. Gosh!” Jesse appealed to his mother.

“Cal was just out here,” Joe said.

“Yes, honey, we were talking about that last night,” Marilyn said.

Jesse gave her exaggerated incredulity. “Stop it,” she said.

“Stop what?” he asked, eyes wide and innocent.

“You know what, and don’t eat so fast,” she said.

Joe pushed his chair away from the table.

“Honey, you hardly ate a thing,” Marilyn said.

“Not really hungry.”

“There’s dessert,” she said. “Bread pudding.”

“No thanks,” he said.

“Where are you going?” Marilyn got to her feet.

“Mare, sit down, eat your supper. I’m just going to go for a little walk.”

“A walk!”

“I’ll be back in a little while.”

“Let him go,” Jesse said to his mother.

"I worry about him," she said, when Joe had gone.

"He's crazy," Jesse said.

"Jesse, don't you say that about your daddy."

"Well, it's the truth."

"Jesse, just be quiet and eat your supper."

"Yes ma'am," he answered with as much sarcasm as he could muster with his mouth full.

On the porch, Joe looked out beyond the ruined trees to the brilliant western sky. The cool evening breeze ruffled his hair. He walked away from the house to the out buildings. Behind the shed he took the pill from his pocket and ground it into the loose soil with his boot heel. He walked on past the barn and leaned over the fence looking out at his fields. Somebody had plowed the stubble under, he didn't know who. People came out, did things. He glanced at the empty hog pens. Somebody had shoveled them out. He guessed the hogs were sold. He couldn't remember. He guessed the maize had been planted, but he couldn't recall exactly when.

He yawned enormously. His head felt stuffed full of cotton. He couldn't get his thoughts in order. One thing he knew for sure, he wasn't taking any more of those goddamn pills.

❧ ❧ ❧

"Mama, you here? Mama!" Renee was practically vibrating with excitement.

"What's wrong?"

"Mama, you will never guess what happened! Mr. Woodson fired Wayne!"

"Really? How come? What happened?"

"Wayne said something bad about Mrs. Woodson, and Mr. Woodson told him to get out of the store and never to come back."

Nadine laughed and coughed. "Something bad about Maureen Woodson? Whoa! What did Wayne say?"

"Well, he was raving about Adam Robbins…"

"Adam Robbins?"

"Yeah, he was going on and on about what a sinner Adam was and how he had committed something, what did he call it, a dull tree? What is that anyway?"

Nadine swallowed hard. "Adultery?"

"Yeah, that's right. He said Adam had committed it with Mrs. Woodson.

What does it mean?"

"Wayne said that?"

"Said it? He hollered it. You should have seen his face when Mr. Woodson leaned over the balcony and told him to get his behind up there. I liked to died, he looked so funny." Renee's laughter faded. "So what is it? Do you know?"

Nadine fumbled, "Well, it's, it's..."

"Is it – is it – sex?"

"Yeah, that's what it is."

Renee's mouth dropped open. "Adam Robbins and Mrs. Woodson? That can't be true, can it? Can it?"

"I think it's highly likely," Nadine said.

Renee stuck out her tongue. "Eww! *Mrs. Woodson*? She is so *old*. Why would he want to do that with *her*? What would he want with an old woman like her?"

Nadine coughed and coughed. Renee banged her between the shoulders. "You sound awful."

"I know," Nadine replied in a strangled voice.

Renee began to pace around the living room. "Why do you think it's true?"

"People have been talking. I think somebody saw them."

"Saw them *doing* it?" Renee clamped her eyes shut to block the appalling image.

"No, but I guess they saw enough to put two and two together."

"But *why*? Why would he want to do it with an old woman? There must be something wrong with him."

"I think you may be right about that," Nadine said quietly.

"*And*," Renee cried, "there must be something wrong with her, too! He's just a boy, and she's a grown woman. *She* should *know* better! Shouldn't she?"

"Renee, sometimes people do things..."

"Well, they shouldn't! They shouldn't do such horrible things. It was horrible, wasn't it? Wasn't it?" Renee was close to tears.

Nadine put her arm around her daughter's shoulders. "Yes, I think it was horrible."

~ ~ ~

Maureen lay on her bed with a cold cloth over her forehead and eyes. She believed that she might have a headache. She thought that Roy would be home by now.

She was utterly bored. Roy probably would want to go out to eat at the Steak House. His idea of a big evening. He was such a stick. She had wanted a glamorous and exciting life, and this is what she got instead. Marilyn might be happy in her little housewife's role, as their mother had been. But it was so dreary being married to Roy.

She thought about Adam. She called him again, but he hung up on her. So that was over. Although you never could tell with men, sometimes they just couldn't stay away. Adam would be going back to Oklahoma City soon anyway, so it was no real loss. Still, he had given her something to look forward to.

I must be getting old, she thought ruefully, if a college boy is all I have to look forward to. The thought brought tears to her eyes. It was so unfair. It was all Roy's fault. He had pestered her until she had agreed to marry him. He had promised her everything and had delivered so little. She needed so much more than Roy could give her.

What if I got a divorce and moved away, she thought. That was what Carolyn Tomlin had done, divorced Daryl and left town. She had seen Carolyn driving down Main Street today in that pretty car with the New Mexico license plate.

She pictured herself, a beautiful, mysterious divorcee. She wouldn't move to Santa Fe – too many cowboys. Maybe New York City? No, she didn't want to live among Yankees and Jews. Now Dallas would be perfect. It was a real city, not a dinky little old town. She could shop at Neiman Marcus.

Roy would be devastated. But she had already given him so much of herself. It was time to take care of Maureen and let Roy look after Roy. She wasn't getting any younger. She rose from the bed to examine her face in the mirror of the vanity table and felt reassured. She was still young and pretty.

First she would have to tell Roy that she wanted a divorce. That would crush him, but he would eventually recover. She would have to see a lawyer. Maybe she should see a lawyer first. A good lawyer would get her alimony and a generous settlement. She would need money to live in Dallas.

She might trade in the El Dorado. It was a nice car, but dark blue was such a somber color. She liked those new little Corvettes. She would drive around Dallas with the top down.

She heard Roy's car pull into the driveway. Should she just tell him now, or should she wait? Maybe it would be best to wait. Maybe she should consult a lawyer first. Tonight they could go out to the Steak House. It would give her more time to plan exactly what to say. She began to brush her hair.

Roy didn't call out to her when he came in the house. That was unusual. She surveyed her closet. She would need an entire new wardrobe for Dallas. She pulled out a flowered silk dress and put it on. Too hot for nylons. She slipped into white mules, admiring her pretty feet. She ran the brush through her hair once more and applied lipstick.

Roy was sitting on the sofa with a highball glass. He looked up when she came in, but he didn't say anything, just drank from the glass.

"Well, can't you even say hello?" she said.

"Hello, Maureen," he said.

"What are you drinking?"

"Bourbon."

She took a cigarette from the box on the coffee table, tapped it on her thumbnail, and waited for him to light it. When he didn't, she sniffed and picked up the big silver lighter herself. She flicked it and applied the flame to the end of her cigarette. "Maybe I'd like a drink, too," she said.

"Help yourself," he said.

This was very strange. Roy didn't seem himself at all. She went into the dining room where the bottle of Jim Beam and the ice bucket stood on the credenza. She made herself a drink in a crystal highball glass, which she took back into the living room. She retrieved her cigarette from the ashtray and sat down opposite him. He drained his glass and took it back to pour himself another drink. When he returned, he didn't sit down, but stood looking down at her.

"Well, you seem to be in a mood," she said.

"I fired Wayne Pickens today," he said.

"You did? Why?"

"That's the sixty-four dollar question, isn't it? Maybe I should have given him a raise instead. He told me I was shooting the messenger. He said I should thank him. I wonder if he was right."

"What happened? You aren't making any sense."

"He told me something I didn't want to hear," he said and sat down again. He held his glass in both hands and turned it, watching the amber liquid roll over the ice cubes. Uneasiness prickled its way up her spine.

"He told me you were having an affair with Adam Robbins. Are you?"

Maureen attempted to remain expressionless, but her face burned. A jumble of memories racketed through her mind, the Packard parked outside their house, her conversation with Wayne Pickens' mother. "Of course not," she said, but her voice wobbled.

"You know, it's funny," he said slowly. "You can know something and not know it at the same time. And then a time comes and everything falls into place. The little pieces that didn't seem to fit before, now they fit. Like a jigsaw puzzle. And then you see the whole thing right in front of your eyes. It's always been there, but you couldn't see it before. Or wouldn't let yourself see it."

"Roy, I don't know what Wayne Pickens thinks he knows, but..."

"So many little pieces. All those times you went out of town. That time I ran into Max Allison and he was so nervous talking to me he sweated through his shirt. All that dental work you said you were having. Then I remembered that day I saw that big old Packard sitting out here in front of the house. I sort of wondered if you had gone out looking for other men, but I didn't think you would have the gall to bring one to our house."

"Roy, you're upset. You're not making any sense."

"Maureen, for the first time in years, I'm making real sense."

"You can't really believe I was having an affair with that boy. Wayne has put nonsense into your head. Roy, I swear..."

"Everybody in town knows about it. I'm just the last one to find out."

"Roy, I..."

"I went over to Don Paulson's office this afternoon. I wanted to know my legal rights. He told me something interesting. He said that in a case of what he called sustained and public adultery, there is no automatic right to division of property or to alimony. I told him to draw up the papers for divorce."

He drained his glass, set it down on the coffee table and got up, went to the door.

"Where are you going?" she cried, her voice high and strained.

"I'm going to go have a steak dinner."

"What about me?" she quavered.

"I don't know about you." Then a harsh bark of a laugh. "Yes, I do. I know all about you."

# CHAPTER ELEVEN

Reverend Dressler had never seen the church so full, not even at Christmas Eve. It seemed that the whole town had turned out for Janice Tuttle's funeral. Stands of flowers crowded the sanctuary, and there was a giant spray of white carnations on top of the casket. Cal and Laura sat in the front pew by themselves, but every other seat was taken including the folding chairs set up. Some people were standing at the back.

The people were subdued, even somber. Almost every Methodist was there, including people he hadn't seen since Easter. Dr. Wright, the First Presbyterian minister, sat near the front, and there were several other pews occupied by members of his congregation. A number of Baptists, but not Brother Robbins. Most businesses had closed for the service. Serving as pall bearers were Pete Mosley, Virgil Harmon, Jimmy Speers, Ray Parker, Tom Reynolds, and Roy Woodson.

Like a great choir, the people sang "Holy, Holy, Holy" with fervent solemnity. Reverend Dressler boomed out the words in his pleasant baritone. "All thy works shall praise thy name in earth and sky and sea. Only thou art holy, there is none beside thee, perfect in power, in love and purity."

After the hymn, Reverend Dressler said, "Our text for today is the 23rd Psalm. We will read it aloud in unison. It is printed on page 2 of your bulletin."

"The Lord is my shepherd, I shall not want. He maketh me to lie down in green pastures, he leadeth me beside the still waters. He restoreth my soul. He leadeth me into the paths of righteousness for his name's sake. Yea, though I walk through the valley of the shadow of death, I will fear no evil, for thou art with me. Thy rod and thy staff, they comfort me. Thou preparest a table before me in the presence of mine enemies. Thou anointest my head with oil. My cup runneth over. Surely goodness and mercy shall follow me all the days of my life, and I will dwell in the house of the Lord forever."

He stepped away from the lectern and began to speak. "My friends, when David wrote these words, he was expressing his deep and unshakeable faith in the presence of Almighty God in his life. Although David was a great and powerful king, in this Psalm he speaks as a lamb with a shepherd who will lead him to green pastures and fresh water, restoring body and soul. The Lord as his shepherd will be with him wherever he goes, whether it be into the paths of righteousness or into the valley of the shadow of death. He will be comforted and spared from fear. The Lord will provide all that he needs and will give him an abundance of life's pleasures and treasures. The cup of blessing will be filled to overflowing. Goodness and mercy will be in plentiful supply, and he will always live in the Lord's house. This is David's statement about his relationship with God.

"Was all this promised David because he was a good man? Did David earn these eternal blessings? Did God single out David as special, as one who could receive such bounty, because David lived a holy and sinless life? Not so, not so at all. You will recall that David committed two grievous sins – murder and adultery – two sins expressly condemned by the Lord's own commandments. Thou shalt not kill. Thou shalt not commit adultery.

"David sent the soldier Uriah into battle knowing he would be killed. Why did he commit murder? Because he wanted Uriah's wife, the beautiful Bathsheba, for himself. That is adultery. In fact, there are three sins here: murder, adultery, and covetousness. He coveted Bathsheba, and that sin led to the others.

"Now, we could ask, how did David get away with all of this? Did David get brought up before a judge or a jury? Was he convicted? Did he receive the death penalty? Did he spend the rest of his life in prison?

"You're probably thinking, well, he was the king, and the king does as he pleases. And you are correct in your thoughts. Nobody put David in handcuffs or led him away to a trial, or prison, or death.

"But God knew, and David knew that God knew of his terrible sins. We know what that feels like, don't we? Even if no one else knows about the wrong we have done, we know it, and we know that God knows it. We know what it feels like to lie down in our beds at night and to feel the weight and the oppression of our sins. During daytime, we could be so occupied going about our business, even doing good works, even going to church, that we could prevent ourselves from feeling the burden of our sins. But at night, in the darkness, they come to rest on our hearts and our minds. And we sweat and we tremble alone there in the darkness under the crushing weight of our own wickedness.

"And we could even plead, well, we haven't committed the terrible sins that David committed. But that doesn't let us off the hook. Because it says in the fifth chapter of the book of Matthew, that to be angry makes us guilty of breaking the commandment against murder. It says that to look with lust makes us guilty of breaking the commandment against adultery. And we know we have indeed been angry, and we know we have indeed been lustful. So in our own ways we could be as wicked as David was.

"But David wrote the 23rd Psalm. How do we reconcile his sinful behavior with this beautiful Psalm? How does a sinful man write these words?

"We learned this Psalm when we were little children. We know it by heart. In fact it is engraved on our hearts. It stands there as a testimony in our own hearts, as a witness to the love and mercy of our Lord. It stands there with us in the night when we sweat and tremble, and it reminds us of the love and mercy of God.

"Our sister Janice walked out to the lake Thursday morning. We don't know what was in her heart or on her mind. We know that for years she suffered a mental illness. We may not know what it was like to suffer in the particular way Janice suffered, but we know what it is to suffer the torments of the mind.

"Our hymn this morning reminded us of that kind of suffering. It says, you remember, Though the darkness hide thee. Our Psalm this morning reminds us of that kind of suffering. The valley of the shadow of death. Not death itself, but the shadow of death. The fear of death. The experience of death looming over us. Darkness and shadow.

"Janice went to the lake Thursday morning. We don't know if she experienced darkness or shadow. We don't know her thoughts. But God knows. Whether Janice realized it or not, God was right there with her, accompanying her through the darkness, through the valley of the shadow of death. Even if the darkness hid him, he was right there beside her. Whether she felt his presence or not, he was there. He was there, just as the shepherd is with the lamb.

"Just as he is here right now with each of us, whether we know it or not. Whether we believe it or not. Whether we feel it or not. The Lord is my shepherd, I shall not want.

"And now unto him who is able to keep us from falling and to present us faultless before the presence of his glory with exceeding joy, be glory, both now and forever."

Fifty automobiles followed the hearse to the cemetery. Maynard Keyes opened the back of the hearse, and the six pallbearers carried the casket and placed it above the freshly dug grave. It was a glorious day. Billowing cumulus clouds hung like snow-filled balloons in the azure sky. The air was warm, not stifling hot, and for once the wind was calm.

For almost fifteen years, the ladies' garden club had tended the cemetery. Trees, shrubs, and rose bushes had been planted and watered. Tombstones dating back to the 1800's, marking the graves of the first settlers, had been straightened, and a record was painstakingly kept, so there were no anonymous graves. Graves maintained by the VFW and the American Legion commemorated those who had died in the two World Wars and in the Korean conflict.

The people walked from their cars to Janice's grave, passing by familiar names carved on large granite headstones. There was a statue of an angel marking the grave of a child, with the words "ASLEEP IN JESUS" at the base.

Reverend Dressler stood near the casket with Cal and Laura at his side. The rest gathered close around to hear him read the rite of burial. After the last Amen, people came up to shake Cal's hand and hug Laura.

Reverend Dressler stood aside. He felt light and cleansed, as if an encumbrance had been lifted. He wondered where that sermon had sprung from. He had written nothing, having only a slight notion of what he would say. He had never before preached extemporaneously. The sermon seemed to unfold before him. He had not once had to hesitate or search for a phrase. It was as if the words had been there all along, just waiting for him to speak them. His eyes burned and his chest and throat swelled with emotion. "Thank you," he said softly.

Deep in his own thoughts, he was startled when people clustered around him, grasping his arm, shaking his hand. Earnest faces leaned toward him, and grateful words surged over him. Some eyes were wet, some voices thickened with tears. "Just want to thank you" and "Meant so much to me" echoed again and again as they pressed against one another in their eagerness to speak to him.

Gradually the people dispersed back to their cars and he and Cal and Laura stood alone, Maynard discreetly off to the side, waiting for them to leave. He saw Emily waiting by their car. He had a great desire to be alone with his wife.

Cal shook his hand. "I never thought about what you said. I did picture her being out there alone, but I never thought about...about what you said."

Laura sobbed quietly. Reverend Dressler put one arm around her shoulders and drew her close to him. With his other arm he gathered Cal into his embrace. The three of them stood together for a moment before he released them.

Dorothy drove with Pat in the front seat and Virgil in back. No one spoke during the ride from the cemetery to Main Street. Dorothy pulled the car into a space in front of the drug store, and turned to look at her brother. He didn't get out of the car. She shut off the engine and rolled down her window. A soft breeze blew.

After a time Virgil cleared his throat and spoke. "I was thinking about

Mama. I remember her in the bed, full of cancer. You know, Sis? I sat there beside her that last night. You were there."

"Oof, when I could stand it," Dorothy said. "I mostly sat in the kitchen with Daddy."

"You remember what she said," Virgil said.

Dorothy reflected. "No, I guess I don't, really."

"Maybe you weren't there. She was laying there, struggling to breathe. I don't think she was hurting so bad, I had just given her the dose of morphine, but she was having a hard time breathing. I couldn't tell if she knew I was there or not. She had been kind of out of her head."

"I remember that," Dorothy said.

"I was just sitting there, watching her. Then it seemed like she got a breath, and she squeezed my hand, hard. She looked right at me. She said, clear as anything, 'The Lord is my shepherd, I shall not want.' A minute later she was gone."

Dorothy mopped up tears with her handkerchief. Pat blew her nose.

"I never remembered that until today," Virgil said. "Well, I better get to work. Thanks for the ride."

❧ ❧ ❧

It was no surprise to Roy that Maureen had not attended the funeral and burial. He had scarcely seen her since Saturday night. He supposed she had gone to Amarillo to get her hair done. As he busied himself in the store, bits of Reverend Dressler's sermon echoed in his head. Roy had been staggered to hear him speak about lying awake at night, sweating. He himself had tossed and turned the past few nights in misery. Although during the day he had presented Maureen with a sternly uncompromising demeanor, the truth was that he was shaky and uncertain inside, especially at night as he sought and couldn't find sleep.

When he wasn't agonizing about Maureen, he replayed the scene with Wayne. He had been so consumed by anger and humiliation that he had to banish that sanctimonious face and wagging finger. But he couldn't eradicate the man from his thoughts. Today at the funeral when he glimpsed Wayne and his mother, Roy had felt embarrassed, as if he was the one who had been caught in wrongdoing.

He had been further discomfited to catch Don Paulson's eye at the funeral. He had been furious with Maureen when he poured out the whole offensive story to Don and was grateful for Don's assurances concerning his legal rights. He had been convinced of his own victimhood and the need to retaliate against both Wayne and Maureen. But that sense of moral superiority had almost immediately faded. His emotions whipsawed him between anger and guilt.

The funeral sermon had captured exactly his experience of being confronted by his own wrongdoing. He lay in bed, trying to convince himself that he was the injured party. But the more he protested, the more guilty and ashamed he felt.

But what exactly was he guilty of? And if he was guilty, what was the penalty? What was he supposed to do, back down and eat crow? Was he supposed to beg Maureen's forgiveness and ask her to forget what he had said? That thought was repellant. He had withstood Maureen's contemptuous treatment of him for long enough. When Wayne said everyone knew that Maureen had been carrying on with Adam Robbins, he could no longer deny his own suspicions. He recalled the day the Packard was parked right there in front of the house. He had been cuckolded in his own house, and the whole town knew about it. So why did he feel so guilty?

As for Wayne, Roy couldn't imagine re-hiring him. He recalled Wayne's final words: "You'll be sorry you treated me this way. I was only doing you a favor." It had been a good turn in its own hideous way, because not knowing about Maureen and Adam Robbins was worse than knowing. But at night he longed for the old days of innocence, when he had been able to sleep.

When he told Don he had found out that Maureen was having an affair, Don said, "I wondered if you knew." That meant that the whole town was in on it. It stung him to realize he had been the subject of whispered conversations and the butt of jokes.

The cycles of rage and retaliation followed by guilt and ignominy continued, night after night. When he finally slept, he dreamed of mortifying situations like being naked in public. When he awoke, he was exhausted.

He had been glad to serve as a pallbearer, but it had been an ordeal to appear in public and to wonder what people were thinking about him.

After Reverend Dressler talked about sweating in the night, Roy thought he had gone on to talk about the remedy for such suffering, but he couldn't recall what it was. Something about God being merciful. He wished he knew how to regain some peace of mind. What if he talked about his plight with Reverend Dressler? No, he couldn't bear to inform one more person that his wife had been unfaithful. It had felt good to pour it all out to Don, but now he wished he had kept it to himself. He felt superior when he told Maureen that she wasn't going to benefit from her infidelity. Now everything pointed to his own inferiority.

# JULY-AUGUST 1954

# CHAPTER TWELVE

The air conditioning kept the examining room cold enough to cause Nadine to shiver in the little cotton gown. Dying for a cigarette, she hugged herself. She had come on an impulse and expected the nurse would tell her to make an appointment and come back another day. But the waiting room was empty, and she had been shown into an examining room to wait for Doc Lomax.

She was never sick, hadn't been to a doctor in years, and wouldn't be here now if it weren't for her pesky cough. It had been especially bad last winter and was no better in warm weather. Sometimes she coughed so hard she couldn't catch her breath.

Ever since Janice Tuttle's funeral, Nadine had been thinking about going to the doctor. She had been surprised to find herself crying during the sermon. Standing at the grave under the brilliant sky, she had felt happy to be alive. Nadine had been thinking about her life since Renee's discovery about Adam and Maureen. Seeing herself through Renee's eyes had startled her. It was true that Adam was just a boy, only a few years older than Renee. Nadine called herself on the carpet. Was she so desperate for sex that she would go to bed with a boy?

Nadine recalled how the affair with Adam had begun. The week before Christmas Adam came into the beauty shop late one afternoon. He told her he didn't want to "get butchered" at the barber shop, so would she cut his hair? She would. They talked and flirted to the point that when he stood up from the chair she wasn't surprised that he kissed her. When she kissed him back, he locked the front door of the shop, turned off the lights, and led her into the back room. She was more than ready for him to start undressing her. Adam was experienced in pleasuring a woman, and Nadine had been thrilled. She was hungry for sex, but for more than just the act. She wanted a man to appreciate her. It had been a long time since she had felt so special. Really, not since Bobby.

But Renee had put her finger on the sore spot and pushed hard. It *was* horrible, what she had done with Adam. What kind of example was she setting for Renee? She had been worrying about Renee's sex life. What about her own?

At the funeral she looked at Virgil, so solemn and sturdy in his navy blue suit with the white carnation in his buttonhole. She had treated Virgil like dirt, for no reason. She had been mean to him about the dance, and he had slunk out of her shop in embarrassment. Why had she done that? Nadine, old girl, it is time for you to turn over a new leaf.

Trouble was, she had been unable to swear off Adam. She planned to say no, but when he called, she said yes. When he left the shop that night, she again pledged to give him up. Until the next phone call.

"Hello, Nadine." Dr. Lomax interrupted her reverie. He washed his hands at the sink. "Beautiful day, isn't it?"

"Sure is," she agreed.

"So, what's the trouble?"

"Well, I've got this cough," Nadine began and the cough began, too.

"So I hear. I'm going to take your blood pressure." He pumped to tighten the cuff and listened through his stethoscope. "That's normal," he said, unstrapping the cuff. He slid a thermometer in her mouth and waited, then took it out and looked at it.

"No temperature. Have you been running a fever?"

"No, not so's I noticed."

"How about chills or night sweats?"

"Nope."

"Have you lost weight recently?"

"I wish."

He was making notes. "Have you ever coughed up blood?"

"No, never."

"How about mucus?"

"Sometimes. Not always."

"Nadine, how much do you smoke?"

"Oh, not much. About a pack a day."

After he listened to her chest for some time, he said, "I'd like for you to have a chest x-ray, and I think while we're at it, I'm going to draw some blood and ask you to give us a urine sample. Plus, I want to do a TB skin test."

"What do you think…." The cough took her voice and breath away.

"I think we'd better find out," he said.

Walking out of the clinic to her car, Nadine started bargaining with God.

Daryl was supposed to be going through the monthly accounts, but the ledger lay unopened on his desk. He had never been so miserable in his life. Having

Carolyn back in town, in his arms at the Rondy-Voo and then later in his bed had been a dream come true. Her abrupt departure had sunk his fantasy of a reconciliation.

Carolyn's cool resolve and certainty about how to handle things had been a consolation to him. When she was in town she took charge, arranging the funeral and the burial. He could never have called up Maynard Keyes and Reverend Dressler in that matter-of-fact way. She had handled Danny, too, made him put on a suit and go to the church and cemetery whether he wanted to or not.

Thoughts of Danny made Daryl grit his teeth. He had never been able to control Danny, or even influence him. With the baby buried and Jeannie gone, Danny had left the trailer and had moved, uninvited, into Daryl's house. He was irregular in coming to the lumber yard. He slept all day and stayed out all night. He merely smirked when Daryl told him he had to straighten up and fly right, and Daryl didn't know what to say next. Carolyn would have given Danny that look, and he would have straightened up.

I have got to get used to the fact that she is gone, he told himself. He had been living his life as if she was due back any day. He had to accept the reality of the situation.

But what was he going to do? He had told Danny to straighten up and fly right. Maybe it was time for Daryl to take his own advice. Should he start dating? He cringed at the thought. No other woman could begin to measure up to Carolyn.

Now, Daryl, he counseled himself, that's the kind of thinking that makes you feel bad. That's the kind of thinking you have to put aside. You have to start thinking in a new way. You have to straighten up and fly right.

The Jaycees' fall dance was coming up in a few weeks. He forced himself to consider getting a date. But who? He paged through the single women in town. Well, there was Linda Stoker. She had flirted with him a few times. But she wasn't much older than Danny. He would feel ludicrous going out with her. Besides, he had heard she was involved in a steamy affair with her married boss at the photography studio. He wrinkled his nose. Little tramp. Like Jeannie. What a relief to have Jeannie gone. He hoped she wasn't ever coming back.

Was there any single woman in town he could take to the dance? Wait a minute. How about Nadine? He liked Nadine, but she was such a pepper pot. She had a wicked tongue, and she might make fun of him just for asking. But she was pretty, almost as pretty as Carolyn. It would be daring of him to ask Nadine. He liked the idea of being a risk-taker.

Before he could talk himself out of it, he picked up the phone and called the beauty shop. No answer. He thought, maybe it's just as well. Maybe I'm not ready yet.

~ ~ ~

"Don't you have any plans for today, Sonny?" Mary Pickens asked.

Wayne finished his dessert instead of answering. Mary looked at him, concerned. He had been glumly hanging around the house since leaving Woodson's. He hadn't even looked for another job. She was a little worried about money. Her meager savings would be exhausted if Sonny didn't get another job.

As if intuiting her thoughts, Wayne said, "I hope you realize, Mama, that I couldn't in good conscience go on working at Woodson's."

"That's what you said, Sonny, but I still don't understand exactly what happened."

"Never mind exactly what happened, Mama. Just take it on faith that I couldn't go on working for a man who consents to his wife's adultery. Makes him as bad as her. You understand that much, I hope."

"Was he surprised when you quit?"

"Not so much. He knows I'm a man of principle. But he was obstinate and refused to accept the truth. I am a prophet without honor in my own country, Mama, just like the Lord Jesus Christ."

"I'm just a little worried..."

"Mama, listen, I've been thinking. You know I'm planning to be a preacher."

"Yes, and go to Bible College."

"Now, Mama, not every preacher has to go to Bible College. When the Apostle Paul talks about gifts of the spirit, he doesn't say that a person who has the gift of preaching has to go to Bible College, does he? Paul didn't go to Bible College. John the Baptist sure didn't. Well, think about it, did Jesus have to go to Bible College before he began his ministry? And he was just my age. I am of the opinion, Mama, and I hope this doesn't sound puffed up, but I believe that I don't require Bible College either."

"But, Sonny, Brother Robbins..."

"Mama, I have to say I am sorely disappointed in Brother Robbins. I used to admire the man, but lately I have come to see that Brother Robbins himself remains willfully blind to sin. I don't believe God would want me to follow a blind man."

"Why, Sonny..."

Wayne rose and spread his arms wide. "I will answer the call. I am ready to set up my ministry and preach the true word of God."

"Sonny, I don't understand..."

"Don't you fear. You are going to see great things, signs and wonders."

"But, Sonny..."

"I have work to do, Mama. Work to do for the Lord."

After Wayne had left the house, his face alight with zeal, Mary washed the dishes in a troubled state of mind. He surely had sounded puffed up. She hoped he would be calmer when he returned home. She counseled herself not to worry. The Lord works in mysterious ways. She knew He had something in mind for Wayne.

~ ~ ~

Dorothy hadn't quite finished her lunch when the back door banged and there was Laura again. She tried to sound welcoming. "Laura, come on in."

"Is Miss Eliot here?"

"Is that Miss Laura Tuttle?" Pat brayed. She enveloped Laura in a bear hug. "Now here's the drill. Dorothy, this will be a bulletin for you, too. We are going to go to Raton to the races. What do you think about that?"

They stared at Pat, Laura with expectation, Dorothy with misgiving.

"I just got off the phone with Spence and he says his big bay is going to run a race on Saturday. Thinks he's got a winner. Plus, he says I can get Silverado registered and talk to some jockeys. Next time we go we'll take Silverado to race. Last time I took a horse to Raton, when was that, she finished dead last. Well, Silverado's going to be a different story."

"When is this expedition scheduled?" Dorothy asked.

"Spence says there are good races all weekend. We'll drive out there Friday morning and come back Sunday evening. What do you say to that, ladies?"

"Me too?" Laura asked.

"Without a doubt you too. We'll stay at the Coachman, like we always do. Remember that restaurant next to the Coachman, Dorothy? We had the best steaks there the last time we went to Raton. Remember, they had a little band playing. I'll call the Coachman to make reservations, but first I got to call Joe and Marilyn. I know they will want to go." She smiled impishly at Laura. "Jesse can't go because of football practice."

Dorothy sat motionless, her arms crossed. "*This* weekend?"

"You heard it right here, madam. This very weekend. Be beautiful in Raton, leaves probably already turning there."

"Pat, school starts in less than two weeks."

"Calendar in your head, that's what makes you special." Pat tousled Dorothy's hair.

Dorothy pulled away. "Pat, there is no way I can get my work done and go to Raton for the weekend."

"Well, if you are not ready, then my message to you is to get ready so we can go to Raton Friday. Now, I need to call my brother."

Laura followed Pat over to the telephone. "I have never been to Raton," she said.

"Then it's time you went. Make sure you ask your daddy. I'll talk to him if he has any questions. Marilyn, put Joe on, would you?" She squeezed the receiver between her head and shoulder and rooted in her shirt pocket for a cigarette.

"Joe? What are you up to this weekend? You don't know? Well, I do. You are going to Raton to the races, what do you think about that? No, but one of Spence's horses is running on Saturday. Yeah, you and Marilyn, too. I'm going to make reservations at the Coachman. We'll drive over there Friday morning and stay the weekend. Sound good to you? Yeah, you tell her. I'll hold on."

She smiled at Laura while she waited. "You never been to the races? High time you did. Nothing like it." She turned back to the telephone. "Yeah, I'm here. She doesn't want to go? Oh, come on. Joe, you twist her arm, okay? Tell her it'll be fun. Listen, I am going to make reservations for y'all, too, so get it in gear."

She hung up the phone. "God Almighty, two wet blankets, what is wrong with some people?" She put her arm around Laura's shoulders. "I went to my first race when I was eight. My daddy put two dollars on a horse for me, ten to one, and it won. I was in hog heaven."

Dorothy said, "I guess I'll have to go up to school."

"You do that, madam," Pat said.

"I'll see what I can get done, but I don't promise anything, Pat."

"You just get it done so we can take off Friday morning."

"Sounds like Marilyn doesn't want to go," Dorothy said hopefully.

"Well, Joe'll twist her arm."

"I was looking at him at the funeral, and I thought he looked a little better."

"Yeah, he sounds better. More life to him. He's all excited about going."

"Well, that makes two of you," Dorothy said.

"So, can I go?" Laura was practically dancing.

Cal said, "I guess so, honey."

"Will you be okay without me?" Laura asked.

"Why sure. Now, you go, have a good time."

"Papa," Laura began and then stopped.

"Yeah?"

"Well, Miss Eliot says at the races everybody wears Levi's, but I should bring a dress to go out to eat. And she says it's cooler in Raton than it is here, so to bring a jacket."

"Yeah?"

"Well, I was just thinking I maybe could get some new clothes, if that's okay with you. For school and everything, I mean. Before I go."

"Okay, why not. You just get what you need and tell them to send me the bill."

Laura hugged his neck. "Oh, thank you, Papa."

He watched affectionately from the front door as she ran out to the car and drove off. She seemed happier than she had been in a long time. He went into the kitchen and paused at the table, where there were plates wrapped in wax paper. People were still bringing food to them. He took a brownie from one plate and ate it with pleasure. He took another and went upstairs.

It had been over a month, and he hadn't gone inside Janice's room. He hesitated outside the closed door. He had rarely been in her room since she set up shop in there a few years back and could only imagine the mess it was likely to be.

He opened the door. Dark. After he drew the heavy curtains away from the window, there was sufficient light for him to take in the whole room. To his surprise, it was immaculate. The twin bed was made up, top sheet crisply folded over the blanket, pillow case unwrinkled. He opened the drawers of the small bureau. The bottom two were empty and the first drawer held only a sparse assortment of underclothes and socks, tidily folded. The drawer of the small desk held a sheaf of blank paper and two pencils. He picked up one by one the books on the desk: the Lincoln Library encyclopedia, Webster's Dictionary, a well-worn copy of Thoreau's *Walden*, and a college textbook – *The Literature of England*. He opened the textbook to where it was bookmarked with a three-by-five card. William Butler Yeats. A poem called "The Second Coming" had been circled in blue ink. He read the poem and then looked at the words Janice had written on the three-by-five card:

"Vico: History proceeds cyclically through three ages – divine, heroic, human. The divine age produces religion. The heroic age produces marriage. The human age produces burial of the dead."

It was a language foreign to him. He knew what the individual words meant, although he had never heard of Vico, but he couldn't discern the meaning. He re-read "The Second Coming," laid the book down, and stuck the card in his shirt pocket.

A few items of clothing hung in the closet. Shoes on the closet floor. He pulled down boxes from the shelf. Inside the first box he found a few photographs and envelopes bound together with a faded blue ribbon. He recognized his own handwriting. Letters he wrote to Janice when he was in college. He studied the photographs – one of him and Janice arm in arm beside his first car, laughing into the camera. Another of their wedding. Laura's school pictures from first grade on up. A sepia studio portrait of Janice's parents on their wedding day, the couple as rigid and sanctimonious as they had been their whole lives. Janice's birth certificate, Laura's birth certificate, and Janice's social security card. A gold pin for perfect attendance in grammar school and the pearl earrings he had given her on their wedding day.

He closed the box and set it on the bed. The other boxes were stuffed with gifts he and Laura had given Janice over the years. Sweaters, blouses, cologne, handkerchiefs, and trinkets of more than a dozen Christmases and birthdays lay embalmed in tissue paper.

He replaced all the boxes, sat dazed on the bed. He pulled the three-by-five card out of his pocket. Burial of the dead. We must be in the human age.

Renee looked at the clock. The afternoon was dragging by. No customers, and Mr. Woodson holed up at his desk, doing nothing as far as she could tell. It was hard to say whether she liked it better without Wayne there. He was a creep, but his presence allowed her to get out of the store for a few minutes. As it was now, she had to hang around all day, unless Mr. Woodson specifically asked her to go to the Post Office. Renee had never before been glad to see school start, but now she was counting the days.

She didn't know what Mr. Woodson was going to do when she went back to school. He was going to be all by himself at the store. She doubted he could do the windows by himself. And he was getting careless. Last night he hadn't even bothered to spread the sawdust and sweep the floor. She wished she had been able to hear everything he had said to Wayne the day he fired him. Well, Wayne deserved what he got. Imagine, hollering and carrying on about Mrs. Woodson. That was just plain stupid.

Mrs. Woodson. And Adam. Every time she thought about Adam, she saw him with a naked Mrs. Woodson. It made her want to throw up. Adam was just plain ruined.

Poor Mr. Woodson. He looked like death warmed over, but Renee had observed a sample of his fury. Mr. Woodson had fired Wayne. He would likely kill Adam. Renee had heard about a man who shot his wife and her boyfriend when he found them in bed together. She wondered if Mr. Woodson owned a gun. Somehow she couldn't picture Mr. Woodson with a gun, let alone shooting somebody, he looked so hang-dog and miserable.

I am bored out of my mind. She wandered over to the ladies' hat counter and tried on a burnt orange number, pulled the veil over her eyes. Close to the mirror, she pursed her lips like Marilyn Monroe. She imagined Adam asking her for a date. She lifted her chin and said haughtily, "I wouldn't go out with you if you were the last man on earth." She dropped her voice an octave and said, "Oh, Renee, please, pretty please, with sugar on it." In her own voice she replied, "Drop dead, sucker."

At the sound of the door chime, Renee whisked off the hat. There was Laura Tuttle.

"Can I help you?" Renee asked, all business.

"I need some Levi's," Laura said.

"Girl's style or men's?"

Laura hesitated. "I don't really know. What's the difference?"

"Well, lots of people like the girl's ones because they have a zipper, but I like the men's ones better. It depends on what you're looking for."

"Could I try on both?"

"Sure," Renee said. She brought a pair of each to Laura and showed her the dressing room.

Laura pulled on the men's Levi's, which hugged her legs and thighs. The buttons up the fly were hard to manage.

"Come on out here and look at yourself in the big mirror," Renee called, and Laura complied. Renee looked her over. "Those aren't bad. They're stiff now because they're new, but they'll get softer once you wash them. Be sure you use cold water or they'll shrink. Go on now and try the girl's."

Laura slipped out of the first pair into the second. Renee was right, the side zipper was much easier to work. She went out to the three-way mirror.

"Now, personally, I like the men's better on you," Renee confided. "They show off your legs, and you've got a little waist and almost no hips. Look at your backside in these, see how they kind of sag. In the girl's, your behind looks like a granny's."

Laura went back in the dressing room and put on the men's. She came back out and turned to see her backside in them.

"See what I mean. Nice and snug. Now here's a cowboy belt." She handed

Laura a western shirt and a carved leather belt. She tied a scarf around Laura's neck. "Now what you need is boots."

"Cowboy boots?"

"Course. What size shoe do you wear? Six? You need a half size bigger in boots."

Renee sat Laura down in the shoe section and helped her into a pair of boots. They felt strange on her feet, but Laura liked the russet sheen and the carving.

Renee brought forward a brown leather bomber jacket. "Try this on."

"It smells good," Laura said.

"Looks good, too. Go look in the mirror."

Renee surveyed the whole picture. "Course, you need to do something with your hair. Personally I think you're a little old for the Alice in Wonderland look. You go over to my mama's shop. Tell her you want a different style. She'll know what to do."

"How much does all this cost?"

"Less than you think," Renee said, borrowing a phrase from Wayne. "You take it off while I add it up."

Laura came out of the dressing room carrying the new clothes and went to the counter where Renee was writing on a pad.

"Cash or check?" Renee asked.

"Charge. My father wants you to send him a bill."

Renee added the figures and showed the total to Laura. "Now that's not so bad, is it? When you think about what you've got here."

"I'll take it all," Laura said, amazed by her own boldness.

Renee put Laura's purchases into two big bags. "Just out of curiosity," she said, as Laura was leaving, "are you going out with Jesse Eliot?"

"Why, no," Laura said, "I thought you were."

"Huh," Renee snorted, "that'll be the day."

# CHAPTER THIRTEEN

Wayne walked up Main Street, hands in his pockets, eyes on the ground. He had just spent a frustrating hour of inquiry about the empty storefront next to Loretta's Dress Shop. The building had been vacant since Franklins Shoe Store went out of business two years ago. You would think they would be anxious to rent it out. He had been to the city hall where he found that the building was owned by somebody from out of town but managed by Don Paulson. When he went to the lawyer's office to ask about renting it, Don at first had seemed interested, but when Wayne told him his plans, Don said no. Just like that, no. Not I'll think about it, or I'll ask the owner. Just no.

After leaving Don's office, Wayne crossed over to the other side of Main Street and walked north. He certainly wasn't going to risk encountering the man he had come to think of as his oppressor. He stopped in front of the vacant store and looked longingly through the window. Not to be, he said to himself. In the next block, he paused in front of Penney's and gave a quick appraisal of their back-to-school windows. Not too bad. Better than Miss Renee Coulter's handiwork. He considered asking Mr. Gus Bell, the manager at Penney's, for a job, but he had more important business. The Lord's business.

Next door to Penney's, he stopped in surprise. Wasn't this Bradshaw's Photography Studio? The sign was missing and the store seemed to be vacant. He peered in through the window. Maybe Mr. Bradshaw had gone out of business. A vacant building.

The door was ajar, and he let himself in. This space was partitioned half way back. Less square feet than Franklins, he thought. That might be better.

"Hello?" he called. "Anybody here?"

Linda Stoker came out of the back room. Pretty, he thought, but in a kind of loose way. Skirt too short and too much makeup.

As she came toward him, he could see that mascara was smeared around her eyes. She looked like a raccoon.

"We're closed," she said.

"The door was open," he countered.

"If you're here for some photographs..."

"No. I wanted to ask about the building."

Linda blinked. "The building? What about it?"

"Is Mr. Bradshaw here? I probably should talk to him."

Linda took a quivery breath. "He's not here."

"When will he be back?"

"He's not coming back," she said. Suddenly, to Wayne's alarm, her face seemed to crack wide open. Her mouth widened, lips taut across teeth. He could see all the way to the back of her throat. Her eyes squeezed tight and tears spurted as she emitted a big, hiccup-like sob.

"Oh, my goodness, don't cry," he said. She began to howl, tears and mascara streaming down her cheeks. "Goodness sakes," he said. "What is wrong?"

She wiped her nose and mouth with the back of her hand, trying to quell her outburst. Wayne offered her his handkerchief. She wiped her eyes, blew her nose. He looked regretfully at the ruined handkerchief. She offered it back to him, but he put his palms out in a gesture of rejection. "No, no, you keep it."

"Thang gew," she said and noisily, productively blew her nose. Words came pouring out while she wiped her eyes and dug in her nose with the handkerchief. "He's not coming back. He's gone for good. Took everything with him." Her eyes puddled up with more tears. "God *damn* him." She looked as if she might start wailing again.

"Now, now," Wayne interceded. "You're upset, but that's no reason…"

"Damn right I'm upset," Linda said furiously. "I am more than upset. I am ready to kill him!"

Wayne watched her with intense interest. No question in Wayne's mind that Linda had been fooling around with Ronny Bradshaw. Ronny wasn't originally from Massey, which made him suspect in Massey, and a lot of people wouldn't put anything past Linda Stoker.

"Vengeance is mine, saith the Lord," Wayne told her.

"What?" she said, wiping her eyes with his handkerchief.

"Come on, let's sit down a minute," he said to her. He latched the front door and led her to the brown vinyl couch, where they sat down.

"Sister, would you join me in a word of prayer? Bow your head." Linda looked mystified but complied.

"Oh, Lord, look upon your servant Linda in her hour of affliction. Forgive her sins, heal her wounds, pour balm on her hurt. Lead her in your way, and cleanse her heart of bitterness. In Jesus' name, Amen."

Linda raised her head.

"Now, then," Wayne said, "why don't you just tell me all about it."

She did. Ronny had insisted on complete secrecy and she had never told anyone. Such a relief to let it all out. She told Wayne everything, from beginning to end. He nodded and occasionally patted her hand. Once or twice he asked a question. When she finished, she was calm and her eyes were dry.

"I've been a fool," she said.

Wayne opened his mouth to say, A fool and worse. He wanted to list the sins she had committed and tell her she was in danger of hellfire. But somehow he just couldn't condemn her. Now that the mascara was transferred to his handkerchief, he could see she had very pretty blue eyes. As she poured out her story, her complexion had alternated between pale white and deep pink. His judicious glance confirmed that her body was alluring. In short, Linda Stoker was one lovely woman.

Wayne cleared his throat. "You got some healing to do," he said. "It takes guts and God to get through a time like this, after you've been betrayed. I know what it feels like to be betrayed. You're angry, and you want revenge. But revenge isn't going to make you feel better. You are going to have to find it in your heart to forgive him."

"Not likely," Linda said, rebelliously.

"The Bible says we are supposed to forgive our enemies. Seventy times seven."

"I can't do it," she said.

"God will help you find a way," Wayne said.

"I don't want to find a way," she said, petulantly.

"I'll pray for you to find a way. God wants you to. I promise, you won't feel better until you do." Linda looked unconvinced, but didn't argue. Wayne took a deep breath. "And, if I may be so bold, there is somebody you need to ask to forgive you."

"What?" she asked, incredulous.

He nodded at her. "Somebody else has been hurt here. You know who I mean."

"Mrs. Bradshaw doesn't know anything about it," Linda said. "I mean, we were discreet. And I never meant her any harm."

"Nevertheless," Wayne said.

Linda shook her head. "I can't."

"Yes, you can. You know I'm right."

Her lip was out and her arms crossed in a posture of defiance, but she began to remember something. Ronny had made her promise never to tell anyone about them. He said it was of vital importance that his wife never find out. Linda began to put two and two together. If his wife found out about her and Ronny, he would have zero chance of ever getting his hands on her father's money. It was true what everyone said about him, that he was a gold-digger. In fact, he was a no-good son-of-a-bitch. The last thing Ronny would want would be for her to talk with his wife.

She uncrossed her arms and looked into Wayne's face. "You probably are right," she said slowly. "I probably do need to talk to her, to Mrs. Bradshaw."

Wayne nodded with satisfaction. "God bless you."

They sat in silence for a minute.

"Well," he said, rising. "I guess I'd better be going."

"Thank you for your handkerchief. I'll wash it and give it back to you."

"You keep it. I've got lots of them. Oh, I almost forgot. Who owns this building?"

"I think Mr. Collier does. You know, Mrs. Bradshaw's father," Linda said.

Wayne looked at his watch. It was almost five o'clock. Too late to see Mr. Collier today. But he felt this was the right place. God had given him a sign here today. He was already saving souls.

"Goodbye for now. Any time you want to talk, Linda, just call on me."

She waved a goodbye at him. My gosh, she thought, I can't believe I told Wayne Pickens about this.

~ ~ ~

"Don't we have any beer?" Joe asked, his head in the refrigerator.

"There's some in the pantry," Marilyn replied, on her way through the kitchen.

Joe took a six pack from the pantry shelf and brought it to the kitchen sink. He put two bottles in the dishpan and dumped a tray of ice cubes over them. The other four bottles went into the refrigerator.

Back in the pantry, he methodically rearranged the canned goods in alphabetical order. He consolidated a nearly empty and a nearly full box of salt. He lined up by height the bottles and jars. Then he swept and mopped the kitchen floor.

He opened one beer and drank thirstily from the bottle. He looked into the refrigerator's depths, threw out some items and rearranged others by height. He drained his beer, threw the empty bottle in the waste basket, and had just opened the second when Marilyn reappeared in the kitchen. "What are you doing?"

"Just straightening things up," he answered, opening a cupboard and taking out cups and saucers.

Marilyn looked at the empty beer bottle in the waste basket. "That's your third beer this evening," she pointed out.

Joe picked up his beer and drank. "And mighty good beer it is, too," he said. "My daddy, that was before refrigerators, we only had an ice box, he would put a case of beer in a big wash pan and chip a block of ice with a pick, and I have to say that was the coldest, best beer I ever drank. It beat refrigerated beer all to hell."

"Joe..."

"Take a look at what I did in the pantry," he said, gesturing. "I don't know how you ever found anything in there, it was so ever-which-way. You had your peas next to your corn. No system. Now if you want peas, you can put your hand right on peas. Take a look, Mare. You need to get mayonnaise next time you're at the grocery store. And beer."

"Well, thank you, honey, but..."

"Get a case next time, would you, Mare." He turned back to the open cupboard.

"Joe, it's after ten."

"I know."

"I'm going to bed. Are you coming?"

"Later, baby, I'm not sleepy. You go on. I'll wait up for Jesse."

"Joe, please don't drink any more beer. You know what Dr. Siegel said."

"Go on to bed. I'll be up directly."

She waited a minute with her hand on the banister, looking apprehensively at him, and then mounted the stairs. Joe was arranging the dishes in the cabinet.

Thirty minutes later, when Jesse came in the back door, Joe had put the kitchen to rights and was rummaging around in the coat closet. He had removed all the empty hangers from the rack and had neatly positioned the coats – first Marilyn's, then Jesse's, then his own – by weight and length.

"Pop?"

"Hey, Jesse, glad you're here. Help me out."

"What are you doing?"

"Right now I am looking for my gun." He was taking down boxes and hats and gloves from the closet shelf.

Jesse stared at him. "How come, Pop?"

"Cause I can't find it. You know the old joke about when you're looking for something, you always find it in the last place you look? You know why? Cause after you find it, you quit looking." He guffawed. "I guess I ain't got to the last place yet."

"No, I mean how come you want your gun?"

Joe turned to him in mock surprise. "Why do you think? Don't you want to know where your things are? Now pitch in, help me look. I don't want to look upstairs, might disturb your mama, she's already asleep. Thought it might be in this closet, but it ain't. Say, this your hunting jacket or mine?"

Jesse reluctantly took a look. "Yours, I think. Mine has a red collar."

"Give that boy sixty-four dollars," Joe crowed. "Okay. So we hang it here, with my other coats and we put the one with the red collar with your coats. Want a beer?"

Jesse's face took on a hunted look. There was no right answer to that question. If he said yes, Joe was sure to give him another lecture about drinking before he was of legal age. If he said no, he might say why not, you already been drinking, haven't you, and give him the third degree about where he had been and where he got beer and threaten to tell Coach to throw him off the team.

But Joe was at the refrigerator, pulling out two bottles, snapping off the caps and handing one to Jesse. Jesse took it in disbelief. If I drink it in front of him, is he going to kill me? But Joe was already drinking from his own bottle. Jesse took a sip of the beer. He didn't really want it; already his head was muzzy from what he had drunk out at the river bottom.

"So me and your Aunt Pat are going to Raton to the races Friday morning," Joe said. "Your mama don't want to go, I don't know why not, but she said no and not to ask her again. Too bad you got football practice, you could go with us, cause your Aunt Pat got a room for your mama and me, but your mama don't want to go, I don't know why not." Joe suddenly frowned and gave Jesse a calculating look. "Where you been tonight?"

"In town," Jesse said.

"Where at in town?"

"Bill Lynch's house." That was partially true. After work he went to Bill's house to pick up Bill and the beer Bill's cousin Charley had bought for them in Sanford. After hamburgers at Benny's, they dragged Main several times and then went out to the river bottom to drink beer and smoke cigarettes. Jesse took Bill home and drove home, expecting to find his parents asleep.

"Doing what?"

"Nothing. Listening to the radio," Jesse said.

"You gonna drink that beer?"

"I don't really want it," Jesse said. "Anyway, Coach don't want us to drink."

"Give it here then." Joe's empty clanked against its fellows in the waste basket. He took Jesse's bottle from him.

Jesse went toward the stairs.

"No, you stay down here and help me find my gun, goddammit," Joe snapped.

"Okay, okay, Pop. Where do you want me to look?"

"If I knew where to look I could of found it myself. So you tell me."

Jesse stood immobile. He knew that his mother had hidden the gun after they took Joe to the hospital, but he didn't know where. Joe had that look on his face, that crafty, focused look he had that morning before he cut down the trees. Jesse felt scared. He didn't know what to do.

As quickly as it had blown in, the storm passed from Joe's face. "Ah, never mind, son, you go on to bed. I'll find it tomorrow. Right now I'm just going to finish my beer. You go on up. I'll be up directly. Don't disturb your mama, she's tired."

Jesse didn't have to be told twice. Joe sat down at the kitchen table and drank from the bottle.

❧ ❧ ❧

It was after ten when the telephone rang, and Renee was already in bed, her hair set in big rollers. Nadine picked up the receiver. "Hello."

"Hi." It was Adam.

Coughing prevented her from speaking.

"Nadine?"

"Yeah," she croaked.

"You ought to do something about that cough."

"I did. Went to the doctor."

"Good. What did he say?"

"Nothing yet."

"Let's get together. Come on downtown."

Nadine tingled at the prospect. She could already feel his hands and lips on her body. It would be so easy, Renee was probably asleep. She could creep out of the house and be back in a couple of hours and nobody would be the wiser. Just this one time, she bargained. This will be the last time. I promise.

She opened her mouth to agree, but the cough began anew. Her lungs felt like they were bursting. Spent, she had to sit down.

"Five minutes?" he said.

She couldn't catch her breath. Okay, okay, I give in. She gripped the receiver, feeling as if she were about to die. "No," she said. She could breathe again.

"What do you mean, no?"

"I mean no, and I mean don't call me again." Her voice had recovered, and no cough came.

"What?"

"You heard me. I am through with this…foolishness. You ought to be, too, for all the trouble you've caused."

"Nadine..."

"I am finished with you."

She banged down the receiver and lay back in the recliner.

Renee called from her bedroom, "Who was that?"

"Nobody. Wrong number."

# CHAPTER FOURTEEN

Ray Parker threw back his shoulders, took a deep breath, and pushed through the door into the diner. Nearly a dozen men sat at the counter and at the big table beside the window. Leroy Talbot, the owner and short-order cook, and Laverne Larimer, the waitress, were serving up coffee, donuts, and conversation.

"Hey, Coach, come on in, have a seat," Leroy invited.

"Coffee?" Laverne asked, holding up a thick white mug and the pot as Ray took a counter seat between Pete Mosley and Virgil Harmon.

"Thanks," he said, and dosed his coffee liberally with cream and sugar.

"Donut?"

"Yeah, jelly, if you've got it," he answered, and she handed him one on a plate.

He lifted his mug in salutation left and right. "Gentlemen, and Lady Laverne," he said and drank. He waited.

"Haven't seen you in awhile, Coach," L.W. Foster said from the elbow of the counter, sandwiched in between Don Paulson and Hugh Hadley, the county clerk. "What's the word this year, ten and oh?"

"Or oh and ten?" put in Jake Mouser, the GM dealer, from the table where he sat with Jim Atkins and Lloyd Tomlin. There was an appreciative chuckle.

"Early days," Ray said, and bit into his donut.

"How's young Eliot working out? He have his daddy's arm?" Leroy inquired.

"Come out to the first game and see," Ray said.

"Oh, we'll be there," L.W. said. "Wouldn't miss it."

Hugh Hadley leaned across L.W. toward Don Paulson. "Say, I hear you got a bite on renting out the old Franklins store."

"You talking about Pickens?" Don retorted. "Oh, hell, no. Not to that fruitcake."

"What's that?" Leroy asked.

"Aah, he had some crazy scheme about that property. I told him we weren't putting any sideshows on Main Street."

Amplification of this tempting tidbit was frustrated as the door opened to admit Roy Woodson. Everybody knew that Wayne had been fired for talking about Maureen Woodson. A few knew, or thought they knew, exactly what had been said. But it was definitely off limits to talk about that with Roy present. Too touchy a subject, and anyway Roy was sensitive as all get out. Never joined in the general ribbing. These days he looked so whipped and raw, nobody wanted to fool with him.

Laverne set a steaming mug in front of Roy and refilled the mugs of the others at the table. "Donut?"

"No, thanks," Roy said.

There was a little pause. "Speaking of Main Street," Jim Atkins said, rising from the table to get another donut from the tray on the counter, "What the hell happened to Bradshaw's? Place is empty."

This was the moment Gus Bell had been waiting for. A dapper little man with several strands of hair plastered over his bald spot, he sat at the far end of the counter next to Forrest Longbrake, editor of the Plains County News. Gus cleared his throat and swiveled his stool so he could face the whole room.

"Guess you didn't hear," he said. "Day before yesterday, Ronny Bradshaw moved out, lock, stock and barrel."

The response was gratifying. "He did?" and "What happened?" echoed through the diner.

"Bout two o'clock," Gus said. "I was out in the alley and here come Ronny and two kids. Bill Lynch and what's-his-name Robbins."

"Adam?" Lloyd Tomlin asked.

Roy stiffened.

"Nah, the middle one."

"Abel," Pete provided.

"Yeah, Abel," Gus said. "Anyways, I was taking out the trash and here come Ronny and them two boys, and low in the hole if they don't commence to load up his truck with all kinds a photography equipment. Lights, cameras, tripods, pictures, boxes, you name it. I wouldn't a thought that little old truck could hold so much."

"Moved the whole studio?" Virgil asked, incredulous.

"Well, looked like most of it. Far as I could tell. So then Ronny he gives the boys some money for helping him and then he gets in the truck and he drives off, bang, just like that."

"You mean left town?" Forrest Longbrake asked.

"That's the way I see it." Gus then played his ace. "Mr. Collier, he thinks the same."

"You talked to Vance about this?" Jim Atkins asked.

"Well, I called him," Gus said. "Thought he ought to know. After all, it's his building."

"And his son-in-law," added L.W.

"That's right," Hugh Hadley chimed in. "Vance owns the whole block. Even Penney's rents from him, isn't that right, Gus?"

"I heard tell that Ronny had moved out of their house to the hotel," Laverne said. "But I didn't hear he was leaving town."

Attention shifted from Gus to Laverne. "He was living at the hotel?" Jim asked.

"You never told me that," Leroy complained to Laverne.

"Well," she said, "I don't like to talk."

"Mr. Collier, he didn't act surprised. Looked like he was expecting something like this," Gus continued, reluctant to cede the floor and willing to embellish.

Here was a new and interesting incident to ponder. Previous topics dissected by those who drank coffee and ate donuts every morning at the diner – such as Jeannie Backus' reputation, Janice Tuttle's drowning, Wayne Pickens' loss of employment – faded into the background. Diner protocol forbade full discussion when someone connected to a sensitive event was present. For instance, both Jim and Lloyd had to be missing in order for Danny Tomlin's sins to be fully rehearsed. Today, Vance Collier's absence allowed the information to be thoroughly chewed on.

Lloyd began. "I never did like that old boy. Something funny about him."

"Everybody said he was after Mr. Collier's money," Laverne said.

L.W. muttered something to Hugh Hadley, and the two laughed uproariously.

"Share the joke?" Laverne said, refilling L.W.'s mug.

Hugh grinned. "Just speculating about who Linda Stoker might go to work for now."

"Yeah, wonder what she charges by the hour," L.W. sniggered.

Merriment engulfed the room.

Ray drained his mug, rose, put some coins on the counter.

"Good luck, Coach. We're all rooting for you," Leroy said.

Ray tipped his cap to the affable farewells and went out the door. Guess today wasn't my turn, he thought with relief.

~ ~ ~

Maureen extended her hand to the tall silver-haired man. "Thank you so much," she said warmly.

"You just keep your chin up, my dear lady, and leave everything to me."

She squeezed his hand and walked out of the wood-paneled office past the bank of secretaries' desks and the receptionist who said a friendly goodbye. Out in the hallway she pushed the button for the elevator. She smiled as she compared the plush workplace of Dugan and Morrison, Attorneys at Law, with the cubbyhole in Massey that Don Paulson called his office.

In Amarillo since Tuesday, Maureen had been staying in a guest room at the country club. It had taken a few days to locate the right lawyer, but it was worth the effort, for Mr. Patrick Dugan had not disappointed. He seemed straight away to grasp her situation and gave her immediate assurances that she was going to get exactly what she wanted out of this divorce. She gave him a sizeable check to retain his services, and he promised to handle the matter personally.

He told her that what Don Paulson told Roy would not stand up in any Texas court. No judge would consider a rumor of adultery. Of course, he added, a lady such as herself would of course be innocent of the charge, and Maureen didn't think it necessary to correct him. She did tell him that the accusation could not be proven. She hoped to heaven that was true, that Adam would be too frightened of disclosure for his own sake. Anyway, she told herself, it was only a few times. What could it possibly matter anyway, now that it was all over?

She told Mr. Dugan that she was only interested in a fair settlement. "I don't come from a wealthy family," she explained. "It's only my sister and me now, and I am doing my best to take care of her, since her husband is mentally unstable. I have given my husband the best years of my life. If he chooses to throw me out on the street, then I must accept that. But I will need some resources in order to begin my life anew." She gave him a pitiable look. "Of course I'll have to leave Massey. He has ruined my good name." Mr. Dugan was compassion personified. Maureen left the building feeling elated. What a lucky coincidence that his office was in the heart of the downtown shopping district. She would need new clothes while she still had access to their joint checking account. She braced herself for a strenuous day of shopping.

Cal sat at his desk with an open file folder and a half cup of cold coffee. The folder contained all the information he had gathered about the death of little Angela Tomlin: Jeannie and Danny's statements; the autopsy report, Pete

Mosley's notes, the missing person report on Jeannie Backus, and the APB to the Highway Patrol. He read through his own notes. It seemed like a year had passed since that morning at Doc's clinic where he had seen the dead child. Images of Jeannie crying and Danny cracking his knuckles arose, and he tasted once again his disappointment in L.W., in Doc, in the whole lot of the Tomlins and Atkinses. He acknowledged his inability to prove any of his suspicions.

There had been no word from or about Jeannie. She had just disappeared. What's more, no one seemed to miss her. He supposed that the Tomlins and Atkinses were relieved. The other night he had seen Danny tooling his car down Main Street with Darlene Shields snuggled up beside him. Clearly Danny had moved on. Carolyn had gone back to Santa Fe. Whenever he saw Lloyd or Jim or Daryl on the street or in the diner, they behaved as if nothing had happened.

It was as if nothing *had* happened. But, he argued to himself, a baby had died. No, more precisely, in his view, a baby had been put to death in some inexplicable way. And no one cared, except himself. He felt pretty sure that no one else even thought about it any more. Even Pete had tired of the matter.

He examined his feelings more closely. He had to admit it would be a relief to stamp "CASE CLOSED" on the folder and stick it in the file with all the other cases that no longer required his attention. It also was true that he had no stomach for any further investigation of this case.

He moved uneasily in his chair. In the cautious manner of someone investigating an aching tooth with a probing tongue, he inquired into the other painful subject that lurked about the edges of his conscious mind: Janice's death.

Everybody had been so considerate, treating him tenderly, as if not wishing to cause him additional distress. Whenever he encountered people, their kind and pitying faces met his glance, and hushed voices asked how he and Laura were doing. Ladies continued to drop by the house with cookies or a casserole, and somebody had mowed and edged his lawn. Pat was preparing a little holiday for Laura, he guessed in part to distract her from her mother's death. Everybody assumed that he was in deep mourning, a man crushed by bereavement.

The truth was, he had never felt better in his life. He had rarely had such a hearty appetite and had never before slept so soundly. Mornings he would find himself humming a tune as he washed and dressed. Clearly, this was no way for a grieving widower to feel and act. He tried to mask his high spirits. In public, he cultivated a sober demeanor and a subdued tone of voice, but it was sometimes difficult to disguise his true feelings. He couldn't count the times somebody had said, "You must miss her." Miss her? he wanted to holler.

Yeah, miss her like you might miss a busted appendix or a tornado. Like you might miss facing bankruptcy or cancer.

Truth was, he felt he had been spared a great catastrophe. His life now spread out before him like a clean sheet of paper. He was free to start all over again. Aside from Laura and his job, he had no responsibilities. He could play golf every weekend. He could take a vacation. Hell, he could have a girlfriend.

A girlfriend. He tried to remember the last time he had sex. Years had passed since he had held a woman, or kissed or been touched. A sudden strong sweet longing welled up in him. He blushed at his vivid thoughts.

This is wrong, he said sternly to himself, and got up so quickly that he knocked over the cup. Coffee surged over the file. "Damn it," he said, trying to wipe it up with his handkerchief. The paper wrinkled and buckled. Coffee and ink ran together, making his notes illegible. He stared for a long minute at the ruined paper, then slapped the folder shut and picked up a stamp. He opened the stamp pad, banged the stamp once against the inky red felt and once against the folder. CASE CLOSED.

❧ ❧ ❧

Daryl put down the telephone and walked outside the lumber yard.

"Eldon," he called.

Eldon Phillips was loading lumber into a truck. "Yeah?"

"I got to go downtown. You answer the phone?"

"I reckon. Seems like I got to do everything else around here."

Daryl climbed in his Pontiac and drove to Main Street. He angle parked in front of Nadine's shop, hopped out of the car and went in the door before he could change his mind. He had never been to her shop before, so he took a look around. On his right was a stuffed sofa next to a coffee table with movie magazines piled on it. Beyond the sofa were two big hairdryer contraptions. On his left a sink and a swivel chair in front of a mirror. There didn't seem to be anybody around.

"Nadine," he called."Nadine, you here?"

She came out from behind a curtained arch at the back of the shop. "Daryl?" she said, surprised to see him.

She had obviously been crying. "Why, Nadine, what's the matter?"

This was not the Nadine he knew, not the smart-aleck with the cutting wisecrack. He had been steeling himself to endure her derisive refusal of his invitation to take her to the dance. He expected to get his head handed to him. Instead, here stood a little girl with about as much ferocity as a wounded doe. Daryl's heart and arms opened to her, and she collapsed against his chest, sobbing.

He held her gently, enjoying the pleasant aroma of her hair, murmuring little syllables of comfort. He led her over to the sofa and sat her down. "Want to tell me about it?" he asked.

Nadine tried but failed to grin. "Oh, gosh, I'm just so scared."

"Scared? What of?"

It came out in bits and pieces as she shredded the tissue. The cough. Going to see Doc. The phone call from the clinic this morning, telling her to come out to get her results. How she would tell Renee she had got cancer.

"Did they say you had cancer?" Daryl interrupted.

"No, they wouldn't tell me anything over the phone. Said Doc wanted to see me. That's a bad sign, isn't it?"

Daryl looked at his watch. He got up and pulled her to her feet. "We've got time to get something to eat at Benny's before we go to your appointment."

"You don't have to do this, Daryl," Nadine said.

"I know that. Better get your key. You need to lock up."

It had been a long time since she had gone anywhere accompanied by a man. Nadine had forgotten how nice it felt to have him open doors and put his hand on the small of her back, gently letting her go first. At Benny's, they chatted comfortably while they ate hamburgers, and Daryl insisted on picking up the check.

Now, idling restlessly in the deserted waiting room of the clinic, she was doubly grateful to him. She could feel a cold lump of fear in her stomach, but Daryl's presence kept her from being petrified. He asked if she wanted him to go into Doc's office with her when the time came, and she readily accepted. "I'll probably be so nervous I won't be able to hear anything he has to say," she told him.

Nadine's knowledge of cancer was based on observation. People got it, had to go to Oklahoma City or Amarillo for treatment, then they lost their hair and got skinny and pale, shortly after which they died. The word "cancer" was usually whispered rather than spoken aloud, and there was another fearsome word – "inoperable." Like when they operated on poor old Mrs. Rogers. They found her so full of cancer they just sewed her back up again, and she died without ever leaving the hospital.

Nadine badly wanted a cigarette, but Daryl didn't smoke, and there weren't any ashtrays in the waiting room, so she bit back her craving. She picked up a tattered Farmer's Almanac from the table beside her and said to Daryl, "Boy,

I'd be out of business if I didn't have something better than this for my clients to read."

He laughed. "What does it predict?"

"Predicts the Germans are going to lose the war," she fabricated, pretending to read. "Says women's skirts are going to get longer. Oh, look here, it predicts that Daryl Tomlin is going to get the Purple Heart for service above and beyond the call of duty, for taking a hysterical person to the doctor."

He looked at the Almanac over her shoulder. "No, it doesn't, it says he's going to get it for having the nerve to invite Nadine Coulter to the Jaycees' dance."

Their laughter stopped when Betty Talbot, the nurse on duty, called out, "Nadine, Doctor will see you now."

They rose and followed her into the doctor's office and sat in the two chairs opposite his untidy desk.

"Take a deep breath," Daryl instructed. She tried to obey.

The door opened and Dr. Lomax came in with a file folder in his hand. He looked surprised to see Daryl, but greeted them both warmly. At his desk, Doc unearthed his pipe from a stack of files and newspapers, poked at its contents with a nail, and struck a kitchen match on the side of his desk. Nadine hungrily breathed in fragrant tobacco smoke.

"Okay," he said, sucking on the pipe. "I got the results of all your tests, Nadine, and I wanted to talk to you about them."

Nadine grasped the arms of her chair with both hands. "Fire away," she said.

"Your tests all came back normal," he said. "What you've got is chronic bronchitis. That's what's causing that cough. And you're not going to get rid of it unless you stop smoking cigarettes."

"You mean," Nadine said, "I don't have cancer?"

"Is that what you thought? No, you don't have cancer." He flipped through the file. "You're a little anemic. I'm going to prescribe some iron pills for that. But the main thing is, you've got to give up smoking." He knocked his pipe against the ash tray, dispelling ashes, and picked up a leather pouch. He loaded loose tobacco into the bowl, tamped it down with his thumb, struck another match, and pulled on the pipe.

Daryl said, "You're saying, if she quits smoking, her cough will go away?"

"It should. See, cigarettes are an irritant, and infection can set up shop in the bronchia for as long as the irritation persists. I'm going to give you a prescription for the infection and for something to soothe your throat." He scrawled on the prescription tablet.

"I thought I had lung cancer," Nadine said.

"Well, you thought wrong. How long you been smoking cigarettes?"

Nadine considered. "Long time. I guess at least twenty years."

"Well, cut it out, and you'll be fine. Any questions?"

She shrugged, shook her head. He handed her the prescriptions and stood up. "Okay, that's it. You come on back in if you have any other trouble."

They shook hands all around and left his office. Outside, the sun was shining.

"What a beautiful day," she said.

"Want to go for a ride?" Daryl asked.

~ ~ ~

"I want to reiterate, Adam, that it seems premature for you to return to Bible College before the new term begins." Brother Robbins had parked the Packard at the Greyhound Bus Station in Gainesville. Wind swirled grit and debris about the car.

Adam shifted restlessly. "Father, I want to get a good start on my studies. This is my last year and I will study advanced homiletics plus Hebrew and Greek. The dormitory is open. I can buy the books and spend my days at the library studying."

"I recall my own days in fervent study of the Lord's word," Brother Robbins reminisced. "I hope you will take my advice and acquire your own copy of Boyce. Nothing is better than Boyce for the preparation of one's mind for writing a sermon. His grasp of theological principles is truly inspired. I wouldn't be without Boyce, Adam."

"No sir."

The bus marked "Oklahoma City" pulled into the station, and Adam opened the car door.

"Adam," Brother Robbins said.

"Yes sir?"

Brother Robbins cleared his throat. "I just want to say what a pleasure it has been to have you home the past few weeks."

"Thank you, Father."

"I just thank the Lord for your faith, Adam. I sometimes am vexed by your brothers' attitudes, particularly that of Abel, and I pray he doesn't lead Seth astray. Perhaps Abel will take you for his example and lead a more God-pleasing life. Why, just the other day I detected the odor of tobacco…"

Adam took his suitcase from the back seat. "Goodbye, Father."

"Goodbye, my son. God go with you," Brother Robbins said, reaching for Adam's hand. But Adam had already closed the door and turned toward the bus, and their hands did not touch. Brother Robbins watched him climb aboard the bus. He craned his neck, hoping to glimpse him, but the bus windows were dirty. He waited until the bus pulled onto the highway, then took out his handkerchief and blew his nose.

Adam hesitated beside an empty seat next to a young woman. "May I sit here?"

She looked up at him, pink-cheeked and smiling. "Sure," she said.

He settled himself in beside her, then turned to her. "How far you going?"

"Oklahoma City," she said. "How about you?"

"Far away as I can get," he muttered under his breath.

"How's that?"

"Oklahoma City." He extended his hand. "My name is Adam," he said.

"I'm Lillian," she said, taking it.

"Lillian," he repeated. "A beautiful name for a beautiful lady," he said.

She blushed and ducked her head down. Adam lowered his head to catch her eye. "Now, Lillian, don't tell me you don't know you're beautiful."

# CHAPTER FIFTEEN

Wayne lay miserably on his bed. His dream was dying. He tried to shore up his deteriorating morale. If at first you don't succeed, he reminded himself. To persist after failure was what made men great. Look at George Washington freezing at Valley Forge. Look at General MacArthur leaving the Philippines. Well, for that matter, look at Jesus hanging on the cross. All of them had appeared to be defeated, and all of them had come back like gangbusters to win the day.

He had to admit he had been greatly encouraged by his conversion of Linda Stoker. That had been effortless; the right words had just come to him, and she had become putty in his hands. He had accomplished all that without Bible College, before setting up his own ministry.

Converting Linda was a sign from God. God wanted to tell him something, sure as shooting. He squeezed his eyes shut and folded his hands in front of his face. As an afterthought, he rolled off the bed and got on his knees. "Speak, Lord, for thy servant heareth," he said.

Immediately came bang, bang, bang! Wayne's heart banged against his chest wall in concert with the noise. It took another bang, bang, bang for him to realize that somebody was knocking on the front door.

When he opened the door, he could hardly believe his eyes. It was Mr. Woodson. Wayne had entertained a number of fantasies about what he would do when he encountered his former employer. He had envisioned himself spitting out words of scornful reproach, or remaining implacably silent.

"Mr. Woodson," he said, opening the screen door. "Won't you come in, sir."

Roy shook his head. "I just came by for a minute." He paused, then said, "Wayne, it looks like we might have had a misunderstanding. I may have been too hasty. Tell you what, I'd like for you to come back to work."

"Why, Mr. Woodson…"

"I know, we had words that we probably both regret, but it seems to me it would be better all the way around if you came back. Let bygones be bygones."

"Why, I…"

"You know, it's probably time for you to be the manager. You've been working for me a long time, and uh well, longevity in a job ought to be…is a factor.

There might be the possibility of a raise."

"Why, Mr. Woodson…"

"So what do you say? Start tomorrow morning? No hard feelings?" He offered his hand.

Wayne pumped it gratefully. "Why, thank you, sir. Thank you. I could come in today, now, this afternoon, if you want me to."

"No, tomorrow morning will be fine. So that's settled." He nodded, turned, and walked back to his car.

Wayne slumped against the open door, weak from happiness, as his mother maneuvered her car into the driveway. She came to the house looking back toward Roy's departing car.

"Who was that?" she asked.

"Well, Mama, believe it or not, that was Mr. Roy Woodson."

"Land sakes, what did he want?"

"He came here on his knees, begging me to come back to work for him."

"He did? Well, if that don't beat the band!"

"He made me such a humble apology that I felt it was the Christian thing to forgive him. He is going to make me manager and give me a big raise. He knows he was in the wrong, and he wants to make it up to me."

Mary Pickens put her hands to her mouth.

"He wanted me to come right away today, but I told him tomorrow morning would suit me better."

"Praise the Lord!"

~ ~ ~

Pat slammed down the telephone just as Dorothy came in the back door with a big sack of groceries on her hip.

"Pain in the patoot!"

"Who?" Dorothy asked, setting the bag on the table.

"Marilyn, that's who. I just got off the phone with her. She doesn't want to go tomorrow, and she doesn't want Joe to go either. She gave me a hundred excuses, but no reason. Some baloney about it costing too much money."

"Well, Pat, that could be the reason."

"No, I told her it was my treat, motel, race course tickets, restaurant, everything but their bets. And they wouldn't have to bet. Plus we can all go in the Buick. It wouldn't even cost them gas. So then she starts in on not wanting to leave Jesse by himself."

"Well," Dorothy said, moving efficiently about the kitchen to put away groceries.

"So then I told her I'd talk to Coach and Jesse could stay with him and Kathryn, or if that didn't work out, I'd talk to the Lynches, and he could stay over there."

"What did she say to that?"

"Said she didn't want to bother anybody. I told her I'd be the one bothering them and that it wouldn't bother them anyway, and even if it did, I didn't mind bothering them. So then she flat out says she's not going to go." Fuming, Pat stopped in her tracks and slapped her pockets. "Where are my cigarettes?"

"Right in front of you. On the table. Here."

Pat lit up and continued pacing.

"What about Joe?" Dorothy asked.

"Yeah, that's what I asked Marilyn."

"Pat, will you please quit stomping around."

Pat threw herself into one of the kitchen chairs and flicked ashes toward the ashtray. Dorothy folded the paper bag neatly and stowed it in the pantry, then sat down at the table.

"Did she say anything about Joe?"

Pat exhaled noisily. "Nothing that made any sense. I think he might have come into the room while we were talking, because she all of a sudden said she had to go, hoped I would understand, cetera, cetera, cetera."

Dorothy considered. "So how did you leave it?"

"I told her we'd be out there to pick them up at eight o'clock tomorrow morning. And then she hung up on me!"

"Well, Pat, if they don't want to go…"

"Course they want to go. It'll be fun! Dorothy, you call Marilyn. Talk her into it. Twist her arm. She'll listen to you."

"Well, I think I might call her. But I'm not going to twist her arm."

"Well, go on, call her."

"Not with you hovering over me."

"Okay, okay, I'll go out back and water the tomatoes. You call her, okay?"

Dorothy met Pat's beseeching eyes. "I'll call her."

Pat stubbed out her cigarette in the ashtray. "Tell her it's all set up."

"Go on outdoors. Shoo!"

Dorothy sat at the table for awhile after the back door banged. Lord knows she wasn't crazy about this trip either, but she wasn't about to let Pat and Laura Tuttle go by themselves. It would definitely be better if Joe and Marilyn would go. It was obvious that Pat was going, hell or high water.

She went to the phone and dialed the number. It rang only once before Joe answered.

"It's your nickel," he said.

"Joe, it's Dorothy."

"Dorothy, how are you, darlin'?"

"Well, I'm fine, Joe…"

"Couldn't be happier to hear that. It's fine to be fine, ain't it? I'm fine, too. Everything's fine. Except just the one thing, and I want your advice about this, Dorothy, because I don't know who else to ask, I have asked Marilyn and she says she doesn't know, so I thought I would ask you, and I know you will tell me the straight-out truth. I think Marilyn might know and just won't tell me. But you will tell me, won't you?" His voice changed from cajoling to threatening when he repeated, "Won't you?"

"Well, Joe, if I know…"

"I knew you would. You have always been a good friend to me, Dorothy. So just tell me. I think you know."

"If I know what, Joe?"

"What I have been asking you, Dorothy, and what I have been asking Marilyn but she won't say. So I need you or somebody to just tell me where it is."

"Where what is, Joe?"

"No games, now. Just tell me straight out where my gun is. Because I need it."

Dorothy had heard tell about the hair rising on the back of the neck but she had never before experienced it.

"Come on," he said, "spit it out."

"Joe, I don't know anything about that," she stammered.

"God damn it, Dorothy, you have got to tell me. I need to know, and I need to know now."

"Joe, can I talk to Marilyn?"

"Go to hell," he snarled and the line went dead.

Dorothy quickly dialed the phone. "Cal," she said, "it's Dorothy. We've got a big problem. Joe is acting crazy again. Can you meet Pat and me out at the farm right away?"

~ ~ ~

As he spread sawdust on the floor and began to sweep, Roy acknowledged that he felt better. Talking with Pickens had gone better than he had expected.

It was all squared away. It wouldn't hurt to make him manager and give him a little raise.

"Can I go now, Mr. Woodson?"

"Oh, sure, Renee, you go on."

"Okay."

"Oh, by the way, Renee..."

She paused, on her way to the door.

"Wayne Pickens is coming back to work tomorrow morning."

Renee gaped at him. "He *is*? How come?"

"Well, yeah. He uh wants very much to put this right. He knows he was out of line. I told him I could overlook it this one time."

"But..."

"It'd be best if you kept this confidential. The less said, the better. I don't want people talking."

"Okay," she said. She felt a laugh welling up, but disguised it by clearing her throat and skipped on out of the store. It'll be all over town in two days, she thought. People in Massey live for stuff like this to happen, so they can talk about it.

Roy latched the door behind her and turned the sign to "Closed." He scraped sawdust and debris into the dust pan and dumped it in the waste can at the back of the store. He turned off the lights, got his suit jacket and hat, and was just about to walk out the back door when the telephone rang. He considered not answering it, but then pounded up the stairs to his office and grabbed the receiver.

"Woodson's," he said.

"Roy, thank God!"

"Maureen?" he said.

"No, no, it's Marilyn. Listen, I can't reach Cal. Can you come out here?"

"What's the matter?"

Her desperate whisper altered to a faked chirpiness. "Yes, ma'am. I'll be happy to bring cookies. You are welcome. Bye now."

Roy said, "Marilyn?" But the connection was broken.

Something bad is happening out there, he thought. He hustled into his car and drove out toward the highway, but then reconsidered and screeched to a stop in front of the court house. The hallway was empty and the door marked "County Sheriff" locked. He banged on the door and called out, "Anybody here? Cal?"

Old Mr. Forbes, the janitor, limped around the corner, carrying a mop and bucket. "How's that?" he asked.

"I'm looking for Sheriff Tuttle!"

Forbes put down the bucket. "Do what?"

"Have you seen Sheriff Tuttle?" Roy bellowed.

Forbes looked thoughtful, scratched his chin. "That there is the sheriff's office," he said, pointing.

"Oh, for God's sake!"

"I think he's probably gone, it being six thirty. But I don't know for sure," he called, but Roy had already left.

"Burr up his ass," Forbes mused, swishing the mop in the bucket. "Well, I guess I might be sore, too, if my wife was catting around." He gave a little cackle and mopped.

Roy floored it all the way to the farmhouse. He was relieved to see Cal's pickup parked there alongside Pat and Dorothy's Buick. The front door to the house was open and light spilled out onto the porch. He hopped out of his car and ran up the porch steps.

The scene inside the house was frozen, like a silent tableau. On one side of the living room, Cal Tuttle stood, hands up. Behind him, Pat was pointing her finger while Dorothy, Marilyn, and Jesse cowered behind her. Alone on the other side of the room, Joe stood with his rifle pointed directly at Cal.

"Hey!" Roy cried and flung open the screen door.

Six heads turned toward him. Joe swiveled toward Roy, aimed the rifle, and pulled the trigger. The blast was deafening. The impact lifted Roy off his feet. He flew backwards off the porch and flopped against the hard ground. He tried to speak, but could only gurgle. He stared upward, pain searing his body. Somebody was screaming. Somebody bent over him. Somebody yelled, "I told you they were coming." Then blackness and silence.

# CHAPTER SIXTEEN

"Well, you're in a good mood this morning."

Renee watched her mother swaying to the song on the radio, belting out a duet with Jo Stafford. Nadine grabbed Renee's hands and swung her out in a happy little jitterbug.

"Come a little closer, make love to me!" Nadine loudly sang.

"Mama! Behave yourself!" But Renee laughed, pleased that Nadine wasn't down in the dumps this morning, as she had been almost all week.

The song ended, and Renee turned down the volume. "Hear you all over the neighborhood," she mock-scolded.

"You want a pancake?"

"Sure." Renee settled herself at the kitchen table. "You want to hear something funny?"

Nadine looked up from stirring together the pancake ingredients. "What, a joke?"

"Not exactly," Renee said. "Well, do you?"

"Fire when ready," Nadine said.

"Wayne Pickens has got his job back."

"You're kidding!"

"Nope. Mr. Woodson told me yesterday. I would have told you last night, but you were out late, gallivanting around somewhere, I guess."

Nadine ignored the invitation to divulge where she had been. "What did Roy say?"

"Just that Wayne apologized and asked to come back and that he was going to let him, but he said that Wayne would have to watch his mouth from now on."

"Well, I never. That *is* funny." Nadine dropped batter in the sizzling skillet.

"Didn't make any sense to me," Renee said. "I thought he'd probably rather shoot Wayne than take him back."

"Did he say anything else?"

"No, but I think Mrs. Woodson's gone out of town. He's been eating his meals at the hotel coffee shop."

"How do you know that?"

"Well, Mrs. Foust came in the store day before yesterday while he was out and she asked me was Mrs. Woodson out of town. I said I didn't know, why? And she said that he'd been at the hotel coffee shop for breakfast and supper all week."

Nadine said, "Well, I heard she went to Amarillo."

"Who told you that?"

Nadine laughed. "Grapevine. Here, take your plate."

"How come you're so happy this morning? Where were you last night?"

"Well," Nadine said, bringing her plate to the table. "I had some good news yesterday."

"What?"

"You could say good news and bad news," Nadine said. "The bad news is I have to stop smoking."

"What's the good news?"

"The good news is my cough is going to go away."

"Well, that is good news. So did you go to the doctor?"

"Yep."

"Did he tell you to stop smoking?"

"He did, he read me the riot act."

"You didn't come home for supper," Renee said. "Where'd you eat last night?"

"Steak House."

"Who with?"

Nadine reached across the table to grasp Renee's arm. "Don't you dare laugh."

"I won't," Renee promised.

"You better not."

"I am not going to laugh. Who did you go to the Steak House with?"

Nadine stuck out her chin. "Daryl Tomlin."

"Why, Mama, you sly dog!" Renee said. But she didn't laugh.

Daryl sat in his kitchen drinking his morning coffee. He reflected on his afternoon and evening with Nadine. It had been a lot of fun. His plan to turn over a new leaf was working out really well. Now it was time for him to take care of another problem.

He drained his cup and marched down the hall. He rapped on Danny's bedroom door and then walked in. Clothes, shoes, dirty dishes, overflowing ashtrays. Looked terrible, smelled worse.

"Daniel Lloyd Tomlin," he said sternly.

The bedcovers shifted slightly.

"My boy, the times, they are a-changing," Daryl said. "Today you are moving out of this house."

Danny rolled over. "What?"

"I want you out of here by the time I get back here tonight. If you're not gone, I will call the law and they'll put you out."

Danny sat up. "What?"

"You heard me. Plus, no more handouts. I am not giving you one more cent. You need to get a job. You are on your own as far as money is concerned."

"But..."

"No buts about it. Now move your sorry ass."

"But...where am I supposed to live?"

"Up to you. The trailer. Anyplace but here."

"I'm not going back to the trailer." Danny glared at him.

"I don't care where you go, as long as you get your butt out of my house." He shut the door on Danny's mutinous face.

Daryl was humming a happy little tune when he got to the lumber yard. He poured himself a cup of coffee and walked out back to find Eldon.

"Eldon, listen, uh, Danny isn't going to work here anymore."

Eldon snorted. "In my humble opinion, Danny hasn't never *worked* here. So far as *I* could tell."

"I know. Now if he comes around when I'm not here, you run him off, okay?"

"You serious?"

"You better believe it. And don't give him any money, understand?"

"You better tell your daddy that, too."

Daryl nodded. "I'm just fixing to do that."

He returned to his office and dialed the phone. When Lloyd answered, he repeated the whole thing to him.

Lloyd said, "Are you serious?"

"Everybody keeps asking me that," Daryl snapped. "Let me go on record. I am damn serious!"

"Okay, okay. I'm just surprised."

"Now I don't want you all coddling him any more. He's got to straighten up and fly right. If he can't stand on his own two feet, he'll have to sink or swim. I wash my hands of him."

"Did he do something?" Lloyd asked.

"No, and that's just the point. He hasn't done shit."

"Well, Daryl, I have to tell you, I think you're doing the right thing," Lloyd said.

"Yeah, it's about time, isn't it."

After he went through the whole thing one more time on the phone with Jim Atkins, he sat back in his chair, satisfied. Jim had agreed about taking a hard-line approach to Danny and said he would try to persuade Mavis.

The phone rang.

"Tomlin's," he said.

"Daryl?"

"Yes."

"Well, finally!"

"Carolyn?"

"Where have you been? I have been trying to reach you for two days now!"

Daryl enjoyed his answer. "Well, I have been busy."

"Well, I am so very sorry to interrupt your terribly busy schedule with my little bitty concerns."

Daryl failed to keep the impatience out of his voice. "What is it, Carolyn?"

"Never mind," she said and slammed the receiver down.

Daryl hung up, rubbing his ear. Then he picked up the receiver and dialed.

"Nadine's."

"Hi, it's Daryl. You busy?"

"Little bit. How are you?"

"Better now. What time are you done this afternoon?"

"Five."

"I'll pick you up at six. Thought we might go to the country club for dinner."

"In Amarillo?"

"Yeah, they have a nice buffet on Friday night and a live band. We could dance. You know, get in practice so we can wow the Jaycees."

"Well…"

"Put on your dancing shoes, lady. I'll see you at six."

"Well..."

"I'm hanging up before you can say no."

"What makes you think I'm going to say no?"

"Say yes then. Say I'd love to, Daryl."

"I'd love to, Daryl."

Grinning, Nadine returned to the chair to roll up Kathryn Parker's hair.

"Was that Daryl Tomlin?"

"My, you have big ears," Nadine said.

"Are you going out with him?"

"My, my, so many questions," Nadine said.

Renee flung open the door to the beauty shop and ran in. "Mama, the terriblest thing has happened! It's Mr. Woodson. He's been shot!"

~ ~ ~

The news that Joe Eliot had shot Roy Woodson spread so quickly that, by noon, when someone tried to pass on the news, that person had already heard.

At 9:30, Leroy Talbot had been in his diner on the phone with his wife Betty, who had just arrived at the clinic. She told him that Roy Woodson had been taken to the hospital in Amarillo the night before. She said he was in critical condition because of a gunshot wound.

Minutes before, Laverne Larimer was gazing out the diner's plate glass window across the street, her attention riveted on Renee Coulter and Wayne Pickens, who were standing outside Woodson's. She wondered why they didn't go on in. And what was Wayne doing there anyway? Then she saw Virgil Harmon rush out of the drug store and say something that made Renee run off in one direction and Wayne in the other. Before Leroy could get off the phone, Laverne stepped outside the diner and hailed Virgil, who hollered the news to her across the street. Those folks lucky enough to be within earshot heard him say that Roy had been shot. He had just had a call from Dorothy, telling him that Jesse wouldn't be at work because they had all gone to Amarillo. A confirmatory statement arrived courtesy of Pete Mosley, who was flagged down by Don Paulson and Mayor Collier in front of the court house. By ten o'clock, when the regulars gathered at the diner, only Gus Bell's ears were virgin with reference to the incident.

The bare fact was firmly established: Joe Eliot had shot Roy Woodson. Folks now could take long-drawn-out pleasure in conjecture about the circumstances. Speculation ranged from the mundane (that it had been an accident) to the fantastic (that it had to do with Maureen Woodson's affair). Several stated that it was no surprise to them that Joe Eliot had gone completely off his rocker. "Just a matter of time" and "Time bomb waiting to go off" were oft-repeated phrases. To make up for a late start, Gus Bell opined that they could have been playing Russian roulette.

Bulletins continued to arrive. Mary Pickens testified that Maureen Woodson had gone to Amarillo Tuesday morning and had not yet returned. Old Mr. Forbes held forth on the state of Roy Woodson's mind ("Burr up his ass! Sore as a boil!") when he had seen him at the court house prior to the shooting.

Beyond the reach of news or gossip, Maureen Woodson decided to stay at the country club for the weekend.

~ ~ ~

Danny Tomlin, barefoot and wearing only a pair of Levi's, stood at the open refrigerator, drinking milk from the bottle. When two slices of Wonder Bread popped up, he knifed chunks of butter onto the toast. He poured Karo syrup over the slices. After he wolfed down the toast, he licked syrup off the plate.

In his bedroom, he stuffed some clothes into a brown paper sack and put on a shirt and his boots. He took his black leather jacket and the sack out to his car and threw them in the back seat. Back in the house, he dialed the phone.

"Hello?"

"Grandma? It's Danny. How're you doing?"

"Oh, Danny…"

"Listen, Grandma, I need a place to stay."

There was a long pause and whispered conversation in the background. "Grandma?"

"Danny?" It was Lloyd.

"Yeah?"

"What is it you want?"

"I want to come over. I need a place to stay."

"Danny, I talked to your daddy this morning. He says it's time you learned to stand on your own, and your grandma and I are going to abide by that. You are welcome to visit any time, but you can't live here. Now, Danny, this may seem hard, but your grandma and I think it's going to be good for you in the long run. We…"

Danny slammed down the phone and fulminated over Daryl's treachery and Lloyd's gutlessness. He could almost cry thinking how unfair it all was and how unlucky he had always been. He had never caught a break, not once. Someday they would all be sorry for the way they had treated him. He would leave this one-horse town. Get away from the lot of them. He would move to Santa Fe and live with his mother. She had always been on his side.

Waiting for her to pick up the phone, he fantasized about life in Santa Fe. He would ride horses. He would get a new car.

"Hello?"

"Hi, it's me," he said.

"Oh, Daryl, I am so glad you called back!"

"Uh, it's Danny."

"Danny? Well, for heaven's sake. You sound so much like Daryl. I was sure it was him."

"No. Uh, look, Mama, I need to talk to you. Something's come up."

"What?"

"You won't believe it, but Daddy has told me I have to move out of the house."

"Why?"

"I don't know. One minute everything is hunky dory and the next minute he has a wild hair up his..."

"Danny," she warned.

"Well, he does. He told me this morning I have to leave. Just like that. Can you believe it?"

He expected her to commiserate, but she said briskly, "So what are you going to do now?"

"Well, I want to make a fresh start. Move clean away from Massey. You know, make a fresh start."

"And go where?"

"Well, I was thinking that I could come out to Santa Fe."

"Santa Fe! And what would you do here?"

"Well, I'd get a job..."

"Doing what?"

"Anything. I could do lots of things."

"Danny, you haven't ever had a real job. You have no qualifications or experience."

"Mama, listen. I would work. Construction, gas station, whatever I could find."

"And where would you live?"

Danny couldn't believe his ears. "Why," he said, "with you."

"Oh, no," Carolyn said. "No, no, that wouldn't be a good idea. No, Danny, I'm sorry, but no."

He felt like crying. "Mama, please. You are my last chance."

"Danny, work it out with your father. You can't just run away every time there's a problem."

"This would not be running away. This would be a fresh start. Please, Mama."

"No, Danny. You can't live with me. I mean it."

He recognized the finality of her tone.

"Call Florence and Lloyd. You can probably stay with them for awhile. Until you make up with your father."

"You're as bad as the rest of them," he sobbed and threw down the receiver. He stomped around the kitchen, muttering curses and threats. After awhile, he collected himself and began to think.

He rooted through Daryl's bureau drawers until he found the leather case. He took Daryl's Masonic ring with the big diamond, the solid gold cufflinks, and the heavy gold pocket watch that had belonged to Lloyd's father. He found Daryl's stash of cash in another drawer and pocketed most of it. Then he went back to the phone.

After the fifth ring came a sleepy hello.

"Darlene?"

"Who is this?"

"Who do you suppose?"

"Danny?"

"Yeah. What're you doing?"

"I *was* sleeping. What are you doing?"

"Well, to tell the truth, I'm leaving town. I just called to say goodbye."

"What?"

"I'm leaving town."

"Oh, Danny, why? Don't do that."

"It's driving me crazy to live with Daryl. So I'm going to leave. I just wanted to tell you goodbye. You are the only person here I will miss."

"Danny, don't go."

"I'm just fixing to leave now. There's nothing for me here. Except you. I will miss you, Darlene."

"Oh, Danny, please don't go."

"I have to. Anyway, I don't have anyplace to stay."

"You can stay here with me."

"I don't know, Darlene…"

"Come on over. Danny, don't leave town."

"Well, okay, but just for a couple of days. I have pretty much decided to get out of here. Maybe move to Dallas, or..."

"Come on over here. You can stay here as long as you want to. Please, Danny."

"Well, all right, you talked me into it."

"Come on over right now."

"Not right away," he said, fingering the jewelry. "I got some business to take care of in Gainesville."

~ ~ ~

The waitress came to the booth and asked, "What can I get you all?"

Dorothy put down her menu. "I'll have a tuna fish sandwich on toast and a Coke. What kind of soup do you have?"

"Clam chowder."

"And a cup of clam chowder."

Pat said, " What do you want, Jesse?"

"Hamburger, fries, chocolate malted," he said.

Pat said, "That sounds good. The same for me. Marilyn?"

"I'm not hungry."

"You have to eat something," Dorothy said. "How about some soup?"

"Okay, a bowl of soup," she said to the waitress. "And coffee."

"I'll be right back with your drinks," the waitress said.

The four of them sat silently. Finally, Dorothy said, "This is a nice little coffee shop. Convenient. I really didn't like the hospital cafeteria this morning. Those eggs had been on the steam table so long, they were petrified."

"The waffles weren't bad," Pat said.

Jesse poured out a little mound of salt on the table and balanced the salt shaker on edge against the salt. The other three watched as he carefully blew away the grains of salt. The shaker remained standing on its edge. "See," he said, "just one grain is holding it up."

When the waitress put their drinks on the table, the shaker fell over. Jesse poured out more salt on the table, but the shaker wouldn't balance. He poured out a mound of sugar on the table and tried to balance both the salt and pepper shakers.

"Jesse, stop it," Marilyn hissed across the table at him.

"I'm not hurting anything," he said resentfully.

"You're making a mess."

"Well, it's a pretty day," Pat said.

"Real pretty," Dorothy agreed.

"We could have been at the races about now if…" Pat began. "Ow!"

"Sorry," said Dorothy. "I was just crossing my legs."

Marilyn looked sorrowfully across the table at Pat. "It's all my fault. He got real upset when I told him I didn't want to go to Raton."

"Oh, Mare," Dorothy said.

"If Roy doesn't pull through, I don't know what I'll do," Marilyn said.

"Now, listen," Dorothy said, "Roy is going to be fine. The doctor said so. The bullet missed all his vital organs."

"That's right," Pat said. "We can probably see him when we go back over there."

"Are they going to arrest Pop?" Jesse asked.

The three of them looked at him, startled.

"No, course not," Pat said.

"Honey, he didn't mean to hurt him," Dorothy explained. "It was an accident."

"It didn't look like an accident to me," Jesse said, raising his voice.

"Well, it was," Pat said, matching his volume.

"Not from where I stood," Jesse persisted.

"Keep your voices down," Dorothy said.

Jesse stuck his chin out. "He meant to shoot somebody. If it hadn't of been Uncle Roy, it would of been Sheriff Tuttle. Or me."

"Jesse, that's bull crap, and you know it!" Pat stormed.

"How can you say that about your daddy?" Marilyn was close to tears.

"All right, hush now, that is enough!" Dorothy said, as if to a room full of rowdy fourth graders.

The food arrived. Jesse glowered across the table at his mother. "He's crazy, and you know it!"

"Jesse…" Pat put her hand on his arm.

"Aunt Pat, you weren't there. When I got in the other night he was acting real funny. He was rearranging the coats. He offered me a beer!"

"Jesse, stop hollering," Marilyn hissed. "People are staring at us!"

Jesse dropped his hamburger on his plate and elbowed Pat. "Let me out," he said.

"Where are you going?" Marilyn asked.

He pushed past Pat and ran out the door of the coffee shop.

Pat said, "I'll go with him. Dorothy, have them wrap up my hamburger. His, too."

Marilyn put her face in her hands. Dorothy patted her shoulder. "Come on, honey, eat your soup."

"Truth to tell," Marilyn said, "Jesse is right. Joe's been like a maniac. The medicine hasn't seemed to help at all. I've been afraid he was going to do something. When he found the gun, I called Cal, but he wasn't there. So I called Roy. If only I hadn't done that, he wouldn't be in the hospital now."

"Now, now," Dorothy said. "We're just going to take this one step at a time. We have an appointment with Dr. Siegel at two, right? And Roy is going to be fine. Now for the love of God, eat your soup."

Pat caught up with Jesse and matched her stride to his. After a couple of blocks, he said, "I hate him."

Pat didn't answer, but her expression was sympathetic.

"He is ruining everything! I missed practice last night! And this morning! Coach is going to kill me!"

"Why didn't you go to practice last night?"

"I started to, but then I got afraid…for Mama. When I left yesterday morning he was tearing the house apart looking for his gun. I thought if he found it, he might…do something. He was mad she didn't want to go to Raton."

"Why didn't you call me?"

"I don't know. I didn't think to."

Pat guided him back to the coffee shop, where Marilyn and Dorothy stood outside, clutching brown paper bags. Jesse shrank away, but Pat muscled him forward. "Come on," she said. "We're going to get through this."

~ ~ ~

"It was providential I still had my key to the store," Wayne said, not for the first time. "Now, Renee, since it's just you and me working here, I hope I can count on you to take on more responsibility."

"Like what?"

"Well, like…well, just be ready when the occasion arises."

Renee snorted. "Are you really going to try to run the store, like it was yours?"

"For sure. That is what Mr. Woodson would want. When he came to me the other day, he told me he was going to make me the manager. He said he should have done it a long time ago."

"Yeah, uh huh," Renee said skeptically. "Well, you know, Wayne, when school starts, I'm not going to be working here anymore."

"We'll cross that bridge when we come to it. Now, I have to go out for a little while. I told Mr. Longbrake that I would come by and tell him the latest. For the paper."

"The latest what?"

"The latest about Mr. Woodson's condition, for one thing, and for another, that the store is going to remain open in his absence."

"Did you hear something about Mr. Woodson?"

"Well, just what Mr. Harmon told me. He said Mr. Woodson is out of surgery and in serious condition, but that there is every expectation that he is going to be just fine and back home within a week."

"Everybody already knows that," Renee said.

"Never mind," Wayne said. "Now while I'm gone, you may as well straighten the piece goods."

Renee began half-heartedly to work at the fabric counter. Wayne was sure full of piss and vinegar today. It was like somebody crowned him king.

She turned when the door chime sounded.

"Hi," said Abel Robbins.

"Hi," she returned.

"How are you?" he said.

"May I help you?"

"No, not exactly. I just came by to ask…"

Somebody else wanting information about Mr. Woodson, Renee thought. Dozens of people had come by the store and stuck their heads in and asked stupid questions, trying to improve their gossip quotient. It was tiresome.

"He's doing pretty well. He's in serious condition, but he's going to recover fully," she said briskly.

Abel looked perplexed. "Who is?"

"Why, Mr. Woodson, of course. Wasn't that who you were asking about?"

"Mr. Woodson? No, I wasn't. What's wrong with him?"

"Have you been living in a cave?"

Abel's eyes widened. "A cave?"

"Okay, let's start over. I thought you were asking about Mr. Woodson. So I told you."

"But you didn't tell me what is the matter with him."

Renee looked at him closely. "You don't know, do you? Well, you must be the only person in town. Mr. Woodson got shot and is in the hospital in Amarillo."

Abel took this in. "Oh," he said. "And you say he's going to be all right?"

"That's right."

"Oh. Well, that's good."

Renee looked at him. He wasn't nearly so handsome as Adam, she thought, hair standing up funny. Totally different type, too. Doesn't know what to say or how to say it.

"So, may I help you?" she said.

"Well," he said, "I came by to ask you something." His ears and cheeks got rosier, as he held her gaze. "I came by to ask you if you wanted to go to the picture show."

When Renee didn't answer, he continued, "With me. Tonight. Or tomorrow night, if you're busy tonight. Or some other time."

Renee narrowed her eyes. "You want me to go to the picture show with you?"

"Yes."

"Why?"

Abel opened his mouth, but nothing came out.

"I suppose you heard something about me. Did somebody tell you something about me?" she asked, angrily.

"Why, no."

"Did your brother say something?"

"Adam?"

"Don't you lie to me, Abel Robbins," Renee flashed.

"I won't," he said. "I'm not. I – nobody said anything."

They faced each other in silence. Then Abel offered, as if he might be able to clear things up, "Adam's gone back to Oklahoma City."

"I don't care where he's gone. He is nothing to me," Renee snapped.

"Oh, okay," he said. "I just thought…" He shrugged his shoulders, gave it up, and turned toward the door.

"Where do you think you're going?"

He turned back toward her.

"Well, just hang on a minute. At least until we're done talking," she said, impatiently. "Okay, I'll go to the picture show with you tonight."

Abel goggled at her. "You will?"

"Yes. You know where I live?"

"Yes."

"Then you come over to my house at seven and pick me up. Okay?"

"Okay. Yes. Thank you." Almost out the door, he added, "I don't drive. We'll have to walk."

"I guess I can put up with that," Renee said. He was kind of cute after all, even when his ears were bright red. I guess I was kind of hard on him, she thought. For awhile there, I thought he was making fun of me.

~ ~ ~

Dr. Siegel paged through his file folder for several minutes. Pat shifted in her chair and cleared her throat. He looked up at her. "So, what's the word, Doc?" she asked.

"You are Miss Eliot?" he said.

"I'm Joe's sister. This is Miss Harmon. This is Joe's son, Jesse."

Dr. Siegel nodded at Dorothy and Jesse. Jesse slunk lower in the chair and began a thorough examination of his fingernails.

"Well," the doctor said, "I guess you all have had quite a time."

"You can say that again," Pat said.

"How is he?" Marilyn asked.

"He's…well, we've put him in the secure ward. He's quite heavily sedated now. He was extremely agitated when he came in last night. According to the attendant on duty, he was fighting everybody."

"Yeah, that sounds about right," Pat said.

"What is going to happen next?" Dorothy asked.

"Well, we are going to try to stabilize him. Mrs. Eliot, do you know if he was taking his medication?"

"Yes, he was. Twice a day. I gave him the pills myself."

"And they didn't help?"

"Oh, at first they did, they really did. He was so much better. He just seemed his old self. It was like a miracle."

Jesse scowled toward her and made a little noise in the back of his throat before going back to his fingernails.

"Jesse?" Dr. Siegel said. "You were going to say something?"

Jesse looked at Pat, who nodded encouragement. "First of all, he was not what I would call better. He acted dopey."

Marilyn intervened, "Now, Jesse…"

"Please, Mrs. Eliot, I'd like to hear what Jesse has to say. Dopey, you say?"

"Yeah, like he couldn't remember stuff, and all the time sleeping and lazy."

"Go on."

"But then it changed. He got different. He wasn't sleeping hardly at all. He got all excited about stuff. And, he offered me a beer."

"That was unusual?"

"You said it. He used to be real strict about it. He would get mad if he even thought I was drinking."

"You say he got all excited about stuff. About what stuff?"

"Well," Jesse said. "He was all excited about going to Raton to the races. I mean, he was like a little kid. Then he started in tearing up the house looking for his gun. He talked about people coming to get him."

Dr. Siegel raised his eyebrows. "That's very helpful, Jesse. Thank you for telling me." He turned to the women. "Did any of you observe the same things in Mr. Eliot?"

Dorothy said, "When I talked to him on the telephone yesterday afternoon, he was in a state, raving and ranting. That's when I called the sheriff and we all went out there."

"And what was he like when you got out there?"

"He had his gun and he was threatening to use it. Said he couldn't trust any of us anymore. Said we were in cahoots with his enemies."

"How about you, Miss Eliot?"

"Yeah, he was sure enough off his rocker."

"But, how about before then? How did he seem to you?"

Pat considered. "At first he was like Jesse said, kind of all slowed down. He complained about feeling sleepy. His golf game was truly terrible."

"What about this trip to Raton?"

"Well, that was my idea. I thought if he could have a little vacation that it would do him good."

"So you had been concerned about him?"

"In a way, yes, I had. But I thought he would snap out of it."

"It sounds to me as if he took the medicine for awhile. That would account for the sleepiness. But then I think from what you all are saying that he stopped taking it."

"But, that's not possible," Marilyn burst out. "I gave him the pills myself, one every morning and one every evening, just like you said."

"Did you actually see him take the pills?"

Marilyn looked frantically around at the rest of them. Dorothy put her hand on Marilyn's arm. "Honey," she said, "nobody is blaming you." She turned to Dr. Siegel. "This has been real hard on Marilyn."

Marilyn began to cry softly into her handkerchief. "I don't know," she said between sobs, "I really don't know if he took them or not. I gave them to him, but I don't know..."

Pat put her arm around Marilyn. "It's okay, Mare, it's okay."

# CHAPTER SEVENTEEN

L.W. Foster sat in Cal's office smoking a cigar. "So when can we schedule the hearing?"

"Soon as he gets out of the hospital, I guess," Cal said. "What are you going to ask the judge to do?"

"Commit him," L.W. said. "Unless Roy wants to file a criminal complaint. You did say Roy is going to be all right?"

"Yeah, he was damn lucky. Bullet went right through him. He lost a lot of blood, but there was no permanent damage. They're probably going to send him home in a few days."

"And what about Joe?"

"I talked to his doctor. They've got him in the locked ward. He's pretty heavily sedated. The doctor said it was obvious he hadn't been taking his medicine."

"In my opinion, they sent him home too soon the first time."

"Looks like it."

"When they get ready to release him, you go to Amarillo and bring him back. You'll have to lock him up until we have the hearing."

"Yeah, I guess."

"What exactly happened out there, Cal?"

Cal rubbed his forehead. "Dorothy called me, said she had talked to Joe and that he was on a tear about his gun."

"His gun? What about his gun?"

"Well, when they took him to Amarillo the last time, I asked Marilyn to put his gun where he couldn't find it. I guess I should have told her to get rid of it altogether. Anyway, I guess he found it and started acting crazy. Dorothy called to tell me and I met her and Pat out there. When we got there, Joe was all strung out. He was hollering, out of his head. He had found his gun and he was accusing Marilyn and Jesse of hiding it. Then things got really tense. He was waving the rifle around. He said he couldn't trust any of us, that we were all against him. I thought I could talk sense to him, calm him down, and get him in the ambulance and back to the hospital. I didn't think he would actually shoot anybody."

"And then Roy showed up?"

"Yeah, Marilyn had called him in a panic and he drove out there. When he came up on the porch and hollered, he startled all of us, and Joe fired on him. I don't think Joe even knew it was Roy. After I got the rifle away from him, he hollered at me that I should have listened to him, that they *were* after him. I had to tie him to a chair so we could concentrate on getting Roy into the ambulance. Then Pat and I wrestled Joe into a strait jacket and I drove him to the hospital and the rest of them followed us in Pat's car."

"Did he say anything to you?"

"He didn't once stop talking, all the way there. Carrying on about the damn medicine and the damn people who were out to get him and how Marilyn and the rest of us were against him. He was out of his head, L.W."

"Yeah. Well, I'm going to file a motion to have him committed. It's a shame."

"A crying shame."

"What is that medicine anyway?"

"Called Thorazine. It's brand new. Miracle drug, they think."

"Didn't work a miracle on Joe."

"No, it didn't."

"Okay, well, you let me know when you're going to bring him back. Take Pete with you. We don't want any trouble between here and there."

"Yeah, okay."

Cal sat at his desk. He felt worn out. He blamed himself for not getting rid of Joe's rifle when he had the chance. He shuddered to think that Joe might have killed Roy. Now Joe would be sent to the state hospital in Gainesville. Cal had seen the ward where the criminally insane were kept. It was like a prison, only worse, because the inmates were so pitiful and scary.

What if the trip to Raton had gone as planned, and Joe had gone crazy out there? He could have hurt Laura. Poor kid, she was all upset when he got home last night. Upset about Roy and Joe, but also disappointed that she couldn't go to Raton, after getting all those new clothes.

Cal realized that he had pretty much turned Laura over to Pat since Janice's death. Seemed like Laura was over at Pat's all the time. Maybe that wasn't such a good idea. She should be with kids her own age. And with him. He felt a sudden urgency to go home to see about his daughter.

She was slumped on the sofa, watching television when he came in the house. "What're you watching?" he asked, coming to sit beside her.

"Kukla, Fran and Ollie," she said.

After a minute he said, "So, which one is Fran?"

"Papa," Laura reproved him.

"Which one is that?"

"That's Ollie."

"What is he, a lizard?"

"Papa, don't be silly. He's a dragon, can't you tell?"

"This is too complicated for me," he said and got up. "You want to go to Benny's and get a hamburger for supper?"

She sat up. "Sure. When this is over."

"Okay, I'm going to get cleaned up. You let me know when you're ready."

Over their food at Benny's, Laura leaned toward him, confidentially. "What are they going to do to Jesse's daddy?"

"Well, there has to be a hearing," he said cautiously.

"Are they going to send him to prison?"

"No, no, probably not. Roy is going to be okay, and you know Joe didn't really mean to hurt him."

"But he did hurt him. Whether he meant to or not."

"I know. But there's a difference between meaning to hurt somebody and an accident. Joe is sick, honey. He couldn't help it."

"That's what you always say." Laura had a new look in her eyes, half-rebellious.

"But..."

"So what then? Will they just let him go?"

"I don't know for sure, honey."

"Well, what do you suppose?" she pressed.

"Well," he said slowly, "what I suppose is that he will have to go to Gainesville, to the state hospital."

"Where Mama was."

"Well, yeah."

"Because he's...insane." She said the word as if it tasted bad.

"Yeah."

"Papa, what makes people turn out that way? Is Jesse going to turn out that way?"

"No, no. Why would you think that?"

"You don't know for sure, do you? I mean, when Jesse's daddy was Jesse's age, didn't it seem like he was fine?"

"Well..."

"And now he's a sick, dangerous person. I've been thinking about it," she said, her brow furrowed. "When Mama was my age, didn't it seem like she was fine?"

"Now, Laura…"

"Well, didn't it?"

"Yes, but that doesn't mean…"

"I really feel sorry for Jesse," she said. "It's going to be real hard on him. People are going to talk about him. Jesse is sensitive. He may not be able to take it. It's awful when you know people are talking about your crazy mama. You know they're thinking that you might be crazy, too."

"Laura…"

"I wish I could talk to Jesse. I know how he feels."

Cal couldn't think of anything to say. He felt a profound sadness take hold of him. Janice hadn't meant to hurt anybody, and neither had Joe. But Roy had been hurt, and could have been killed. And here was Laura, hurt. There was Jesse, hurt. What could he, what could anybody, do about that kind of hurt? The point she raised, whether insanity could be inherited, troubled him. Would Jesse one day grab a rifle and shoot at imaginary enemies? Would Laura one day walk out to the lake and into the water? Dread and sadness and anger wrangled within him. Finally, unable to bear the growing disturbance in his breast, he threw his napkin on the table and got up.

"Let's go," he said shortly.

Surprised, Laura stumbled to her feet. She grabbed out for his arm. "Papa, I'm sorry, I'm sorry. I didn't mean it. Please, don't be mad at me." Tears gathered and overflowed down her cheeks.

"Oh, honey," he said, grabbing her in a bear hug. "I am not mad at you. Don't cry, honey, please don't cry." Over her shoulder, he stared down the inquisitive faces turned toward them. "Come on, let's get out of here."

In the pickup, he tried clumsily to talk to her, to reassure her. She wasn't crying any more and she said she understood, but Cal felt her retreat into a remoteness which he could not penetrate. He drove them home in silent melancholy.

❧ ❧ ❧

"It seems wrong," Nadine said in Daryl's car.

"What does?"

"To feel so happy when there's so much misery in the world."

Daryl reached for her hand. "You should always feel happy," he said.

"Course I'm about to die for lack of a cigarette," she said. "That's the fly in the ointment."

"How's your cough?"

She coughed in response. "As you can hear, it's still with me," she said. "You never smoked, did you, Daryl?"

"No, I tried it a couple of times, but I never got the hang of it."

"Lucky you. I started in junior high school. I'd steal a pack of my old man's Luckies, and me and Tina Forbes would go down by the creek and smoke after school."

"If I'd done that, Florence would have killed me."

"My folks never figured it out."

"Couldn't they smell it on you?"

"I guess not. They both smoked."

"Florence made Lloyd give it up when they got married. She has some kind of religious conviction about it. Thinks it hurts God's feelings for people to smoke."

"Well, you can poke fun at her, but at least she kept you from getting chronic bronchitis."

"Have to thank her some day for that."

"You were such a straight arrow, you probably wouldn't have smoked anyway."

"Straight arrow? How come you want to insult me?"

"Well, you were, Daryl. You know, boy scout, honor roll, never in any trouble. Squeaky clean. Now other boys were not straight arrows."

"Like Bobby."

"Bet your boots like Bobby. He was about the crookedest arrow of them all." Nadine laughed, remembering. "He'd put me on the back of that motorcycle and we would go places and do stuff that sometimes even scared me."

"Like what?"

"Well, he drove that thing like a wild man. But other stuff, too, like stealing beer and cigarettes right out from under the clerk's nose. And, well.... I shouldn't shock you with tales from my wicked past, Daryl."

"I heard about you and Bobby out at the river bottom."

"Yeah, I reckon you did."

"Some day I'll take you out to the river bottom and you can tell me all about it," Daryl said, lightly stroking Nadine's thigh as he drove.

"Maybe I can do better than tell you about it," Nadine said.

Daryl pulled the car into the parking lot of the country club and turned off the engine. He pulled her into his arms. They kissed. A few minutes later, Nadine said, "Whoa, Daryl."

"Probably you better fix your lipstick before we go in."

She pulled out her compact. "Yeah, you've ruined it."

"I'll ruin it again later," he said.

"Promise?"

"Promise."

"Daryl! Look!"

"What?"

"Look at what I see. That is Maureen Woodson getting out of her big old Cadillac!"

Daryl looked. "Wait a minute. You think she knows about Roy getting shot?"

"You think she cares?" Nadine said.

They watched Maureen run up the steps to the entrance of the country club. She almost immediately returned with a young man in tow. He took several packages from her car and carried them inside.

"Looks like she's been shopping," Nadine commented.

"You ready to go in?" Daryl asked.

"What are we going to say if she sees us?" Nadine asked.

"We're going to say, 'Hello, Maureen. How is Roy?'"

"Oh, that's perfect," Nadine said. As she waited for Daryl to come around and open her door, she practiced: "Hello, Maureen. *How* is Roy? How *is* Roy? How is *Roy*?" She laughed as they went up the steps, arm in arm.

~ ~ ~

The nurse said, "You can see Mr. Woodson now. But just one of you. And just for a few minutes."

"You go, Marilyn," Dorothy said.

"Are you his wife?" the nurse asked.

"No, I'm his sister-in-law."

"Is his wife here?"

Marilyn said, after a glance at Pat, "We haven't been able to reach her yet."

"He's been asking for her."

Pat humphed but Dorothy elbowed her and said, "Marilyn, you go on in. Tell Roy we're here, too."

They walked over to where Jesse sat, scowling at a magazine.

Marilyn entered the hospital room timidly. Roy's eyes were closed. He was bandaged around his chest and left shoulder. She went over to the bed and took his hand.

"Roy," she said.

"Maureen?"

"No, it's Marilyn."

He stared woozily up at her. She bent over him. "How do you feel, Roy?"

"Lousy," he said. "Where's Maureen?"

"She'll be here soon. Roy, I am so sorry."

"I need to talk to Maureen."

"She'll be here soon. Don't worry."

He moved restlessly, grimaced in pain, and lay still. Marilyn stood awkwardly beside the bed, still holding his hand.

"Can I do anything for you?"

"Just get Maureen." He closed his eyes.

"Okay, I will," she said. She let go of his hand and backed away. He didn't open his eyes.

"He wants to see Maureen," she told Pat and Dorothy.

Pat lighted a cigarette to keep from humphing.

"Well, where do you suppose she is?" Dorothy asked.

"I don't know. There's no answer at the house," Marilyn answered.

"Well, if she's not at home, where would she be?"

"Okay, let's think now," Pat said. "Would she just take off for parts unknown?"

"I don't know," Marilyn said.

Pat snorted. "Not without a big fat settlement, she wouldn't." Dorothy frowned at her. "Oh. No offense, Marilyn."

"It's okay, Pat."

"Does she have a lawyer?"

"She doesn't really confide in me, Pat," Marilyn said. "But I doubt it'd be anybody in Massey."

"That's just what I'm thinking," Pat said. "She probably has a lawyer here in Amarillo. In fact, I'll bet she's staying here."

"At a hotel?" Dorothy asked. "Oh, I bet I know…"

"At the country club!" Pat boomed. "They've got those what-do-you-call-em…"

"Guest rooms," Dorothy supplied. "We stayed in one last year. Real fancy."

Pat stubbed out her cigarette in the smoking stand. "Where are the phones? I'll call out there."

"Maybe you'd better talk to her," Dorothy said to Marilyn.

"Oh, gosh," Marilyn said. "What am I going to say?"

The three of them moved toward the bank of pay phones. Dorothy found the number in her pocketbook, and Pat dialed.

"Yeah, hello," Pat said. "I'm trying to reach Mrs. Roy, uh, Mrs. Maureen Woodson. Yeah, if you would." She handed the receiver to Marilyn. "They're ringing her room."

Marilyn took the phone and put it to her ear. "Maureen? It's Marilyn. Listen, I've got some bad news."

~ ~ ~

Daryl sat in his office, the phone at his ear. When Carolyn answered, he said, "Hi, it's me."

"Daryl? Well, you sure took your own sweet time calling me back."

"After you hung up on me, I wasn't sure you still wanted to talk." He leaned back in his chair and put his feet up on the desk.

"Didn't Eldon tell you I called again?"

"Okay, I'm here now. What's on your mind?"

"Well, I've been giving a lot of thought to what you said," she said.

"What I said about what?"

"What you said about us. I've been thinking that you might be right. I might have been in too much of a hurry. Maybe it was wrong to walk away."

"But you said when you were here…"

"I know what I said, but…well, today I'm seeing things in a little different light."

"What do you mean?"

After a long pause, she said, "I have some news."

"News?"

Another pause. "Daryl, this isn't easy for me. Give me a minute." She blew her nose.

"Have you got a cold?"

"No, I haven't got a cold," she answered. "I've got something…I guess you might say, something a little more significant than a cold."

"Are you crying?"

"A little bit," she said.

"Carolyn, what's going on?"

"Now, promise me that you will just listen, okay? Don't say anything, just listen."

Mystified, Daryl said, "Okay, I'm listening."

"Well, I guess there is no pretty way to say it. Daryl, I think I'm pregnant."

"Pregnant!" His sudden involuntary jerk almost catapulted him out of the chair. "My God, Carolyn!"

"I know."

"Pregnant! Well, what...what does this mean?"

"That's what we need to talk about. I've been thinking about what would be best, and it seems to me the best thing now would be for me to come home."

"You mean...here?"

"Well, yes, there, where do you think? I just can't have a baby way out here and be alone, all by myself." She sniffled. "It wouldn't be fair to the baby, or to me. Or for that matter to you."

"To me!"

"Well, yes, I mean, after all, it's your baby, too."

Daryl didn't know where he got the nerve. "Are you sure about that?"

"Why, Daryl, it's obvious. I...why, you remember when I was in Massey..."

"I remember, but...." His mind was racing. He took a deep breath. "Carolyn, are you telling me you haven't...been with anybody else?"

"Daryl, what are you insinuating?"

"I'm not insinuating anything. I'm asking a question."

"Well, of all the questions you might have asked me! This is highly insulting, Daryl Tomlin, and I think you had better start apologizing to me right now!"

"Well, I didn't intend to insult you."

"You are so mean, Daryl! I don't know how you can be so mean. With all I'm going through."

"It's just that...well, this comes like a bolt out of the blue to me."

"To me, too. I never intended it."

"I thought that's why we used a rubber."

"Well, they don't always work, I guess."

"Carolyn, I don't know what to say."

"I thought maybe you might be a little bit happy, but you sure don't sound like it."

"I'm surprised. I'm shocked. It takes some getting used to."

"Well, what do you think about me? I'll have to sell my house. My beautiful, beautiful house."

Daryl tried to hang onto himself. "Carolyn, let me ask you something. Have you thought about… I mean, are you sure you want to go ahead and have this baby?"

"Why, Daryl! What are you suggesting?"

"Well, aren't there ways to…do something else if…"

"Daryl, I just can't believe how mean you are. I don't think I can talk to you about this any more. I'm getting too upset. You seem bent on making me miserable." She sniffled again.

"But I'm just saying…"

"Okay," she said, and now her voice was steely, "now I think I understand. I'm so slow, sometimes it takes me awhile to get the message. You don't want this baby and you don't want me. I guess you probably think I deserve that. Then just forget it. Never mind. I'll stay here and get along the best I can. You go on and have a nice life."

"Carolyn, wait a minute…"

"I am hanging up now."

"Carolyn, don't hang up."

"You better think through what you've said to me today, Daryl. Goodbye," she said and broke the connection.

# CHAPTER EIGHTEEN

"Okay, Linda," Wayne said. "I'm going to show you the ropes before any customers come in. Most of the menswear is located on this side of the store, and most of the ladies' clothing is located in the back, next to the shoe department. Up front here opposite the menswear is our notions and piece goods departments."

Linda followed Wayne around the store as he spouted volleys of information. He showed her how to work the cash register and write up sales slips. He continued, "As I told you, Mr. Woodson will have the final say about your employment. But I think you can be confident that if you please me, he will be pleased. You see, as manager of the store, I am totally in charge while Mr. Woodson is recuperating."

Linda asked, "What actually happened to Mr. Woodson?"

"You mean you didn't hear about it?"

"Oh, I know that Joe Eliot shot him, but I never understood the reason why. Folks say it wasn't an accident."

"Well, you see," Wayne said, "that's how rumors get started. People start speculating and before you know it all kinds of stories start floating around. That's one of the things I just have to deplore about a small town like this. People have got nothing better to do than gossip and spread rumors."

"So what exactly did happen?" Linda asked.

"I am not at liberty to say," Wayne snapped. It was a sore point with him. Lord knows he had pondered that very question a hundred times. He and his mother had speculated endlessly about the situation. He had even asked Miss Harmon, straight out, but she had the nerve to tell him she wasn't at liberty to say.

"I am not at liberty to say," he repeated. "And it would be best if you refrained from any frivolous discussion of the subject, at least while you are our employee."

"I guess sooner or later it will all come out in the wash," Linda said.

"Be that as it may. Now, we are open from 9 till 6. Saturday nights we stay open until 8. Some Saturdays you will come in at 9 and leave at 6, and some Saturdays you will come in at 11 and leave at 8. We'll work that out week by week. Do you have any questions?"

"What is the salary?" Linda asked.

Wayne hesitated. He had no idea what Mr. Woodson paid Renee, although he had tried to find out. But Mr. Woodson's desk and files were locked. Wayne didn't even know what his own salary would be after Mr. Woodson returned.

"What did you make at Bradshaw's?" he asked.

She told him.

"Well, I'll take that into consideration when I make my recommendation about you to Mr. Woodson. He will have to make the final decision, you understand. Now, let's get you started. You can begin by straightening up this counter. Some high school kids were in here yesterday and tore it all to sunder. Fold these sweaters nicely, like this, and put the smalls on the left, the mediums in the middle, and the larges on the right. Okay?"

"Okay," Linda said.

"That's right," he said, observing her. "Welcome aboard, Linda."

The door chimed and Renee walked in. She looked at Linda and then at Wayne.

"A little tardy this morning, aren't we?" Wayne asked her. "Say hello to our new employee, Renee."

"Hi," Linda said.

"I didn't know you were working here."

"She just started this morning," Wayne said.

"Does Mr. Woodson know?" Renee asked.

"Renee, that's not your concern. You go on back and unpack that box of men's undershirts."

Renee shrugged. "I guess you're the boss, Wayne."

Pale and sweating, Roy waited at the curb outside the hospital while Maureen wheeled the El Dorado into the driveway. She leaned over to open his door, and he crawled in awkwardly, trying to protect his left arm, which was in a sling. With difficulty he settled himself in beside her and closed his door.

"Okay?" she said.

"Fine," he said. "Let's go."

She pulled the El Dorado out onto the street. Roy cradled his arm and tried to brace himself. He made a little grunt as she took a corner.

"Easy," he said.

"Sorry," she said and slowed the car.

She said, "I wonder what they are going to do to Joe."

Roy frowned. "To Joe?"

"I suppose they will have to lock him up somewhere. I have been warning Marilyn about him, and now I guess finally everybody can see my point."

"Joe didn't intend to shoot me," Roy said.

"Well, that's very generous of you," Maureen said, but it didn't sound like a compliment. "Nevertheless, whatever he may have intended, he did shoot you. He might have killed you."

"Well, he didn't."

They rode on in silence.

Roy shifted uncomfortably in his seat. Maureen asked, "Do you want to stop?"

"No, I need to get back to the store," he said.

"Surely that can wait."

"No, it can't."

"Roy, you're in no condition to work today."

"I'll be all right," he said. "You just take me to the store."

"Have it your way," she said.

After awhile, she glanced at him. He was turned away from her, gazing intently out the side window. "What are you looking at?" she asked.

"Nothing out here to look at. Just flat land. Like they say, miles and miles of nothing but miles and miles." After a pause he added, "I was thinking about my grandfather."

"Your grandfather?"

"Yeah. He came out west to make his fortune. Settled near Massey. What do you suppose he saw in this country? No trees, damn little water. What made him think he could make a go of it? What made him want to live out here?"

She didn't answer.

"Why would anybody want to live out here?" he went on, speculatively. "Farmers scared every year there won't be enough rain to grow their crops. Wind blows everything away. Take you, you've never liked it out here. You've been wanting to get away from here for years."

She looked at him.

"You know, being in the hospital gives you a lot of time to think," he said. "I've been thinking. Finally, I've begun to understand."

"Understand what?"

"Not what, who. I think I've finally begun to understand you."

"Me?"

"You're unhappy, restless. You want something. Something different from what you have."

She made a slight noise in her throat, but he continued before she could speak. "I remember before we got married, your daddy said something to me. I didn't understand what he meant by it at the time."

"Daddy?"

"Yeah, he said something to me. Just before we got married. It was the night before the wedding. We were out at your folks' house, after the rehearsal. He took me aside. He said, 'Mo's hard to satisfy.' Then he put his hand on my shoulder, confidential-like, and he said, 'Don't take it personal.' That was all he said. I hadn't thought about that in years. But while I was in the hospital, it kept coming back to me."

"Roy, I…"

"Let me finish," he said. "He was trying to give me some advice. Problem was, I didn't follow it. I did take it personal. I knew you were an unhappy girl, but I thought I could make you happy. Then, later, I thought you were unhappy because of me. Now, I am beginning to believe that your unhappiness has nothing to do with me. That I shouldn't take it personal. That was what your daddy was trying to tell me."

"Why, Roy…"

He continued, as if she hadn't spoken. "So, I've been thinking. Here's what I've come up with. I'm going ahead with the divorce, Maureen, but I'll give you whatever you want, as far as a property settlement goes. You'll have plenty of money. You'll be able to go wherever you want and do whatever you need to do to find happiness. Maybe you can find it somewhere else. With someone else."

"Roy, I…I don't know what to say."

"No need to say anything. Just pull up here in front of the store," he said. He opened the car door and hoisted himself out onto the street. He bent down to look at her, smiled, and gave a little salute with two fingers at his right temple. Then he turned, closed the car door, and walked toward the store.

He was surprised to see the store open for business. Everything was much the same, except there was a new display of men's fall-to-winter dress trousers on the front counter. A vivid painted sign, with curlicues and exclamation points, announced their brand and price. His attention was drawn to several bolts of corduroy in vibrant colors arranged on the piece goods counter. Here was another sign featuring a cartoon figure with a bolt of cloth for its body and a balloon coming out of its mouth with the words, "WEAR ME THIS FALL!" He looked around, bewildered.

Wayne hurried up the aisle. "Well, look who's back!"

Renee scampered up from the back of the store. "Hi, Mr. Woodson!" she said.

Wayne pumped Roy's arm so vigorously that the movement caused a sudden sharp crack of pain. Roy winced.

"Oh, sorry," Wayne said contritely. "Renee, bring Mr. Woodson a chair. You should probably ought to sit down, Mr. Woodson."

"I'm all right," Roy replied, but gratefully accepted the stool that Renee dragged over from behind the counter. The two of them stood smiling at him.

"You kept the store open," Roy said.

"Why, certainly I have," Wayne said. "It was providential that I still had my key. Yessiree, we've been open for business every day since you've been gone." He dropped his voice. "We've taken in a fair amount of money, Mr. Woodson. I made regular deposits at the bank. I put all the deposit slips up on your desk, along with the tickets. I would have entered the tickets into the ledger, but I couldn't find it."

"Well, that's fine, Wayne."

"I was just telling Renee that we probably need to order some more of those bomber jackets. Plus, a whole truckload of wetbacks going up north for the harvest came in yesterday and about cleaned us out of work pants."

"You feel okay, Mr. Woodson?" Renee asked. "You look a little peak-y."

"I'm just so surprised," Roy said.

"Well, the show must go on, right?" Wayne said.

"You better tell him about Linda Stoker," Renee prompted.

"In good time," Wayne said, frowning at her. "Man's been in the hospital. Can't bother him with every little detail. Take a look at the new merchandise, Mr. Woodson. I thought we ought to get those new trousers out where people can see them just as they walk in. And I wanted to showcase the new corduroy. Already sold some of it."

"That was my idea," Renee said.

"Well, that's right, Renee has been helping me," Wayne allowed generously. "Course you know with school starting Renee isn't going to be here much longer."

"I can come back afternoons and weekends," Renee said, "to do the windows and other projects. I've taken over doing the signs."

"They sure are eye-catchers," Roy said.

"That was my idea, to make the signs more, uh, eye-catching," Wayne said.

"No, it wasn't," Renee argued. "You fought me every step of the way."

"Looks to me like I owe you both a debt of thanks," Roy said, staving off more debate.

The door chimed and Linda Stoker came toward them, the canvas bank deposit bag in her hand.

"Oh, hi," she said to Roy, handing the bag to Wayne.

"Linda," he acknowledged.

"Told you, you ought to tell him," Renee hissed at Wayne.

"Tell me what?" Roy asked.

Linda and Renee both looked at Wayne. "Well," he said.

~ ~ ~

Maureen relaxed in the tub, foamy bubbles up to her chin as she stretched out full length and rested her head against the little pillow. It felt so good to lie in the warm fragrant water. It had been impossible to have a good bubble bath at the club's guest room without her special bath salts and the pillow.

When I move to Dallas, she thought, I'll get a really big bathtub. She smiled. Big enough for two people. She experienced a brief pang about Adam Robbins. What a perfect young body he had. Oh, well, she thought, there will be others.

Roy's capitulation had come as a complete surprise. She expected he would stick to his guns, and Mr. Patrick Dugan would have to weigh in before surrender. Now it looked as if there was nothing between Maureen and her fondest wishes. Images like shiny bubbles floated before her eyes: a grand house with a red Corvette in the driveway; a big bathtub and a handsome young man.

Hard to satisfy? That was nonsense. Roy completely misunderstood her. Her father, that dried-up failure, had spent his whole life trying to wrest wheat from a paltry fifty acres of dry land. Mean and stingy, he had never wanted to provide anything beyond the basics for his daughters. Marilyn never complained, but Maureen fought him. She learned early on to enlist her mother in subverting his control. Her mother secretly spent egg and heavy cream money on new clothes for Maureen and, less often, for Marilyn.

Her father had begrudged every cent spent on Maureen. "You are going to send us to the poor house," he would warn her. "See what fancy clothes they let you have there."

The biggest battle had been waged over Maureen's desire to go to college. Her father had objected vehemently, saying it was a waste of money to educate a girl. But help had arrived in the person of Aunt Mo, her mother's sister, after whom she was named. Aunt Mo had paid for room and board at Texas Tech after Maureen won a tuition scholarship. Maureen worked at various jobs to get money to improve her wardrobe. Over time she was able to acquire many flattering outfits. At graduation, her parents had been an embarrassment, her father silent and glum in work boots, her mother nervously clutching a cheap white patent leather handbag with her red-knuckled hands.

Maureen couldn't wait to get away. After college she rented a tiny apartment in Massey and taught high school English. She didn't liked teaching, but she enjoyed her independence. Many men came courting, but she was discriminating. It wasn't in her plan to marry poor. She encouraged Roy Woodson mostly because he came from wealth.

Hard to satisfy? The truth was, she wanted so little. It was galling to learn that her father warned Roy against her. Roy had seemed so different from her father, but under the skin they were brothers. It was high time to get away from Roy, just as she had escaped from her father.

She rose from the cooling water and toweled the foam off her body. In the bedroom, she surveyed with satisfaction the new dresses, shoes, hats, and purses she had bought during her stay in Amarillo. She didn't know where she was going to put everything, the closet was so small. She imagined the closets and dressing room she would have in her house in Dallas.

The little princess telephone rang. "Hello?"

"Maureen, it's me, Marilyn."

Maureen frowned. I should have let it ring, she thought. "Oh, honey, I was just fixing to call you."

"I wondered if you were home yet."

"I only just got here."

"Did you bring Roy home? How is he feeling?"

"Oh, he's fine. I left him off at the store."

"Really? I would have thought he would want to rest."

"Guess not."

"Well, I just wanted to tell you. They're going to go get Joe Monday."

"Who is?"

"Cal and I think Pete. There's going to be a hearing. L.W. called me to tell me about it. Did he call you?"

"Why would he call me?"

"I think he wants to know if Roy is going to file criminal charges."

"I don't know. Probably not. Roy seems to think it was an accident."

"Oh, I'm so relieved. I guess that's the first good news I've had."

"So what's supposed to happen at the hearing?"

"Well, I think," Marilyn said, and her voice broke, "I think they're going to ask to have him committed. I just don't know what I'm going to do."

"Now, honey," Maureen said. "You mustn't get so upset. This will be for the best, don't you think? All the way around."

"They'll send him to Gainesville," Marilyn sobbed. "He will just hate that."

"Well, it..." Maureen reconsidered. Probably not wise to tell Marilyn that it served Joe right, even though that was the honest truth. "It might be for the best, in the long run. They can help him there."

"You don't know what it's like there."

Maureen attempted to keep the exasperation out of her voice. "Listen, honey, I just got out of the tub and I'm getting chilled. Can I call you back?"

"Oh, sure, I'm sorry, that's fine," Marilyn said and hung up.

Maureen put on some of the new lingerie. After slipping into a white silk dressing gown, she began the agreeable task of putting away all her new things.

~ ~ ~

"Hi, it's Nadine."

A second went by before Daryl returned her greeting. He sounded oddly flat.

"Thought you might like to know what I got today," she said. The new green velvet dress hung on a padded hanger on the door of her bedroom, where she could see it from the telephone.

"Wait a minute," he said, and there was a scuffling noise. "Sorry. Go on."

"I just was saying that I bought something pretty today," she said.

He didn't answer.

"Daryl? You there?"

"Yeah, I'm here. How're you doing?"

"I'm doing fine. You busy?"

"Well...kind of. Go ahead, what you were saying?"

"I just wish you could see what I bought to wear to the Jaycees' dance," she said.

"Uh huh," he said.

"You must be busy," Nadine said. "You want to call me back later?"

There was a long pause. Nadine fidgeted. She reached for a piece of candy.

"Cat got your tongue for sure."

"Uh," he said.

"You call me back when you've got a minute," she said.

"I will, I will."

"Okay. Bye then," she said. Well, he was in another world.

"What is this?" Renee stood transfixed in front of the green dress.

"You like this little number?" Nadine asked.

"Like it! I love it! Is it for you?"

"Well, who do you think it's for, silly?"

Renee touched the lustrous fabric. "It is gorgeous. What's it for?"

"So many questions," Nadine said.

Renee held the dress up to her own body. "Can I try it on?"

"No, you cannot." Nadine took the dress away and hung it in her closet.

"Where'd you get it? Loretta's?"

"Yep."

Renee took a Coke out of the refrigerator and snapped off the cap. "Tell me," she persisted. "What's it for?"

"The Jaycees' dance," Nadine said.

"Ooh," Renee said. "Is Daryl Tomlin taking you?"

"Yes, ma'am," Nadine said. She leaned back in her recliner. "Boy, I'm tired. Shopping really takes it out of me."

"What else did you get?" Renee perched on the footstool.

"Isn't that enough? Lordy, it was likely the most expensive dress in town."

"What about shoes?"

"I haven't decided yet. I have black suede heels."

"Mules. Get some mules," Renee suggested.

"No, mules are tacky. Maybe high heeled sandals," Nadine said.

"Mama," Renee said, with a coy smile. "Are you sweet on Daryl Tomlin?"

Nadine grinned. "Mind your own beeswax, Renee."

"Oh!" Renee said. "I like to forgot! Guess what?"

"What?"

"Mr. Woodson is back in town. He came to the store this afternoon."

"Is that right? How's he feeling?"

"I think probably not so good," Renee said. "He looked real peak-y to me, and he needed to sit down. His shoulder is all bandaged up and his arm is in a sling."

"When did he get home?"

"Today, just this afternoon. He said that he hadn't even been home yet."

"My goodness," Nadine said. "Well, it's a miracle he's still alive."

"I know," Renee said. "Listen, he really liked my signs."

"Did he?"

"He said so. Said they were eye catchers. It about killed Wayne when Mr. Woodson complimented me on the signs. Wayne is such a creep."

"Well, you've got to hand it to him for keeping the store open and all, while Roy was in the hospital."

"I guess, but now he acts like he owns the place. But it was funny," Renee said and giggled at the memory. "You should have seen his face."

"Who?"

"Wayne. He was bragging on himself about how he had done this and done that and then here comes Linda Stoker. She had been to the bank, and so she comes in with the deposit bag and hands it to Wayne, and Mr. Woodson looks at her and she looks at him, and I tell Wayne he'd better explain why she is there, and Wayne just stands there with his face all hanging out. It was so funny I had to laugh."

"So what did Roy say?"

"Why, he didn't say hardly anything. He just sat there and listened to Wayne's whole made-up story about how he had had to take charge in the crisis – that's what he called it, the crisis – and that it was providential that he had found Linda, who needed a job, and on and on. Mr. Woodson, he just said okay, and that was that. I thought sure he would ream Wayne out, but he didn't."

"Well, Roy is probably going to need some help, at least until he gets on his feet again. When school starts, you won't be working there."

"I told him that I'd come back and do the windows," Renee said.

The phone rang. "That's probably for me," Nadine said.

But Renee got there first. "Hello? Oh, hi! Nothing. Well, I suppose. Give me about 30 minutes. See you."

"Who was that?" Nadine asked.

"Mind your own beeswax," Renee trilled.

"Smarty pants," Nadine said. "Who was it?"

"Abel Robbins," Renee said.

"My oh my," Nadine said. "You going out with him again?"

"I sure am. I better get ready."

What an unlikely couple, Nadine thought. Abel so serious and such a straight arrow. Could never have predicted Renee would like him. Opposites attract, I guess. She had been wary about Abel, because of Adam, until the first time he showed up for his date with Renee. He came inside, all knees and elbows, and made polite conversation until Renee was ready. Since he didn't have a car, they had to walk everywhere they went. At least I don't have to worry about them being parked out on some country road.

After Renee and Abel had gone, Nadine wandered restlessly about the house. She took the green dress out of the closet and swirled it around. She found her grandmother's gold hoops in the jewelry case on her dresser. She surveyed the suede heels and decided that she would definitely go to Gainesville or maybe Amarillo to get shoes.

The phone rang. She rushed to answer it. Wrong number. She thought that Daryl would have called back by now. She went back to the recliner and picked up a magazine. Boy, she thought, would I love to have a cigarette.

# SEPTEMBER 1954

# CHAPTER NINETEEN

~

"Laura, you up?" Cal called up the stairs.

"Yes, Papa."

Cal returned to the kitchen table and finished up his Wheaties. He was on his second cup of coffee when Laura finally appeared.

She spun around and the new dress flared out from her legs in a panorama of autumn colors. "Do you like my dress?"

"You bet. Want some Wheaties?"

"Sure."

He poured out some in a bowl for her and pushed the milk and sugar closer to her.

"Senior year," she said.

"You excited?"

"Kind of. I hear it's the best year of high school – parties, the prom, and stuff."

"Yeah, that's probably right." Cal finished his coffee and picked up his hat. "Well, I got to get going. Listen, I may be late tonight. I have to go to Amarillo."

"To get Jesse's daddy?"

"Yeah."

"I wonder if Jesse will be in school."

"Probably so. First football game coming up."

"I think I'm going to talk to him," Laura said.

~ ~ ~

Outside the high school building, Renee smoothed the new poodle skirt she had been saving for the first day of school. She stole a look through her eyelashes at the gang of boys laughing and horsing around outside the front door and saw Abel detach himself from the other boys and move toward her. She swung her hips to make the skirt billow.

Abel fell into step alongside her. "Hi," he said.

"Hi," she responded.

"You look pretty."

"Thanks."

"Got your schedule?" he asked.

"Right here."

"When do you have lunch?"

"After third period."

He grinned. "Me, too." He leaned over her shoulder to look at her schedule. "Who's your home room teacher?"

"Mrs. Bradshaw."

"Oh, I got Coach Parker."

The first bell rang, and the students streamed into the building, jostling against each other and talking excitedly.

"I'll see you third period," Abel said, and turned to go up the stairs.

"If I don't see you first," Renee said.

He looked perplexed.

"Joke," she reassured. "Just a joke, silly."

ᕼ ᕼ ᕼ

Bill Lynch caught up with Jesse at the lockers and watched him swear and struggle with the combination lock. "No, man," Bill instructed. "Remember, you got to go all the way around once and then go left to your first number."

Jesse followed Bill's advice, and the lock popped open. He stowed a couple of books and his letter sweater in the locker, then turned and challenged, "What are you looking at?"

Bill blinked. "Nothing," he said. "Who you got for home room?"

"Mr. Mathers," Jesse said.

"Me, too. Come on, second bell's gonna ring."

The hall was quickly emptying as students entered their home rooms. Laura saw Jesse and Bill Lynch coming toward her. Maybe he had Mrs. Victor for home room, too. As they passed her, she called out, "Hi, Jesse," but he didn't answer.

ᕼ ᕼ ᕼ

Coach Parker stood at the door of his room. "Come on, stragglers," he said to the last two students who hurried into the room just as the second bell rang.

"Okay, people," he said. "Take your seats and settle down."

The loud speaker system droned, crackled, and whistled as a prelude to Principal Pointer's voice. "Boys and girls, your attention, please. I want to welcome you to the first day of the 1954-1955 school year at Massey Senior High School. For those of you just entering senior high, and for those people with bad memories, we have particular rules here which we expect you to follow. One of these rules is that everyone must be seated before the second bell rings. The first bell rings at 8:55 a.m., and the second bell rings at 9 a.m. I have instructed home room teachers to report as tardy any students still lingering in the hallways after the second bell rings. Three tardy reports will count as one unexcused absence. Home room will end at 9:15 a.m. and you will be dismissed to your first period classes. Running in the hallways is strictly forbidden. Now please stand for the Pledge of Allegiance."

The students rose from their desks to face the American flag at the front of the room. They put their hands over their hearts and recited the pledge.

Principal Pointer continued, "You may now be seated. Bow your heads for the prayer." There was a pause, and he growled, "Start it now!" A needle scratched a record, and a baritone voice sang the Lord's Prayer.

When the record ended, Principal Pointer said, "Announcements. There will be a pep rally in the gym on Friday afternoon at 2:30 p.m. Sixth period teachers should plan accordingly. Your homeroom teacher will have other announcements for you." The loudspeaker emitted a shriek before it went dead.

After Coach Parker took the roll, he said, "Okay, people, hands up if you are coming out to support the team Friday night."

Every hand but one went up. "Abel Robbins?" Coach said.

Abel looked up from his English textbook. "Yes sir?"

"You coming to the game Friday night?"

"Yes, sir."

"Well, then, I guess you can raise your hand, too."

Abel looked around, blushed, and raised his hand.

"Like for you people to pay attention. Hate to have to single out those who don't seem to be paying attention," Coach said with heavy sarcasm. "Okay, so that looks to be one hundred percent coming to the game. The team welcomes your support."

The bell rang, and the students scrambled to their feet and poured out into the hallway.

~ ~ ~

"So, we still following our original plan?" Nadine asked, running the comb through Kathryn's hair.

"Well, I still don't look like that picture."

"In its own good time," Nadine said.

The telephone rang. "Nadine," she lilted. But then her shoulders sagged. "I'll put you down for four o'clock." She replaced the receiver and popped a piece of candy into her mouth.

"You still not smoking?" Kathryn asked.

"Nope."

"Well, good for you."

"Yeah, I hope so," Nadine said.

"Isn't your cough better?"

"I guess."

Nadine snipped at Kathryn's hair and then combed it out. She moved the tray of big rollers closer.

Kathryn said shyly, "Nadine, I've got some news."

"Well, lay it on me, honey," Nadine said.

"I went to see the doctor yesterday and…well, we're going to have a baby."

Nadine turned the chair so Kathryn could face her. "Why, Kathryn, that's wonderful! I am so happy for you!" They hugged.

"You're the first person I've told," Kathryn confided. "I can't quite believe it's true."

"How are you feeling?"

"Fine. I haven't had any morning sickness. I feel good, raring to go."

"Well, that is such good news. Are you telling people?"

"Well, you're the first one. I guess I'll start telling now."

"Is Ray excited?"

"Oh, you bet. He's expecting a boy."

Nadine patted Kathryn on the shoulder. "You're going to be a great mother."

"I hope so. I love babies." She patted her stomach. "I just hope it will love me, too."

"Course it will," Nadine said. "Come on, let's get you under the dryer. You want a manicure?"

"If you've got time."

Nadine wheeled the manicure table over to the dryer. She took the little bowl and filled it with soapy water and put Kathryn's hand into it. The phone rang and she jumped up to answer it.

When she returned looking glum, Kathryn asked. "Something wrong?"

"Why?"

"Well, you seem a little down in the mouth."

Nadine considered. "Well, I've been expecting a call, and every time that phone rings, I think it's…"

"Daryl?"

Nadine frowned. "How did you guess that?" she asked.

"Wasn't a guess. Why, is it a secret?"

Nadine snorted. "Try to keep a secret in this town," she said. "Who told you?"

"Gosh, I can't remember. Everybody's talking about it. We all think it's really nice. It's about time Daryl stopped mooning around over Carolyn."

~ ~ ~

Leroy Talbot poured himself a cup of coffee and rested his backside against the counter. The breakfast bunch had dispersed and the morning coffee and donut crowd hadn't yet begun to trickle in. "He there?" he asked Laverne Latimer, who was positioned at the diner's front window.

"Can't tell," she replied. "He might of come in from the back. Wayne opened up, and he and Linda Stoker went in the front a few minutes ago. Oh, see, there goes the sheriff and Pete in the sheriff's car."

"Probably on their way to Amarillo to get Joe Eliot."

"Poor old Joe," she said. "What do you suppose they are going to do to him?"

"I don't see they got any choice but to lock him up."

"You mean jail?"

"Likely," Leroy answered. He finished his coffee and turned his attention to the griddle, shoving leftover grease into the back pan with a metal spatula. He opened the big oven; the aroma of roasting meat escaped. "You want to write the specials on the board?"

Laverne erased the blackboard in front of the register and wrote with chalk: "LUNCH SPECIAL: ROAST PORK, PAN GRAVY, MASHED POT." She hesitated. "Corn?"

Leroy looked at the big cans over the stove. "Green beans," he answered.

She finished up: "GREEN BEANS, ICE TEA OR COFFEE, PIE OR CAKE, 45 CENTS" and resumed her vigil at the front window.

"Why wouldn't they send him to Gainesville?"

"Well, they might, at that," Leroy acknowledged. "L.W. said it would depend on whether Roy wants to make a charge against him. You want to put out the donuts?"

Laverne opened the grease-stained cartons which had been trucked in from Sanford early that morning and arranged the donuts on a tray with tongs. She began making a fresh pot of coffee.

"Reckon what Marilyn will do then?" she mused. "Figure she can run the farm by herself?"

Leroy shook his head. "It's a damn shame. Nice woman like that running a farm on her own."

"Well, she could get a hired hand. Plus, Jesse's old enough to help out," Laverne said.

Leroy smiled wryly. "Maybe her sister'll help out."

"Huh!" Laverne snorted. "Maureen's about as much use as tits on a boar. Besides, I don't see her sticking around here much longer."

"You hear something?" Leroy asked.

"Well," Laverne said, "I don't like to talk, but Doris, you know her sister Thelma works over to the court house? Well, Doris said that Lenore in Don Paulson's office said it's only a matter of time before Roy gives Maureen her walking papers."

"Wouldn't surprise me none," Leroy said, scraping more grease off the griddle. "Say, did you hear tell that Daryl threw Danny out?"

Laverne turned from the window. "Well, I was wondering. His car's been parked night and day in front of Darlene Shields' house. I knew they were hot and heavy, but I didn't know if he was living there."

"Her daddy will like to have a fit if she's shacking up with Danny Tomlin," Leroy said.

"Believe you me, Darlene hasn't paid attention to Reverend Shields since she was a tot," Laverne said.

The door opened to admit Gus Bell and Forrest Longbrake, talking as they entered. "Yeah, he's back," Gus said. "I seen him in the store. Got his arm in a sling."

"I heard so," Forrest said, as they took stools at the counter.

Laverne took two mugs from the shelf and filled them with coffee. "Morning, gentlemen," she said. "Would y'all care for donuts?"

~ ~ ~

Brother Robbins sat at his desk, leafing through Boyce. Usually by this time he would have finished his sermon for prayer meeting, but he had not yet found a text. Boyce could ordinarily move him to great heights of sermon composition, but he had been searching its pages for more than half an hour, and nothing had inspired him. He supposed he could go into his filing cabinet and choose a sermon he had already preached, but he deplored such a lazy practice.

He opened the Bible at random. Jeremiah, Chapter 24. He was partial to the book of Jeremiah, not only because he was the prophet's namesake, but also because the book contained such stirring condemnation of sin. Much more satisfying than Isaiah which, when you came right down to it, could be a little ambiguous about the consequences of wrongdoing. When as a young man he had read the first chapter of Jeremiah, he had marveled at its aptness to his own life. That passage from Jeremiah had been prophetic, figuring heavily in his decision to answer the call to be a minister of God. He paged back to the first chapter and fondly read the familiar words.

"Then the word of the Lord came unto me, saying, Before I formed thee in the belly I knew thee; and before thou camest forth out of the womb I sanctified thee, and I ordained thee a prophet unto the nations. Then said I, Ah, Lord God! Behold I cannot speak: for I am a child. But the Lord said unto me, Say not, I am a child: for thou shalt go to all that I shall send thee, and whatsoever I command thee thou shalt speak."

He supposed he could fashion a sermon from that. He paged forward to Chapter 24, which was unfamiliar to him. It was short, only ten verses. The chapter heading read, "By good and bad figs, the prophet foreshows the restoration from captivity, and the desolation of Zedekiah and the residue of Jerusalem." Figs. He had never eaten a fig. The Lord had made aprons from fig leaves to cover Adam and Eve's nakedness in the Garden of Eden. Jesus had once cursed a fig tree for failing to provide Him with fruit. He read:

"One basket had very good figs, even like the figs that are first ripe; and the other basket had very naughty figs, which could not be eaten, they were so bad. Then said the Lord unto me, What seest thou, Jeremiah? And I said, Figs; the good figs, very good; and the evil, very evil, that cannot be eaten, they are so evil."

The word "naughty" floated up to him from the page, setting off a train of thought. He had just that day reprimanded Abel for naughtiness. He sighed. Abel was indeed cause for worry. Here he was, a mere boy, not yet finished with high school, and already wanting to go on dates with girls. Premature and naughty. Brother Robbins had not exactly wished to forbid Abel to be in the company of girls; rather, he had hoped that Abel would not harbor such a desire and that the subject would not arise. But it had unfortunately already arisen, and Brother Robbins could not in good conscience condone the idea, especially when it involved Renee Coulter. If Abel wanted a girlfriend, why could he not have chosen a wholesome Baptist girl? But no, he had chosen that young hussy, Renee Coulter.

Brother Robbins had deplored Renee's mother's scandalous behavior for years, and he recently saw Renee flouncing about town with her red fingernails and her scanty clothing, a veritable Jezebel in the making. Abel was impressionable, desiring fleshly pleasures, uncommitted to living a holy life. Brother Robbins had worn himself out admonishing Abel about the snares of the flesh, but he had made little headway.

In fact, Abel had remained implacable to Brother Robbins' entreaties. He listened patiently to his father's arguments against going to moving pictures (bad enough in itself) with such a girl. Abel had not budged. He said that he had his own money and that it was his intention to go, whether or not his father approved.

"This is naughty, Abel," Brother Robbins had said.

"I am sorry you think so, Father," Abel had responded.

Brother Robbins yearned for Adam. Adam had never once gone against his father's wishes. In fact, Brother Robbins was confident that Adam sincerely shared his own values about a Godly life. If Adam had wished to attend a moving picture, he would have presented good, Scripture-based reasons for doing so. Adam would shun trash such as (Brother Robbins shuddered) *How to Marry a Millionaire*. Abel had not produced for his father one compelling reason to see such an abomination. Brother Robbins had explained to him that Marilyn Monroe was an embodiment of Satan, but Abel had only smiled.

Good figs and bad figs. Adam was certainly a good fig. Was Abel a bad fig? Brother Robbins trembled at the notion that Abel was on his way to hellfire. But more unsettling was the realization that everyone in town would know that Abel had attended this motion picture with Renee Coulter. What would people think?

Agitated, Brother Robbins paced about the small office, feeling anger and frustration at Abel's intransigency. He had told Abel no, and Abel had disobeyed. That was a grievous transgression, a sin against the Fourth Commandment. Brother Robbins experienced confusion. He had failed to train up Abel in the way he should go. But what did Scripture say about the child who refused to be trained up? What about a child who caused his parent intolerable pain?

"It is sharper than a serpent's tooth, to have a thankless child," he muttered, and then marveled. There it was, there unexpectedly was his sermon text. The Lord had provided. The sermon would reassure people that he was not to blame for Abel's public transgressions. He reached for his concordance.

Hmm, not under serpent, nor under child. If only Adam were here! Well, he could locate the verse later. He began to write on a clean sheet of paper.

# CHAPTER TWENTY

Daryl sat hunched over the newspaper at the kitchen table, as if reading, but his eyes were unfocused and his face drooped. He fingered the stubble on his cheeks and chin, realizing that he hadn't shaved. He got up from the table and shook a couple of aspirin out of the bottle. He cupped water in his hand from the faucet and washed them down. Ugh.

The telephone rang, shrilly and insistently. He walked away from it. It continued to ring and he continued to walk, faster and faster, until he was in his bedroom. He slammed the door against the ring. He grabbed a pillow and thrust it over his head as he threw himself on the bed. After an eternity the phone stopped ringing.

Pete stood at the door of Cal's office. "I put him in the cell," he said. "He's probably still cussing me out. You talk to Marilyn?"

"Yeah."

Pete scratched his head and stared at the floor. "I just want to say," he began slowly, "it don't seem right to me, locking the man up. You saw that he was perfectly fine all the way here from Amarillo."

"Well," Cal replied, "L.W.'s leading the way on this."

"You think it's right?" Pete persisted, taking a chair in front of Cal's desk.

Cal said, "Doesn't matter what I think. You either, for that matter."

"Joe thought we were taking him to the farm. Nearer we got to it, the happier he got. He was all relaxed and cheerful. You should of seen his face when you drove on past the turn and brought him in here. That's when he got excited. If we'd left him off at the farm, he would have been mild as a lamb. Mind you, I'm not saying what he did was right, I'm just pointing out…."

"I know what you're saying," Cal said. "I don't altogether disagree with you. Still, we did what we were told to do. Put him in the jail until the hearing."

"And what's going to happen at the hearing? They're going to send him to Gainesville, aren't they? Then he'll be in another kind of jail, right?"

Cal didn't say anything.

"Plus," Pete said, "Roy isn't going to press any charges, is he?"

"Said he wasn't."

"Don't that count for something?"

"Well, Pete, you know the prosecution has a duty, whether or not the victim presses charges."

"Well," Pete said, his voice rising, "in my humble opinion, this here prosecution plays favorites. You know it, too, Cal. I see Danny Tomlin out there free as a damn bird. This prosecution never did nothing to him about his baby, did they? Wasn't even a hearing. You call that fair? You call that justice?"

"Pete..."

Pete sagged in his chair. "I'm just thinking about Marilyn. And Jesse. First football game's around the corner. How's that boy going to play football with his daddy locked up? For that matter, what's Marilyn going to do now? Run the farm by herself?"

Cal had never seen Pete so worked up. He couldn't recall a time when Pete had put so many words together at one time.

"I know, Pete. It's hard on Marilyn, too."

"Well, I been asking around and I think if she was to ask him, Buster Edelman would work the farm for her."

"You're a good man, Pete."

"Well," he said, "somebody's got to do something right for a change."

~ ~ ~

Nadine laid the green velvet dress on the tissue paper on the bed. She carefully folded the paper and put the swathed dress into the shopping bag.

From the radio, "And now, for the tenth week in a row, number four on your hit parade, Miss Jo Stafford singing, 'Make...'"

She switched it off. Don't want to listen to that. She set the bag down beside her purse so she would be sure to take it to town in the morning. Might as well get it over with, she thought. At least she hadn't made the trip to Amarillo for new shoes.

Nadine was a little surprised by the extent of her disappointment. After Adam, she had vowed never again to let a man interfere in her life. Now, after only a few weeks, she had allowed herself to get sappy over Daryl Tomlin, who had for some damn reason disappeared. She guessed he had changed his mind about the dance. Didn't even have the courtesy to tell her in person. It shouldn't bother me, she admonished herself. It's his loss. But the words rang hollow in her head. It did bother her. She had let herself get a little used to the idea of a boyfriend. One she could be seen with. It had been comforting to have Daryl with her at the clinic that day. Making out in his car like randy teenagers had been a delight. She had allowed herself to make plans. I got way ahead of myself, she thought ruefully. I should know better.

It about killed her to think about returning the dress. But what good is a dress if you don't have anyplace to wear it?

A familiar dialogue began like a game of ping pong in her head.

I wish I had a cigarette.

Well, you don't. And you don't need one.

I could buy a pack. Just a pack. Not a carton.

Bad idea.

Just a pack. And then I'll quit for good.

She was out of the house with her purse and the car keys before she could talk herself out of it. It was kind of late. Would the drug store be open?

She pulled the car into a space in front of Harmon's and was relieved that the lights were still on. But the door was locked. She banged on the glass.

"Virgil!" she cried. "You in there?"

Virgil came slowly to the front, wiping his hands on a towel. "Nadine?"

"Oh, I'm glad you're still here. I just need a pack of cigarettes." She couldn't meet his eyes.

"Come on in," he said and relocked the door behind her.

"I'm glad you were still here," she said, digging in her purse for a quarter.

"You know what I was doing when you knocked?" Virgil said, conversationally. "I was just about to make myself a banana split. Couple of bananas won't last another day, and I thought I'll just make me a banana split."

"That's nice. Just give me a pack of Luckies."

"Okay, fine, but I've got two bananas. They'll be bad by morning. Can't you eat a banana split? On the house."

She looked into his round friendly face. "Why, sure, I guess. I can't remember the last time I ate a banana split."

"Come on, sit down, make yourself to home." He took two metal oblong bowls from the shelf and peeled and sliced two bananas down the center. He placed them carefully in the bowls and scooped up balls of ice cream from the freezer. "Vanilla, chocolate, and strawberry," he said.

"Sounds good," Nadine said.

He ladled chocolate, pineapple, and strawberry syrups over the round balls of ice cream, heaped on whipped cream, and added a maraschino cherry. He placed the bowls on the counter and came around to sit on the stool next to hers.

"Cheers," he said, saluting her with a spoonful.

"To your health," she responded, digging in.

They consumed the gooey concoction in companionable silence, eating slowly enough to savor the combination of flavors.

Nadine put down her spoon down and sighed contentedly. "Virgil, that hit the spot."

"Nothing like a banana split, I always say," he said. He slid off his stool, taking the bowls behind the counter to dunk them in soapy water. He wiped his hands. "You said Luckies?"

"No, I…I changed my mind," she said.

He looked at her and smiled. "Good girl," he said.

Nadine wiped chocolate syrup off her mouth with a napkin. "Virgil," she said, "You'll have to forgive me for unladylike behavior, but I was wondering. Would you like to take me to the Jaycees' dance?"

~ ~ ~

"I don't altogether approve of eating meals in a restaurant," Wayne said.

"Really? Why?" Linda asked.

Wayne peered around the Steak House. "You can see that there's little respect for the Lord here. Nobody says grace, for one thing."

"Maybe they say it without showing everybody that they're saying it," she suggested.

"See," Wayne said, "that's what I mean. If people can't honor their religion in public, then they're ashamed. The Apostle Paul told us not to be ashamed of the Gospel."

"Well, if you're not comfortable here, Wayne, we could leave."

"No, no, I didn't mean *we* shouldn't be here," he said. "Just talking about other people. I'm perfectly comfortable here. I wanted to bring you here this evening."

"Did you? How come?" she asked.

"We'll get to that after we decide what to eat." He surveyed the menu. "Now, Linda, you just order whatever you like. This is my treat."

Linda pretended to look at the menu, but in fact she was studying Wayne. She felt a little self-conscious and wondered what people would say. She guessed they were on a date; he had asked her and he was paying. However, they had come in her car since Wayne didn't drive. She thought they probably looked like a cute couple. She knew the color of her dress made her eyes look like sapphires. Dressed up, Wayne was handsome. She liked the way his hair curled. It was only when he started preaching that he looked a little strange.

Truth was, she was grateful to him. She liked working at Woodson's now that it was just the two of them, Renee Coulter back in school and Mr. Woodson mostly in his office upstairs. Wayne had taught her how to tag and display merchandise and how to treat customers. She had learned to say, "*And* what else?" and to suggest items. Wayne made sure Mr. Woodson knew how much merchandise she sold.

But beyond that, Linda was thankful that Wayne had helped her get over Ronny so easily. That day she bawled her eyes out, she was sure her heart was permanently damaged. Whatever it was Wayne said to her, it seemed to have cured her. These days if she even thought about Ronny, she felt contempt. He had no right to prey on a vulnerable young girl. Wayne had assured her that Ronny had done most of the sinning and that she had been a victim in his snare. It had even felt good to apologize, even though Mrs. Bradshaw had thrown her right out of her house. Some people didn't want to be helped.

It had been a long time since Linda had been out on an actual date. Ronny had certainly never taken her anyplace. Plus, Wayne was a real gentleman. He opened the car door for her and took her elbow as they climbed the steps to the Steak House.

She put her menu down. "What are you going to have, Wayne?"

"Well, I was thinking about the chopped sirloin," he answered.

"That sounds good to me," she said. "Why don't you order for both of us." She had seen that done in a movie and thought it romantic.

"Okay," he said. "You want mashed potatoes or French fries?"

"Whatever you're having," she said. "And iced tea." She knew that Wayne never touched alcohol.

After he placed their order, she smiled at him. "So, how come you wanted to bring me here this evening?"

She was pleased to see him look a little shy. "Well," he said, and the skin over his cheekbones turned pink, "partly to reward you for being such a fine employee."

"Partly? What's the rest of the reason?" she asked, flirting a little.

Blushing, he looked young and vulnerable. She had never before noticed his long eyelashes. "Linda," he said, "you are a fine-looking woman. No, you are beyond that. You are mighty pretty. It is a pleasure to be in your company."

"Why, Wayne," she teased, "are you sweet-talking me?"

"It is not good for man to be alone," Wayne said solemnly and took her hand.

"Or woman either," Linda said. She squeezed his fingers.

Later in her car, parked out at the lake, they kissed. She electrified him when she guided his hand inside her dress to her breast. His manhood strained powerfully against his trousers as he eagerly kissed her.

"Lay back a little," she murmured.

"Oh," he cried, as she unzipped his pants and took him in her mouth. "Oh, Linda. Oh, please. Oh, sweet Jesus! Oh, merciful God in heaven!"

❧ ❧ ❧

Carolyn looked down. There was bloody water in the toilet. Another cramp made her gasp. She held onto the sink with both hands and took several deep breaths. She eased herself down on the toilet seat and braced herself against the next cramp.

After a few minutes, when the cramps seemed to be easing up, she leaned over the side of the tub and turned on the tap. She undressed and threw her bloody underpants in the wastebasket. She eased herself into the warm water.

Well, she thought, this simplifies matters considerably.

Presently, feeling much better, she got out, dried herself, and inserted a tampon. In her bedroom, she donned a turquoise chenille robe. She brushed her hair back from her face and dabbed perfume onto her pulse points.

Better, she thought. She still felt a little tug in her belly, not exactly a cramp. Well, I know what will make that go away. Carolyn had discovered a surefire remedy for cramps when she was in junior high school.

She picked up the telephone. "Hi there. What are you doing? Me? I was just wondering if you want to come over. I'm just lying here in bed by my little old self." She giggled at his response.

She made another call. "Hello, it's Carolyn Tomlin. Is Melissa there? Well, would you give her a message for me? Yes, that's right, T-O-M-L-I-N. Tell her I've changed my mind about selling my house. That's right. Well, she can call me if she wants to, but there's really no need now. Thank you."

When she heard the key turn in the lock she lay back against the pillows and closed her eyes. He came into the room and sat on the bed.

"What's wrong, baby?" he asked.

"Oh, Johnny, I have the worst cramps," she said.

"Can I do something to make it better?" he asked.

"Well," she said, "there is one thing that usually helps a lot." She explained and lay back against the pillows. When she finished, she sighed, flushed and glowing.

"My turn," he said.

"Not today, Johnny. I told you I had my period. Just take care of yourself."

After he finished he said, "I missed you."

"I thought you had forgotten all about me."

"Not likely," he said. "I thought you forgot me."

"Well," she said. "I just had a little complication."

"What kind of complication?"

"Never mind. It's all over now."

He looked at his watch. "Uh oh, I got to go."

"Already?"

"She'll wonder where I am."

She sighed. "When can you come back?"

He was dressing. "Well, you *are* friendly. I wondered why you hadn't called me."

"I've been preoccupied. But things have eased up now," she said. "Can you come over tomorrow?"

"Will you still be on the rag?" he asked.

"Crude," she said. "You are crude, you know."

"Will you?"

"Yes, but tomorrow I might feel like…you know," she said.

"I'll try to get away."

"Such a devoted husband," she said as he bent to kiss her goodbye.

# CHAPTER TWENTY-ONE

~

"You think Marilyn is doing okay?" Pat asked, shoveling eggs into her mouth.

"We can go out there after I get out of school, if you want to," Dorothy said. She rinsed Jesse's plate at the sink. "He didn't eat much."

"Said he was going to go out and throw the football," Pat said. "He's all pumped up about the game."

"Well, I for one will be glad when this game is finally over. Whole town is standing on its head, holding its breath for the event of the century."

"I truly believe they can beat Sanford. Coach is looking pretty happy these days."

"Well, he ought to be, with Kathryn expecting."

"I didn't mean happy about that. I meant about the team."

"Lordy, Pat," Dorothy said, shaking her head. "Now, do you want to go out to Marilyn's? Or are you going down to the…to see Joe again?"

"No to both. No time. We're going to go out and see Silverado. Then it'll practically be time for the game."

"We who?"

"Me and Laura. She hasn't been out there for a long time. Spence says he thinks he's about ready to run a race."

"Pat…" But Pat had left the kitchen. and it was too late to start that conversation now.

~ ~ ~

L.W. Foster looked up from his desk. "Morning, Cal," he said and clamped his cigar in his mouth. "How's our star prisoner?" L.W. sniggered. "He happy with the accommodations?"

Cal came into the office and closed the door behind him. He bent and laid his palms on the desk and looked directly into L.W.'s face. Startled by his proximity, L.W. rolled back his chair.

"I got something to say to you." Cal's eyes were narrow and his jaw thrust out.

L.W. managed a sour smile. "Go ahead, speak your piece."

"I got an appointment with Judge Randall this afternoon."

"And why would that be?"

"I figure the district judge will be very interested to hear about the state of affairs in this county. I hear he already has some notion of what a sorry son of a…"

"Now, wait just a minute, Cal…"

"…bitch you are. I think he'll be interested to hear how you handled the Tomlin baby's death. He'll likely want to conduct a general audit. You recall, don't you, what happened when the county attorney over in Range County got caught taking a bribe."

"Now, Cal, just hold on a damn minute," he said. "You don't want to do something you might regret."

Cal straightened up. "I wasn't asking for your advice, I was just giving you some information."

"Wait a minute!" he cried, as Cal turned to leave. "What is it you want?"

"Want? Why, there isn't a damn thing I want… from you." He opened the door and walked away.

❧ ❧ ❧

Laura watched Jesse come into Mrs. Victor's English class and throw himself into his desk. He kept his head down and slid way into his seat, legs and feet straddling the empty desk in front of him.

Mrs. Victor was a tall woman, white hair swept into a French twist. She wore big black rimmed reading glasses and paged through *Shakespeare's Plays for High School Students.* She looked up after the final bell rang and said, "Class, today we have a shortened period because of the pep rally, so we won't assign the parts to *Romeo and Juliet* until next week. Today I will introduce the play and…"

The loud speaker buzzed and whined. Mrs. Victor took off her glasses and frowned up at it. After a metallic shriek, Principal Pointer said, "May I have your attention, please. I have a few corrections to make to the announcements concerning the pep rally. The warning bell will ring at 2:15. At that time, the football team is to report to Coach Parker in the locker room. Members of the pep band will collect their instruments and proceed directly to the gymnasium. The cheerleaders will report to Miss Garber's room, not the gymnasium. Abel Robbins will be dismissed to take yearbook photographs. The rest of the student body will proceed to the gymnasium when the bell rings at 2:30." He said, away from the microphone, "Is that it? Well, I hope so." He turned back to the microphone. "Thank you for your attention."

Mrs. Victor looked at the clock above the blackboard. "How many of you have to leave at 2:15?" she asked.

Abel Robbins, Jesse and two other team members, one cheerleader and four pep band members raised their hands. "Half the class," she said. "I think we'll leave *Romeo and Juliet* for Monday's class. You may talk quietly until the bell rings."

Laura took a deep breath and moved from her desk to the empty desk in front of Jesse. She turned in the seat to face him. He looked up at her.

"Hi," she said.

"Hi."

"Are you excited about the game?"

He shrugged. "Not so much."

"Everybody is sure we are going to win," she said.

He crossed the fingers of both hands and held them up.

"Everybody says those Sanford boys just don't have a chance," she said.

"People," Mrs. Victor's voice rang out, "I said quietly."

"I just wanted to let you know, Jesse," Laura whispered, "that I am rooting especially for you tonight."

Her knuckles shone from clutching the back of the desk chair. Her face and neck were pink. She looked very pretty.

"Well, thanks," he said.

"Maybe I can buy you a Coke sometime, you know, to celebrate the victory."

"Sure."

The bell rang and he got up, collected his books.

"So," she said, looking up at him. "Just call me when you want that Coke, okay?"

He grinned. "You bet."

"Good luck, Jesse," she said.

Mary Beth Vinson slipped into the desk Jesse had vacated and put her face close to Laura's. "What did you say to him?"

"Oh, not much, just wished him and the team luck," Laura said.

"Well, whatever it was, he sure looked happy. He's been looking real bad, but while you were talking to him, he looked real happy."

~ ~ ~

"Hey, Dorothy," Cal said. "Where you going?"

"Oh, Cal. I was just down to the jail to take Joe some cookies," she replied.

"Yeah," he said. " Say, Dorothy, come on into my office. Something I want to ask you about." Cal had been looking for an opportunity to consult Dorothy for some time.

"Sure, okay," she said and seated herself in the chair in front of his desk.

Cal pulled a 3 by 5 card from his shirt pocket. "Dorothy, I found this card in one of Janice's books. I can't make heads or tails out of it. Thought you might have an idea about it."

Dorothy took the card and read it twice.

"Thought maybe you might recognize this guy, what's-his-name, Vico. Or maybe might tell me why you think it might have been important to Janice."

Dorothy shook her head. "I never heard of him, Cal. But I have to say, it seems kind of like Janice."

"Really?"

"She used to come up with the darndest stuff."

"She did?"

"Well, you were older than Janice. You probably didn't ever have any classes with her. But I remember one time in biology class. Mr. Wells was telling us about an experiment somebody did with rats."

"With rats?"

"Yeah. He said some scientists had run some experiments and had found out that some rats were really smart at getting through a maze and other rats were really dumb, you know? So they started mating the smart rats with the other smart rats and the dumb rats with the other dumb rats until they had two distinct groups of rats, the smart ones and the dumb ones."

"Yeah?" Cal couldn't imagine what she was talking about.

"So Mr. Wells said that the smartest of the dumb rats had about the same intelligence as the dumbest of the smart rats. And then Janice asked her question."

"What?"

"She asked whether it was better to be the smartest of the dumb rats or the dumbest of the smart rats. So then Mr. Wells asked the class to vote which they would rather be, and why. Turned out that everybody in the class wanted to be the smartest of the dumb rats. Everybody except Janice, that is."

"Janice voted different?"

"Yeah, she said it would be better to be the dumbest of the smart rats, because you belonged to a superior group. Said you would probably try to be smarter. She said nobody would have expectations of you, and that meant you could be more of your own person." Dorothy laughed, "Only she said, more of your own rat."

Cal laughed too. "That does sound like her."

"Well, a lot of the class thought she was crazy. Oh, I'm sorry, Cal."

"That's okay. I know what you mean."

"But she really got me to thinking. Janice had that kind of mind, Cal. So I'm not surprised she was interested in this Vico person. Kind of makes me want to look him up, find out more."

"Thanks, Dorothy. By the way, I want to thank you for everything you and Pat are doing for Laura."

To his surprise, Dorothy's face darkened. She looked at him for a minute and tried to smile. "Laura's a sweet girl, Cal. But sometimes I wonder..."

Puzzled, he waited for her to finish. When she didn't, he asked, "Wonder what?"

"Oh, just whether she might be better off with people her own age."

Cal said, "Say, I hope she hasn't been making a nuisance of herself."

"That's not what I meant, Cal," Dorothy said.

~ ~ ~

When Virgil saw Dorothy enter the drug store, he beamed. "Howdy, Sis."

"Hi, Virgil."

"How you doing?"

"Oh, I'm okay. I just came downtown to see Joe for a minute. I'm on my way out to Marilyn's."

"How is Joe?"

"Purely miserable. Have you seen him?"

"No," Virgil said. "I should go over there."

She sat on a stool at the soda fountain. "Well, I don't know if you should or not. He would hardly look at me, let alone have a conversation. I just left him some cookies and told him I was going out to Marilyn's."

"How long they going to keep him in there?"

"Well, the hearing is Monday."

"What a sorry state of affairs." Virgil shook his head.

"Ain't that the truth," Dorothy said.

"You want something to drink?"

"Coke, I guess."

He shoveled ice into a glass, added syrup, filled it with seltzer water and stirred vigorously.

"Have you seen Roy?" she asked.

"Not to talk to," Virgil said. "He never shows up for coffee at the diner any more. I went in the store the other day, but he wasn't there. Just Wayne. And Linda Stoker."

"Linda Stoker?"

"Yeah, she's working there now."

"I didn't know that."

"I hear Wayne hired her before Roy even got back from the hospital."

"What's the deal with Wayne working there anyway? I thought Roy fired him."

"Well, he did, but after a while he took him back. I heard Roy even apologized."

"That's hard to believe."

He came out from behind the counter to sit next to her. "Maybe you already heard. Maureen's left Roy and they're getting a divorce. They say he's going to give her everything she asks for. Which is a surprise, given her infidelity. Now, some folks say he never figured out that she was unfaithful. Others say he knew, but didn't mind about all her catting around."

"Why, Virgil, you are a veritable fountain of information."

"Well, you tend to hear things at the diner," he said.

"What else do you hear?"

"Well," he said, and smiled, "I didn't hear it at the diner, but there is some news."

"What?"

"I'm going to the Jaycees' dance."

"You are? With who?"

"Guess."

Dorothy drew a blank. "Is it somebody I know?"

"Sure is."

"Virgil, I have no idea. You have to tell me."

He grinned broadly. "Nadine," he said.

"Nadine? Why, I thought..." She stopped. "Why, Virgil, I didn't know you were going out with Nadine."

"Neither did I," he said. "Until she asked me."

"She asked you?"

"Yeah," he said. "Don't tell anybody that part, okay? It might embarrass her, you know?"

"Your secret is safe with me." Dorothy smiled back at him. "Well, Virgil, I can tell you're happy."

"I am."

"I'm glad." She drank from her Coke and sighed.

Virgil looked at her. "What's the matter?"

"Nothing," she said, her eyes on the counter.

After a pause he asked, "Pat okay?"

Dorothy hesitated a bit and then said, "Virgil, what do you hear, you know, in town, about…." Her voice trailed off. She began again, "You know, when you're at the diner, or…." Again she bumped to a stop.

"About what?" he prompted.

"Do you ever hear anybody talk about…me and Pat?"

Virgil reached down and re-tied his shoe lace. "What about you all?" he said, his voice muffled.

She looked away, her face red, then plunged ahead. "Virgil, tell me, what do people think? That we're just a couple of homely old maids? That we're together because no men would have us? Virgil, look at me!"

He couldn't. "Nobody's never said nothing to me."

"Well, nobody would ever mention infidelity if they were talking about us, would they? They wouldn't even think it was possible, right?"

"Sis, I don't know what you're talking about." He had always looked up to Dorothy. She was the smartest person he knew. And Pat was family. He knew that Dorothy and Pat shared a bedroom, but he tried never to think about that. He also knew that folks sometimes did say things about Pat.

"Sis, nobody's never said nothing about you." At least that was true.

"Oh, Virgil," Dorothy said, love and irritation blending, "you are the limit."

❧ ❧ ❧

Junior Thompson brought the horse out of the stable with pride. "Me and Spence think he's got what it takes," he said to Pat.

Pat reached in her pocket for an apple, and the horse nuzzled her hand. "Hey, boy, how you doing," she said, cradling the horse's head against her shoulder. "He looks real good, Junior. Come here, you rascal, let me see your mouth. Junior, I want you to watch that bit when you put it on. There isn't any call to give him a sore mouth, you understand?"

"Yes, ma'am," Junior said.

"You're a beauty, aren't you? Regular old champion, aren't you?" she crooned to the horse. She threw the reins over the horse's head, put her foot in the stirrup, and hoisted herself up into the saddle. She gave a little click-click with her mouth and turned him with the reins, then dug her heels into his sides. The horse took off down the path past the stable and out into the open field.

Laura and Junior watched her go. "Course," Junior said, "a jockey won't weigh half that."

Laura smiled in spite of herself. "Can he win a race?" she asked.

"Depends on the track and who he's up against," Junior said. "Still, me and Spence think he's got something special in him. She ought to take him up to Ruidoso or Raton and find out."

"That would be so exciting," Laura said.

Junior nodded. "Nothing like it." He looked at her curiously. "You still ride?"

"Not for awhile," Laura said.

"Miss Harmon, she don't ride," Junior said. "Even when they lived out here, to my recollection, she never rode none of the horses, not even once. Course, Miss Harmon, she took care of the house. And the garden. Grew vegetables and flowers right out there in that there little patch." He gestured and Laura looked over at the little patch, now choked with weeds.

"Yeah," he said, "that's pretty much gone to pot since they moved to town. Miss Harmon, she don't hardly never come out here. I reckon she likes town better."

Laura said, "I guess."

"Course that's their deal, you know. Miss Eliot, she does the man thangs, and Miss Harmon, she does the lady thangs. Miss Harmon, she used to get on Miss Eliot all the time for wearing her muddy boots into the house, tracking up the floor. Without she didn't have Miss Harmon, I reckon Miss Eliot, she'd just live like any other old bachelor."

Laura blinked.

"Well, I got chores to do," Junior said and moved away.

Uneasiness took up residence in Laura's stomach. Junior talked like they were a married couple. But women married men, not other women. The part about Miss Eliot doing the "man thangs," and Miss Harmon doing the "lady thangs" seemed true. Plenty of times Laura had heard Miss Harmon criticize Miss Eliot's messiness. Miss Harmon dressed so frilly and dainty, wore high heels, had her hair fixed every week. Laura had never seen Miss Eliot wear anything but Levi's, and she went to the barber shop instead of Nadine's.

One thought followed another, like boxcars on a freight train. Thoughts heretofore unthought pulled up in front, demanding to be considered. One thought in particular popped out. Miss Harmon seemed to resent it that Laura was over at their house all the time. It was like she was jealous of Laura. Miss Eliot had asked all those questions about Jesse, like she was jealous of him.

Face burning and stomach churning, Laura recalled Miss Eliot's questions about Jesse and kissing. She had touched Laura's mouth and had told her she loved her to pieces. That had been enormously exciting. The truth was, it had been like being with a boy. Laura realized that she had been hoping that today Miss Eliot would touch her mouth again.

Laura felt guilt and shame. She pictured Miss Harmon, sitting alone at home, like a wife with a cheating husband. It was like that movie, where Burt Lancaster fell for Terry Moore and started drinking again and Shirley Booth went crazy. Distressed, Laura felt as if she had been involved in something nasty.

"Here she comes," Junior said at her elbow, and Laura jumped. "I scare you?"

"No, not really," she croaked. She did feel scared, but not by Junior.

Pat rode back into the stable yard and climbed down from the horse.

"How was he?" Junior asked.

"He is a champion," Pat said, happily. "We got to take him to Raton. Laura Tuttle, you're looking at a winner here."

Laura tried to make her mouth smile.

Junior moved to take the reins from Pat. "No," she said, "that's okay. Laura can help me put him in the stable. You just go on about your business. Come on, Laura."

Laura took a deep breath and doubled over, clutching her abdomen. "Oh," she cried. "Oh, golly!"

Pat and Junior stared at her. "What's wrong?" Pat asked.

"Oh, my stomach hurts!" Laura cried.

Pat threw the reins to Junior and strode to Laura's side. She tried to put her arm around Laura's shoulders, but Laura shied away. "You sick?" she asked.

"Yes," Laura said. "I think I need to go home."

"Why don't I take you in the house? You can lie down for awhile," Pat said.

"No, no, I just want to go home."

"Maybe I ought to take you to the doctor," Pat said.

"I'd just like to go home. I think it's my period," she whispered.

"Oh, well, then. Junior, you put Silverado away. We got to go back to town."

Laura hurried into the pickup and crouched tensely on the seat. Pat started the engine and headed toward town.

"You hurting pretty bad?" Pat asked.

"Terrible." Laura bent over, clutching her stomach.

"Cramps, huh?"

Laura made a carapace of her rounded back all the way to town. Once when Pat touched her shoulder, she shrank away, trying to make herself smaller. When Pat pulled up in front of the Tuttle house, Laura jumped out.

"Hey, wait," Pat said. "I'll go in with you. I know a real good remedy for the cramps."

"No!" Laura shouted and ran up the sidewalk to the front porch. She let herself into the house, slammed the door behind her and locked it. She stood, breathing hard, her back against the door, until she heard the pickup drive away.

~ ~ ~

"Okay, Lenore, you notarize this," Don Paulson handed his secretary the sheaf of papers. "Signatures are on the next to the last page. All copies. And close the door."

Lenore Waters stole a glance at Roy and Maureen Woodson before returning to her desk.

Don continued to Roy and Maureen, "Now that you have a property settlement, there won't be anything you need to do until the divorce hearing. I'll send the judge a petition and then one or both of you can show up for the hearing, and it'll all be over. Now, Maureen, like I said before, you have the right to retain counsel of your own."

"I don't believe that's necessary," Maureen said. "Do you mean it's not required for both of us to be at the hearing?"

"Correct. Whoever comes has to bring a witness. I did explain that part to you, didn't I?" They nodded. "Okay, then, whenever the six-month period is up, you just let me know and I'll send the petition."

Lenore knocked at the door and came in with the notarized copies. Don handed each of them a copy and gave the third back to Lenore. "For the file," he said. "That's all, Lenore. And close the door."

Lenore sat down at her desk with the document titled "Property Settlement." She read through it again. Woo-ee, he's signed it, given her the whole shebang. Wait'll Sis hears about this.

"What do I owe you, Don?" Roy asked.

"I'll send you a bill at the end of the month."

Maureen rose from her chair. "Well, are we through?"

The two men got up. "Yep, we're done," Don said. He offered each of them his hand and they shook it. Maureen walked out of the office.

Roy stopped. "About that other matter," he said to Don.

Don handed him a file folder. "All drawn up. Sure you want to do this?"

"I'm sure," Roy said, accepting the folder. "Thanks."

At the house, Roy loaded four big suitcases into the trunk of Maureen's car.

Maureen surveyed her bare bedroom. She picked up her overnight kit, gave one last look around, and joined him at the front door. "That it?" he asked.

"That's it," she answered. "As soon as I get settled, I'll let you know where to send the rest."

"That's fine."

Without lingering, she left the house. From the porch he watched the big tailfins disappear. It had cooled off, and a nice breeze was blowing. He noticed how quiet it was, and how peaceful he felt. It hadn't been difficult to sort out the problems between him and Maureen. Once he had faced the facts, it was easy to cut her loose. But discerning his own future took time. Now he was content. Maureen wasn't the only to get a fresh start.

In the hospital, he had been plagued by worries about the store and his responsibilities. Gradually he admitted his reluctance to return to the store. Finally he had to confess that he hated running the store. That had been an eye-opener.

When he returned from Amarillo to see that the store was getting along fine without him, he was initially startled. Then an idea had begun to form. He was only minutes away from making that idea a reality.

~ ~ ~

Elated, Maureen headed south on Main Street and turned onto the highway, intending to stop for a minute at Marilyn's. She planned to overnight at the club, and head south the next morning after getting her hair and nails done. She had reservations at the Adolphus Hotel in Dallas and would stay there until she found a place to live. After saying goodbye to Marilyn, Massey would be permanently behind her.

"Maureen, I'm so glad to see you!" Marilyn said, opening wide the screen door. "I'll get you some coffee, honey."

"No, don't," Maureen said. "I can't stay. I just came to say goodbye."

"Goodbye?"

"I'm leaving Massey. I'm moving to Dallas."

Marilyn stared at her. "Moving to Dallas? But…what about the store?"

"I said, I'm moving. Roy is staying here," Maureen said.

"Oh," Marilyn said, still staring.

"We're getting a divorce."

"But you don't know anybody in Dallas," Marilyn ventured, still stunned.

"Well, of course I don't, now. But I intend to meet people. I've visited there quite a few times, you know."

"But why would you move there?"

"Because I'm tired of living in a small town. Finally, I have a chance to live a different kind of life. You know it's what I've always wanted." Maureen chafed under Marilyn's uncomprehending gaze. "I thought you might be a little bit happy for me."

"Oh, well, sure, if it's what you want. If it makes you happy…"

"Well, it does."

"Well, I'm happy if you're happy," Marilyn said, looking perplexed and unhappy.

"I *am* happy," Maureen snapped angrily.

"But…what about Roy?"

"Marilyn, what does it matter about Roy? Or his store? Is that all you can think about?"

"Mo, I'm sorry. I didn't mean…. It's just…I'm so surprised."

"*Please* don't call me Mo."

"I'm sorry, I forgot. Maureen. Don't be mad."

"I come all the way out here to tell you goodbye and all you can do is worry about Roy and his damn store. I guess you care more about him than you do about your own sister."

"Mo…Maureen, please, I'm sorry, really I am."

"Well, never mind. I guess I couldn't really expect you to understand." She headed for the door. Marilyn followed, wringing her hands.

"I'll let you know my new address," Maureen said. "I'll be staying at the Adolphus Hotel until I get settled. Roy has the number."

"Maureen, I really am sorry."

"Oh, all right, it's okay."

Marilyn wrapped her arms around Maureen and held her tight. Maureen endured the hug for a few seconds, then broke away and smoothed her dress. "Now," she said gaily, "don't you worry about me. I will be just fine."

ᨐ ᨐ ᨐ

Roy parked his car in the back of the store and went inside, taking the folder with him. "Pickens?" he called.

"Just a minute," came Wayne's voice, followed by Wayne himself, flushed and sweaty. "Just unpacking some merchandise," he explained.

"I see," Roy said. "Where's Linda?"

"Back there. She was assisting me."

Linda came out smiling. "Hi, Mr. Woodson," she chirped.

"Hi, Linda," he said. "Wayne, I need to talk to you. Come on upstairs."

"Why, sure, Mr. Woodson." Wayne was filled with consternation. He was still mortified by the memory of the last time he had been ordered up to Mr. Woodson's office. Now, reeling from Linda's kisses, he feared a second punishment. Was there lipstick on his mouth? The image of Brother Robbins and the phrase "the wages of sin" alarmingly joined forces in his head. Experiencing dread, he followed Roy upstairs.

"Sit down, Wayne," Roy offered, nodding to the straight-backed chair near his desk. He put the folder on his desk and sat in his desk chair, cradling his left arm.

"Your arm's bothering you," Wayne said, noticing.

"Not so much any more," Roy said. "Little tender."

"I imagine," Wayne said.

Roy leaned back in his chair and looked at the ceiling. He didn't speak, just sat there, absently stroking his elbow, rocking a little.

Wayne couldn't have suffered more acutely if fire ants had been crawling up his body. He tried his utmost to sit still, but the air was so close and his body was so hot, he was about to combust. His body felt slimy and itchy.

After what seemed a very long time, Roy leaned forward. "Wayne," he said.

"Yes, sir," Wayne answered, in an agony of not scratching.

"Wayne," he said, "I'm going to give up the store."

"Sir?"

"I've had a lot of time to think, and I have decided to give it up."

Wayne's throat constricted. Here indeed was punishment. He felt crushed, overwhelmed. The store would close, and once more he would have no job. He would not be manager.

"I'm going to turn it over to you."

Wayne squinted. "Turn it over to me?" he croaked.

"I'm giving you the fixtures and the inventory, free and clear. Of course, you'll have to pay the rent and utilities and for new merchandise. But I don't think that'll be a problem, if you keep on selling like you have been."

"I don't think I understand," Wayne said.

"We'll put your name on the lease. I've calculated what the current inventory and the fixtures are worth. It's all laid out in this folder. That is, if you want it."

"The store?"

"That's right," Roy said. "I've got the papers all drawn up. I'm giving it to you."

"Giving it to me?"

"That's right. How do you like the sound of Pickens' Department Store?"

Wayne's face turned a pasty white. His eyes rolled up into his head and he began to slide out of the chair. As he fell, he cracked his temple against the edge of the desk and then lay sprawled across the floor.

~ ~ ~

Daryl pulled out his wallet. "How much do I owe you, Mary?"

"Oh, just the regular," Mary Pickens replied.

"But you did a whole lot more today," he said. "I'm going to add something extra." He took several bills from his wallet and gave them to her.

"Well, thank you, Daryl," she said, putting the money in her apron pocket.

"Thank *you*," he said. "Place looks great."

"Danny isn't living with you any more?" she asked.

"No," Daryl said, moving away toward the door.

"Well, young folks," Mary said, not moving. "They have to lead their own lives, that's what I always say."

Daryl held open the screen door. Mary picked up her bucket of cleaning supplies. "I'll come back for the vacuum cleaner," she said.

"I'll take it out for you."

Daryl loaded the old Hoover into the trunk of her car, and Mary put the bucket in beside it. He closed the trunk and started back toward the house.

"Well," she said, "you just let me know if there's anything else you want done before the big day."

"The what?" he asked.

"I thought you might want to replace that shower curtain. For that matter, I could get you a new one, if you don't have time before she gets here. Although, Carolyn might like to pick it out herself."

"Goodbye, Mary," he said.

"Just let me know," she called after him. She settled herself into her car. "I thought so," she said with satisfaction. "Why would he want all that extra cleaning done if she wasn't coming back. He had me do all the things she used to want done."

In the house, Daryl scratched his head. How the hell did she know? He hadn't told a soul that Carolyn was coming home. Well, everyone would know soon enough. The last time Carolyn called, it looked like everything was set for her to come soon. He wanted to get the house in order for her, make it just the way she had left it.

At first, he hadn't exactly cottoned to the idea. It had gone against all the plans he was starting to make with Nadine. The thought of Nadine caused him to tense up. He should call her, or maybe even go to see her, and explain. But he didn't think he could face her. Nadine probably already figured it out. When Carolyn came home, Nadine would know the whole story without him having to tell her.

He and Carolyn would make a whole new start. With Danny out of the house, it would be just the two of them and their baby. Having a baby at their age! People would talk, but so what. We're not that old. In fact he felt youthful, ready for anything. He could hardly wait.

He picked up the phone. "Hi, it's me," he said when she answered.

A pause. "Daryl?"

"Yessum," he said. "I was just thinking about you."

"Oh, dear, I was about to call you," Carolyn said. Another pause. "Daryl, you're going to have to try to understand. Promise me you will try to understand."

"Understand what?" Icy fear crept close to him.

"Just listen. I've...I've thought it over, and well, the bald truth is that I just can't come back. I was mistaken to think it was even a possibility. I guess I was just scared and...well, impetuous. You were wiser than I -- you saw from the first that it was a crazy idea."

"What are you saying?"

"It was sweet of you to agree to let me come back, but I think we both know it just wouldn't work. I really should apologize for being so silly."

Daryl fell into a chair. "But what about the baby?"

"Oh. Well, I guess I should have started with that. I…I got my period. I'm not pregnant."

"But the last time we talked…"

"It just happened. I was about to call you."

"You're not pregnant?"

"No." She laughed. "Not even a little bit."

"But that doesn't matter, does it? We were going to make a fresh start. It would even be easier without a baby. You can still come home, can't you?"

"Daryl, I am home. Right now. Here in Santa Fe."

"You said you were selling your house."

"Daryl, I know this has probably come as a shock to you. But I just wasn't thinking straight when we talked before. Now I've had time to think everything through. I know you will agree, when you give yourself time to think about it."

"I don't need any time to think about it. I want you here. Carolyn, I can't believe you are doing this. You are turning my life upside down again. When you left, it about killed me. When you decided to come back, yes, I admit I was shocked. But I was happy, too. I have got everything ready here for you. You can't do this to me again, Carolyn. You have to come back."

"Daryl, once you calm down, I think you will understand it's better this way."

"Better for who? It's never been better for me. You are killing me, Carolyn."

"I think we had better hang up now until you are calmer."

"No, don't hang up!"

"I will call you in a couple of days and we can discuss this like adults. I know you will feel different then."

"I will never feel different!"

"We can talk later." The line went dead.

❧ ❧ ❧

Cal had rarely felt better in his whole life. His head was clear and he felt strong and purposeful. He had left Judge Randall's office with the signed subpoena, which he locked away in his safe.

Pete put his head in the door. "You're back," he said.

"Yeah."

"L.W.'s been looking for you all afternoon. Told me to tell you to talk to him before you did anything."

Cal smiled.

Pete continued, "He was all excited, came running down here, asked me where you were and when you would be back. What's he in such a sweat about?"

"Well, Pete, I got to thinking about what you said."

"What did I say?" Pete took a chair.

"As I recall, you said the prosecution plays favorites."

Pete nodded. "That's what I think, Cal."

"Well, that's what I think, too. Now we're going to find out whether that's the fact, or whether you and me are just imagining things. I'm reopening the Tomlin baby matter."

Pete stared at him.

"I've been to Judge Randall's office. He and I had a long talk this afternoon. I got a hunch that somebody may have made it real attractive for L.W. to look the other way. Anyway, we'll find out."

Pete didn't speak, just stroked his jaw, pulling the flesh around his mouth down to his chin with even, steady strokes. Finally he said, "You saw Judge Randall?"

"Right."

Pete pulled hard on his lower lip, elongating his whole face. Then he released his grip and grinned widely. "I be damned."

"Yeah."

"Listen, Cal, I went ahead and talked to Buster. He said he'd go out there and talk to Marilyn. You know, about working the farm, while Joe is…away. I told Buster that he ought to talk to Joe, too. Out of courtesy, you know."

"Good idea."

"Buster looked like I was asking him to go talk to Hitler."

"Yeah, he's probably scared of Joe."

"I'll tell Joe myself. He deserves to know what's happening on his farm."

"There's the matter of the mortgage," Cal said.

"It's paid off."

Now it was Cal's turn to stare. "Paid off? The whole thing?"

"Yeah. Virgil got everybody at the diner to pony up, and then Pat and Roy wrote out checks for the rest. With the money she got for the hogs, I think Marilyn will do just fine. Virgil and me, we're going to keep an eye on things out there till Joe comes home."

"Good man, Pete." Cal looked at his watch. "You going to the game?"

"You bet."

They walked out of the court house together. The sky was high and clear, with a few cirrus clouds skimming the surface, waiting to pick up the sunset's brilliant color show. The air was mild, hinting at fall.

At home, Cal picked up the mail from the hall table and took it into the kitchen. Nothing here worth keeping, he thought, and pitched it in the wastebasket, which was overflowing. Time to take it out to the trash can in the alley. Wedged in the basket were three record albums. Glenn Miller. These were the albums Pat had given Laura. She had been playing them constantly.

"Laura," he called.

"What?" she appeared at the head of the stairs.

"Why you throwing these Glenn Miller albums away?"

"I don't want them any more."

"Thought you'd be at the game."

"I'll go later," Marilyn said. "Right now I'd rather sit here with you."

Joe shrugged. "No place for you to sit."

"Yes, there is." She dragged a metal folding chair outside his cell.

She was wearing denim pants and jacket and cowboy boots. Her hair fanned out becomingly around her face and she was wearing lipstick. "You look pretty," he said.

She smiled. "Why, thank you, sir."

One of the drunks in the cell next to Joe's called out unintelligibly in his sleep and the other one snarled, "Shut up, asshole."

"Nice neighbors," Marilyn whispered.

Joe brought the low stool from the center of his cell and put it near the bars. He sat on it, his legs bowed out.

"How's Jesse?" he asked.

"I think he's fine. He's been staying with Pat and Dorothy all week. For practice sessions, you know. Pat says he's all pumped up for the game."

"Yeah, she said the same to me. Bet he's eating them out of house and home."

"I think they're happy to have him."

"He mad at me?"

Marilyn blinked. "Mad at you?"

"Yeah. Ashamed. You know."

"Honey, nobody is mad at you. Or ashamed. Everybody is on your side."

"Roy came to see me this afternoon."

"Did he?"

"I didn't know what to say to him." Joe got up from the stool and paced around the cell. "What was I going to say to him? That I was nuts? Well, I guess I was. Probably still am."

"Honey…"

"You know what he told me? I don't know whether to believe him or not. You know what he said? He thanked me. He said I helped him. Said he was confused before and now everything was real clear."

"Oh, my," Marilyn said softly.

"I don't know whether to believe him. I don't even know what he was talking about."

"Maybe I do. Maureen's left town. She's moving to Dallas," Marilyn said.

"He didn't say anything about her. He said he wanted to shake my hand and thank me. Can you believe that? I put a bullet in him, and he wants to thank me." Joe shook his head.

"Sit down again. I want to tell you something."

"Okay."

"Buster Edelman's going to work for us at the farm as long as we need him."

"Yeah, I know. Pete came by, told me the same thing. I guess it's a good idea. Don't know how long I'm going to be gone."

"Probably not long. But he'll work for us, he says, as long as we need him. He takes care of his sister's spread near Morgan, but he says he has time to help us out."

"Pete said it would be good to have him for awhile. You think so?"

"Yeah, I think so."

"Well, that's good, then."

Joe wiped his face with both hands and sighed.

"How do you feel, honey?"

"Oh, I don't know. Taking those pills, but only one a day now. The doctor said probably one would do me. I feel okay. It's just…you know, being in here…. I don't know what's going to happen at the hearing. Don said the fact I'm doing okay on the pills is a plus. Still, the judge could send me to Gainesville, you know, make me go." He got up again, moved restlessly about the cell.

"We're going to get through this," Marilyn said. "Everybody's rooting for us."

"You ought to go to the game," he said.

"After awhile. I just want to sit here with you awhile. If you'd sit."

He sat on the little stool again. She reached through the bars and took his hand. She held her face up close to the gap between the bars. "Come here," she said.

He leaned close in toward her. She smelled like flowers, or fruit, real sweet. He touched her hair. It was silky. She reached for his shoulder. Between the bars, they kissed.

# CHAPTER TWENTY-TWO

The Sanford team had brought a good-sized crowd with them for the game, including their pep band and cheerleaders, who were decked out in black and orange, making the visitors' bleachers more than half full.

The people of Massey packed the home team stands. Seemed like everybody in town had come to the game. The pep band in maroon and gold uniforms blared the fight song relentlessly, and eight cheerleaders in maroon circle skirts and gold sweaters turned cartwheels and shook pompoms. "Gimme a B, gimme an E, gimme an A, gimme an R, gimme an S, whaddya got? BEARS! BEARS! BEARS!" they screamed and the crowd joined in. The marching band was ready to put on a halftime show which would involve flag twirling and intricate formations, concluding with GO BEARS spelled out across the field. The team's mascot, Ricky Talbot, in spite of practically being suffocated in his wooly brown bear costume, ran playfully among the cheerleaders to help inspire the crowd.

When the Massey team ran onto the field to the accompaniment of the fight song, the home crowd stood and screamed out the words: "We will fight, fight, fight, for Massey High. Our boys will win this game, they'll do or die."

Some of the girls were planning to walk their sweethearts off the field at the end of the game. Mary Beth said, "Laura, why don't you walk Jesse off the field?'

"I don't know if he would want me to," Laura said, looking down at the field where she could see Jesse, number 8, splendid in his maroon and gold uniform and helmet, throwing a football in tight spirals to Bill Lynch.

"You ought to," Mary Beth urged. "How will it look if the quarterback doesn't have anybody to walk him off the field?"

"I might," Laura said.

"I double dare you," Mary Beth said.

"Ladies and gentlemen, please stand for our national anthem." The marching band, in formation between the home goal posts, began to play. Men removed their hats and women put their hands over their hearts while everyone fervently gave voice to "The Star Spangled Banner."

The cheers that followed were quelled when the announcer continued, "We now call on Dr. George Wright of the First Presbyterian Church to offer a prayer." Heads bowed and hands folded. Dr. Wright gave lengthy thanks for the beautiful weather, the prosperity of the United States, peace in the world, and especially for the young people gathered here tonight. He implored blessings upon the teams, the schools, the towns, the nation. He ended with a benediction and an amen, and the crowd roared as the pep band blasted out the fight song.

Massey won the toss and elected to receive, and the teams lined up for the kickoff. The game was underway. Jimmy Don Griggs returned the kickoff to the thirty-three yard line where he was driven out of bounds. First and ten on the thirty-three. In the huddle, Jesse called for a pass in the flat to Bill Lynch coming out of the backfield to his left. Up they came to the line of scrimmage. Over the center, Jesse took the snap, moved to his left and tossed a perfect spiral to Bill at their own forty-five yard line. First down.

Wayne and Linda sat together in the stands. He had a bandage over his left eyebrow and was still a little pale. They had spent an hour at the clinic where Dr. Lomax stitched up the cut in his forehead. Linda took his hand. "You just tell me if you feel too sick to stay," she whispered in his ear.

"I'm fine," Wayne insisted. "Long as you're here with me."

L.W. Foster pushed past them, knocking against their knees in an attempt to get down the row to where Lloyd and Florence Tomlin were seated.

"Rude," said Linda, loud enough for him to hear.

"Lloyd." L.W. squeezed in between Lloyd and Jake Mouser.

Lloyd's eyes were glued to the field. He didn't speak.

L.W. leaned closer and whispered, "Just wanted to let you know I've got a handle on it. Don't you worry."

The crowd stood to cheer as Jesse completed another pass to Bill, giving the Bears a first down in Sanford territory.

"Tempest in a teapot," L.W. continued, at Lloyd's elbow.

Lloyd gave a low growl, "Be better if we talk some other time."

"Okay, all right." L.W. pushed past the Mousers to get to the end of the row.

"What did he want?" Florence asked.

"Nothing," Lloyd said.

"What did he mean, tempest in a teapot?" she pursued.

"Nothing."

Two rows above Lloyd and Florence, Jim Atkins watched L.W. sit beside Lloyd and then leave. "Hope that's all taken care of," he muttered.

"What is?" Mavis asked.

"Nothing," he said.

Way up in the stands, Betty Talbot chirped to Lenore Waters,"Look down there just in front of the cheerleaders."

"Where?" Lenore craned her neck.

"It's Wayne Pickens and Linda Stoker," Betty said. "You should of seen them out at the clinic this afternoon. Quite the lovebirds."

"Out at the clinic?"

"Yeah, apparently he fell down at Woodson's, cut a big gash in his forehead. Doctor had to sew him up. She was right there beside him the whole time, holding his hand."

"I knew she was working there, but I didn't know they were…"

"You should of seen them. Totally gaga about each other."

"My, oh, my," Lenore said. "Wonder what his mother thinks."

"Do you have to take pictures all night?" Renee asked Abel.

Abel pointed the big camera from the high school audio-visual department at her. "Give me a smile," he said.

She struck a pose, one hand behind her head, the other on her hip, and smirked into the lens. The bulb flashed.

"You're going to get in trouble taking a picture of me," she said.

"Mrs. Victor told me to get some candid shots for the yearbook," he said, putting another bulb into the flash attachment.

"Abel, Abel, take our pictures!" Abel's brother Seth and his friend Peter Mathers dashed up from behind the stands.

Abel didn't want to waste a flashbulb on grade school kids, but good-naturedly pretended to take a picture of the boys standing with their arms around each other's shoulders.

"I have to get some more action shots," Abel said. "Wait here for me."

Renee stuck out her lower lip. "Don't be long."

"I won't." He squeezed his lanky body between the railings and jumped down onto the field to walk behind the players who were standing at the edge of the field. He captured Coach Parker yelling and gesturing with his clipboard. Downfield, he changed to a wide angle lens to get a sweeping shot of the two teams facing each other at the scrimmage line. He snapped Jimmy Don Griggs breaking through the Sanford line and carrying the ball for another first down.

He aimed his camera again at the line of scrimmage and waited until Jesse stood up, moved back out of the pocket and delivered a short pass into Bill Lynch's waiting hands. When they lined up again, he pointed the camera at the end zone and waited. Sure enough, after a few seconds, Abel found Bill there with the football. Touchdown! Everybody stood and screamed the fight song.

Abel made his way back to Renee in the stands and sat down with her. "I got some good shots," he said.

"Now maybe you'll pay some attention to me." When he didn't speak, she taunted, "Cat got your tongue?"

Abel reverently touched her hair and said, "But soft, what light through yonder window breaks? It is the east, and Renee is the sun."

"What is that?" she asked, smiling delightedly.

"That's Romeo, talking about Juliet. Or Abel, talking about Renee."

"Ooh," she said, wriggling her shoulders. "That is pretty. Say it again."

She nestled against him while he said it again.

Danny told Darlene, "I'll be right back." He ducked beneath the bleachers and took a pull from his flask, then walked around the end zone over to the visitors' side. He scanned the Sanford crowd. A young woman disengaged herself from a group and moved toward him. "Hi, Danny," she said.

He took her hand and pulled her behind the stands.

"I was looking for you," she said.

"Now you see me," he said, pulling her close. He kissed her. He put his hands on her buttocks and pulled her tight against his body. She thrust her hips against him. They kissed again.

"Come on," he said.

"Where to?" she asked.

"My car's right outside." He took her arm and led her out of the gate.

Virgil waved to Nadine and patted the cushioned seat beside him. He had brought two cushions with him just in case. She waved back and started to make her way over to him."Hi," she said.

"Hi," he answered. "Sit yourself down."

"Hi, Nadine," Dorothy greeted her from Virgil's right.

"What's the score?" Nadine asked.

Pat leaned across Dorothy to answer. "Seven zip. Sanford's about to give us the ball again. Looks like our boys showed up tonight."

"How's Jesse doing?" Nadine asked.

"Threw a touchdown. Looking good."

"These seats saved?"

The four of them turned to see Marilyn and Roy on Pat's right. "Sit down, sit down," Pat roared. "You just missed seeing your son throw for a touchdown."

"Maybe he'll throw another one," Marilyn said.

"Without a doubt," Pat crowed as Sanford's punter came out on the field.

Virgil stood to shake Roy's hand over the women's heads. "How you feeling?"

"Good," Roy said. "Better than ever."

The final score was Bears 28, Hornets 6. Massey held Sanford to two field goals, completely dominating the game. The last quarter Coach Parker sent in the second string, and the team scored its fourth touchdown. At the final whistle, the Massey crowd cheered mightily and surged down from the stands.

Kathryn Parker ran onto the field to hug Ray. "You did it!" she cried.

"Well, we missed a couple of opportunities, and I'm not altogether satisfied with the blocking," he said.

"Ray, it was great," she said.

"Yeah," he answered, watching the team hustle off the field. "I guess it was."

Laura caught up with Jesse. "Can I walk you off the field?" she asked.

"Sure," he said and linked arms with her. His uniform was filthy and he smelled hot and sweaty and delicious.

"You were wonderful," she said.

"Everything worked," he said happily.

"I about lost my voice screaming," she said.

"You want to wait for me to get changed?" he asked. "We could go out to Benny's or something."

"I would love that," she said.

Pat and Dorothy watched Laura walk Jesse off the field. "She's a nice girl," Pat said. "Jesse is a lucky boy."

Dorothy looked at her.

"Come on, precious," Pat murmured in Dorothy's ear. "Let's go home."

Carrying the camera equipment on one shoulder, Abel put his free arm around Renee's shoulders. "You mind walking?" he asked.

"Not so long as I'm walking with you."

"You know what I'm thinking about?" Nadine said.

"What?" Virgil asked.

She gave him a wicked smile. "Bananas. You got any bananas?"

He laced her fingers through his. "You bet," he said. "You bet I do."

## Also Available from Genoa House

| | |
|---|---|
| ***Feasts of Phantoms*** by Kehinde Ayeni | ISBN 978-0-9813939-2-6 Literary Fiction |
| ***Main Street Stories*** by Phyllis LaPlante | ISBN 978-0-9813939-1-9 Literary Fiction |
| ***The RR Document*** by J.G. Moos | ISBN 978-0-9813939-0-2 Literary Fiction |
| ***Requiem*** by Erel Shalit | ISBN 978-1-9267150-3-2 Literary Fiction |
| ***Sulfur Creek*** by Thad McAfee | ISBN 978-0-9810344-8-5 Literary Fiction |
| ***Timekeeper*** by John Atkinson | ISBN 978-0-9776076-5-5 Literary Fiction |
| ***Dark Shadows Red Bayou*** by John Atkinson | ISBN 978-0-9810344-7-8 Literary Fiction |
| ***Journey to the Heart*** by Nora Caron | ISBN 978-0-9810344-3-0 Literary Fiction |
| ***The Malcolm Clay Trilogy*** by Mel Mathews | Literary Fiction |
| ***LeRoi*** | ISBN 978-0-9776076-0-0 |
| ***Menopause Man*** | ISBN 978-0-9776076-1-7 |
| ***SamSara*** | ISBN 978-0-9776076-2-4 |
| ***Beyond the Mask: Part I*** by Kathleen Burt | ISBN 978-0-9813939-3-3 Astrology |

Phone Orders Welcomed
Credit Cards Accepted
In Canada & the U.S. call 1-888-298-9717
International call +1-831-238-7799
books@genoahouse.com
**www.genoahouse.com**

Lightning Source UK Ltd.
Milton Keynes UK
UKOW050725170911

178833UK00002B/68/P